The Lying Guest

ALSO BY MAHI CHESHIRE

Deadly Cure

The Lying Guest

MAHI CHESHIRE

Harvill
Secker

1 3 5 7 9 10 8 6 4 2

Harvill Secker, an imprint of Vintage, is part of the
Penguin Random House group of companies

Vintage, Penguin Random House UK, One Embassy Gardens,
8 Viaduct Gardens, London SW11 7BW

penguin.co.uk/vintage
global.penguinrandomhouse.com

First published by Harvill Secker in 2025

Copyright © Mahi Cheshire 2025

Mahi Cheshire has asserted her right to be identified as the author of
this Work in accordance with the Copyright, Designs and Patents Act 1988

Penguin Random House values and supports copyright. Copyright fuels creativity, encourages diverse voices, promotes freedom of expression and supports a vibrant culture. Thank you for purchasing an authorised edition of this book and for respecting intellectual property laws by not reproducing, scanning or distributing any part of it by any means without permission. You are supporting authors and enabling Penguin Random House to continue to publish books for everyone. No part of this book may be used or reproduced in any manner for the purpose of training artificial intelligence technologies or systems. In accordance with Article 4(3) of the DSM Directive 2019/790, Penguin Random House expressly reserves this work from the text and data mining exception.

Typeset in 11.7/16 pt Calluna by Jouve (UK), Milton Keynes
Printed and bound in Great Britain by Clays Ltd, Elcograf S.p.A.

The authorised representative in the EEA is Penguin Random House Ireland,
Morrison Chambers, 32 Nassau Street, Dublin D02 YH68

A CIP catalogue record for this book is available from the British Library

HB ISBN 9781787304505
TPB ISBN 9781787304512

Penguin Random House is committed to a sustainable future
for our business, our readers and our planet. This book is made
from Forest Stewardship Council® certified paper.

To my family

Prologue

Sri Lanka

The house stands at the end of a wide, empty road, flanked by gnarled palm trees. It was a colonial mansion, once. Now the whitewashed walls are yellowed, the carvings along the edge of the roof are crumbling and the windows are opaque with dust. Despite everything, it has an air of faded elegance. The pale glow of moonlight casts shadows on the cracked pillars that adorn the entrance. It's in need of restoration and some care. That's not what it's going to get.

There's a word my parents used to call me when they were angry. *Yakkā*. Demon. I hated them for that – and for many other things – but they were right. For what I'm about to do, I must be a *yakkā*.

In the distance, night creatures call. The wind picks up, rattling the foliage that grows through the cracks of the porch railings. Untended and unloved. An owl hoots. In the distance the sea crashes. I open the door.

Prologue

PART ONE
The Night Shift

1

Anika

Perched at the workstation in the corner of the operating theatre, I steal a glance at the screen. On the computer in front of me, in between tabs about today's surgery, I have a holiday website up. The page offers me deals in Greece, Jamaica, the Maldives. The glittering hotel pools and beach cabanas are enticing but I keep scrolling; none of these are what I'm looking for. I haven't had a holiday in over a year. My hospital rota has been relentless and I did extra shifts in my leave, to save up for my flat. Whenever I think about a holiday, which is a lot, there's one place I always come back to. The one place I can't go.

A nurse rattles a tray of equipment as she stocks it for the next surgery. Within minutes I'll be scrubbing in for the final procedure of my shift. I hesitate. Then I type a destination into the search box on the top right of the screen. *Sri Lanka.*

It's been such a long night. Longer than usual because my night shift technically ended thirty minutes ago. I should be in my car, halfway home by now. But today's operating list is due to start and because of yet another rota mix-up, there's no surgeon to operate. It's a routine procedure. At my level, nearing consultancy, I've done many of these. It will take me twenty minutes, max, between the first incision and closing up. I could let them cancel a patient who has been waiting months for their operative date, add them back to the end of the too-long list. Or I could do it. It's the simple solution. Easy, almost. Or it would be if I was running on more than zero hours' sleep.

The page populates with images and I find the one I'm looking for. A beach with white, a sweep of sea, a little surf shack made of driftwood. I remember this area well, it's near where my family's house used to be.

One more patient, one more surgery, then I'll be home, in bed. One more hour. For now, I let myself escape. I imagine myself far from the sterile walls of the hospital, the hum of the heating unit replaced by the gentle lapping of waves. This is the photo I come back to whenever I need to feel better. I stare at the screen hungrily. I want to fall into it.

'Sri Lanka? Nice.' The scrub nurse looks over my shoulder. 'You going on holiday?'

Reality jars as I pull myself back to the present. The space at the centre of the operating theatre is still empty. I close the tab down.

'I wish.'

'I'd say you earned it after tonight. We went last year.' He starts talking about the beaches, the food, the friendly locals. I nod and smile. I remember those things too. The other memories, the ones I most need, are buried so deep in my subconscious I don't think I'll ever get them back.

'Five minutes,' another nurse calls. The patient is on the way down.

I start scrubbing in. My hands shake as I open the packet containing a fresh surgical gown and mask and empty the contents onto the sterile table. The ward manager walks over. I shove my hands in my pockets before he notices.

'You're really helping us out, Anika. Though . . .' He puts a hand on my shoulder. 'Are you sure it's okay? It's a lot to ask after a long shift.'

'It's no bother, honestly.' I pour some disinfectant gel from the dispenser onto my hands. 'Sleep is overrated anyhow.'

The nurses laugh, the ward manager mumbles another apology even though it's not his fault. I stare at my hands, mesmerised by the suds on my knuckles. Grogginess hits me. It's been a busy night in the emergency department, the ward and in theatre. It's catching up with me now. My eyelids are heavy. It's an effort to keep my eyes open. *Keep going.* I wash off the suds, turn off the tap with my elbow.

Then something strange happens. A jarring feeling. Like suddenly I'm looking at myself from outside myself. I'm standing by the bank of sinks, putting on my surgical gown. My long wavy black hair is in a collapsing ponytail; it had been high and jaunty at the start of shift. *Why am I doing this?* I don't need to stay.

The double doors of the operating theatre open. Wheels squeak on the linoleum as the stretcher comes to a stop.

I want to leave. But my feet don't move. I keep standing there obediently as a nurse fastens the ties on the back of my surgical gown.

'We're ready,' the scrub nurse calls from the table.

My gown is tied too tight. It feels like a straitjacket. I finally move, stopping at the table. The patient is unconscious, under anaesthetic already. In pre-op clinic earlier this morning, the anaesthetist would have discussed the complications, the many things that could go wrong. A surgeon would have, too, in another, routine pre-op clinic a week before. Not me. I was on nights then too. I wasn't the one to take this patient through all the potential complications. Now the anaesthetist sits on a stool by the patient's head calmly checking the monitors showing the patient's breathing rate, heart trace, blood pressure. All good numbers and even, regular lines.

I get that feeling again, like I'm looking at all of this from afar.

I see myself at the operating table, the patient lying in front of me. The patient looks to be asleep, a bare hand flops by the side of the bed. All the patient's jewellery and personal attire have been removed in pre-op clinic. They sit in a bag in a locker. Waiting.

'Anika?' The anaesthetist is watching me with an expectant expression. They all are.

'Scalpel.'

The nurse passes me one. I hold it tight, feel its familiar cold weight in my hand. It grounds me. A little while longer. I make the first incision.

2

One second is all it takes. One millimetre. A knife's edge, separating life and death.

'Anika.'

A ringing noise fills my ears. On the floor, blood pools and puddles. A trail leading back to the operating table. There wasn't supposed to be so much blood. It's on my shoes too. Fresh splatters covering the old bloodstains on the toes of the Crocs, borrowed from the box of disgusting communal surgical shoes in the female changing room. I can't take my eyes off a drop of blood that trickles off the edge and onto the white-tiled floor.

'Anika.' A hand on my shoulder. The scrub nurse looks at me, eyes full of concern. Behind them, something else. Numb shock.

'We have to clean up now.'

'There's nothing more we can do,' says a voice that doesn't belong in the operating theatre. The hospital's chief executive beckons me to the side of the room, away from all the blood. When she put that cream skirt suit on this morning, I doubt she expected to be called in here. But what just happened is more than enough to bring hospital management out of their offices and onto the front line.

'. . . as the operating surgeon . . .' she says. I am the operating surgeon. I'm the one responsible. Panic sets in.

'. . . not your fault.' Now she puts her hand on my arm. 'We'll need you to sign off on the paperwork. Later. Go home now. Get some rest.'

I look back down at my blood-splattered Crocs. *I should go home.* 'I – I can't. I have to stay.'

'There's nothing you can do,' she says more firmly.

The swish, swish of a mop reverberates in my head. They're cleaning up. Now I force myself to look at the table. First the base, surrounded by wires and all the blood. Then the hand that dangles off, lifeless. Feet sticking out from under the sterile drape. The suture line, made with shaking hands as I sewed the patient back up, knowing it was futile. As the blood pressure had dropped, the beeping monitors fell silent. That was the worst part. I force myself to keep looking, at the face, pale and lifeless. The eyes closed. Nausea builds in my throat. No, this, this is the worst part.

'I have to go.' My shoes skid on the slippery floor as I rush for the changing room.

'Anika,' someone calls after me. I tear off my soiled gown and gloves, stuff them into the bin by the door. I barrel through the doors of the changing room, into the nearest toilet cubicle. Slamming the door shut, I heave into the recently bleached toilet.

Under the cubicle door, disembodied feet exchange trainers for surgical shoes. Clean, unlike mine. It's early, the day staff have started to come in. I stay there on the floor of the cubicle until all the feet have gone.

Adrenaline ebbs out of my system and reality takes its place. A patient just died. On the operating table. With an effort I drag myself out of the cubicle. My face looks back at me from the clouded mirror above the bank of sinks. I'm pale, clammy. Sweaty. I don't look like myself.

'Anika.' It's Sara Peele, the consultant. She came in, had to, when it became clear I couldn't manage. It didn't make a difference, in the end.

'You should go home now,' Sara says, sitting next to me on the changing-room bench. Her scrub-clad legs are clean. After the surgery, she was as covered in blood as the rest of us. She must have showered and changed. When did she have time to do that? How long have I been here?

'Okay,' I say, staring at the floor. Going home involves showering, putting my clothes back on. Getting in my car, driving. A lot of steps, requiring energy I just can't imagine having right now. So I keep sitting here.

'You mustn't blame yourself,' Sara says. Her usually curt tone is tempered today. Gentle. I've never heard her anything but stressed and snappy before. That anomaly, more than anything, tells me how bad this situation is.

'It happens, sometimes. However hard we try, patients do die on the table.'

I wince.

'Sad as it is, they do. You know that. You, we, did everything we could. We tried our best.'

But our best was not good enough.

'We move on,' Sara says. 'That's all we can do.' She rests her hands on her knees. 'I had a case too, when I was a little more junior than you. Also a haemorrhage . . .' She keeps talking but my brain catches on the word haemorrhage. Repeats it over and over like a broken record. Amplifies it, so I can't focus on anything else. How could I have let that happen?

'Anika?'

I close my eyes, then open them.

'Yes, I'm listening.'

'You're an excellent surgeon, Anika. This is no reflection on your abilities. It is the risk of surgery. It could have happened to anyone.'

'I . . . Sure.' Then I remember what must come next. A new sick sensation makes itself known, writhing around in my gut. 'The relatives.' My voice catches.

'They're on the way,' she says.

I have to break the news to the family. Who didn't expect this. I have to look them in the eyes and tell them their loved one is dead and it's my fault. Tears stream down my face. I wipe my cheek with my arm. I must have had blood on my arm because it comes away diluted, mixed with tears. Sara's apprehensive expression confirms, I now have blood on my face.

'I'm sorry, I'm a mess.'

'It's been a shock for you,' she says, not even trying to deny it.

'I'll be okay, talking to them. Just let me clean up.' My voice gets choked up again.

'No,' Sara says quickly. 'I'll speak to them.'

'Really?'

'I have to be there anyway – intraoperative death requires a consultant be present when speaking to the relatives. It's hospital procedure. So I'll do it.' My relief at not having to face them is immediately followed by guilt, for feeling relieved in the first place. She's being so nice but I don't deserve this kindness. *I* did this. *I* should be the one to tell the relatives. Deal with the shock, disbelief, despair that follows. I've seen it before but I've never been the one responsible. I should be the one to tell them. But I can't. I'll take the easy way out she offers instead.

'Thank you.'

Sara nods.

'There needs to be a debrief for all staff involved. Ordinarily we'd have it the same day but—' Her eyes flick over my bloodied scrubs. 'Given how long you've been here already. Go home. We'll have an informal debrief when you're back.'

'Thank you.'

'We do need a written statement from you. Your account of events, for the root-cause analysis.'

'Now?'

'As soon as you can. If you don't feel able to write it now, then email me as quickly as possible.'

'Okay.'

'Take some time to recover. It's all staff's personal responsibility to seek help via their GPs if they need it so I recommend you do that too.'

It's cold in the changing room. I wrap my arms tight around me.

'I don't need to see my GP.'

Sara doesn't look convinced. 'Go home, take a day or two. When you're ready, you come back to work and carry on. Got it?'

I nod mechanically. It won't be that easy. This night is never going to leave me. I already know that to be true.

The door slams open. It's Eliza. She's on day shift today, her face is still morning fresh. Seeing my best friend here is a relief. And it's not. I don't want her to see me like this.

'I heard . . .' She takes in my appearance, from stained scrubs to bloody clogs. 'So it's true?'

I nod.

Sara backs away, Eliza takes her place on the bench next to me. 'What happened?'

'It was a routine procedure. It was fine. Then it wasn't.'

'A major haemorrhage, they're saying upstairs.'

Word has spread to the wards already. Of course it has.

'It came out of nowhere. I couldn't stop it. Suction, suturing, nothing helped. They transfused four units but it just kept coming.' I bite my lip, hard. The reality of it all hits me again. How could a routine procedure go so wrong? 'I thought it would be a quick surgery. That I'd be out in twenty minutes.'

She sucks in a breath.

'So you had to operate after your night shift?'

I nod.

'You weren't even supposed to be here. What shitty luck.'

'I shouldn't have offered to stay. It might have gone better if it were someone else—'

'Don't do that. You're one of the best surgeons I know. From the sounds of it, no one could have stopped what happened.'

She squeezes my shoulder and again I want to let it out, to cry until I can't breathe. I won't, though. I don't deserve to.

People come and go around us. More day-shift staff arriving. I catch whispers. Furtive glances in my direction that tell me they've heard about what happened.

'I have to get out of here.'

'You going to be okay, driving home?'

'I'll have a shower, and . . . I'll be fine.'

Eliza chews her lip like she does when she's worried.

'You haven't slept in, what? Twenty-four hours?'

'Something like that.'

'I'll call you a taxi.'

'No point, I have my car. If I leave it here, I'll just get a ticket or get towed or something.'

Eliza's pager bleeps. She checks it then silences it.

'You should get that.'

'You sure you're able to drive?'

'I've managed after longer shifts.'

'I know but . . .' She sighs. 'Let me know when you get home.'

'Sure.'

'Listen to me. It's going to be okay,' she says.

It's not, though. There's before this surgery. And there's after. Things won't, can't, be the same, ever again.

I walk towards the showers. Staff look up from changing, ask me if I'm okay. I mutter *yes, I'm fine*, keep my head up until I turn the corner, out of sight. I head for the furthest shower cubicle and shut the door. Then I turn the tap left until the water runs as cold as it will go. I stand under it, fully clothed. Blood streaks the water on the tiles, runs down the hair-clogged drain and swirls away. When the water coming off me finally runs clear, I strip off the scrubs. I stand under the frigid water until my fingers are wrinkled and my teeth are chattering.

3

The hospital already looks different. It's a clear early-autumn day; crispy brown fallen leaves decorate the steps of the entrance. People walk in and out, the automatic doors sliding between footfalls. It's a normal day, but something feels off. My feet drag as I approach the front steps.

'Anika.' Rosa waves from the entrance. Her dark hair is neatly pulled back, and she's already in her blue scrubs. Usually we both come in early but today I couldn't face the six thirty start so I said I'd meet her here instead. Getting a coffee on the way to handover is our ritual when we're on shift together but it feels foreign to me now. Even though I haven't been away long. The rest of the week, at the insistence of the consultants and hospital management. I wanted to come back right away. Awful as being here in the immediate aftermath of what happened would have been, being away turned out to be worse. Being alone with nothing to distract me from the awful thoughts clashing in my head, and worse, the nightmares? Being back in the hospital is preferable. At least here I can work. I can try and return to normal.

'I missed my morning latte partner,' Rosa says, taking my arm. 'How are you doing?'

During the day I've been racked with anxiety and at night, I'm barely sleeping. 'I'm okay,' I say. 'In a way, glad to be back.'

'It's for the best. Rip the plaster off quick, right?' She hesitates. 'Eliza said the autopsy results came back.'

The fish tank by the reception desk catches my eye. The stones on the bottom of the tank glow red under the strip lights. The autopsy is standard procedure after intraoperative death. I got an email from management, when the results came out. The autopsy stated, Cause of death: haemorrhage. What it should say is, Cause of death: me.

'Anika?'

Rosa is a little ahead of me now. I realise I'm standing still, with my face close to the glass.

Rosa pulls me gently away from the fish tank. 'Are you sure you should be back?' She's using a guarded tone I've heard her use with difficult patients, ones who might lash out at any moment.

Get it together. I nod.

'I'm fine. So what's been going on with you? Is wedding planning any better?'

She frowns slightly.

'You want to talk about that?'

'Of course. What have I missed?'

'Well, Ravi's mother is still a nightmare – never mind. We haven't talked about the autopsy. Or how you're doing. You haven't been picking up my messages or calls. You really want to discuss my wedding planning?'

I couldn't bring myself to answer my friends' well-meaning messages. Their lives have carried on as normal while mine feels like it's stopped.

'I'm sorry, I didn't feel up to talking much. Please, hearing about your control-freak future mother-in-law would be a great distraction.'

She laughs.

'In that case. Ravi's mother has lost the plot. She wants to ship in peacocks for the reception.' She launches into the story as we walk to the coffee shop, under the chandelier that dominates the entryway. It's busy this morning, patients and staff mill in different directions. It's a normal day, even if it doesn't feel like one for me. How am I going to get through today?

'Anika?' Rosa asks, and again, I realise I've lost track of the conversation.

'Sorry.'

'Okay, we have to talk about what's going on with you.'

'I'm fine.'

She doesn't look convinced.

'It will get better. The autopsy is done now. Then there will be the internal review and the other paperwork.'

Paperwork. The incident form and my account of events that Sara, the consultant, has been pushing for. I left her emails unanswered.

'And then it will be over,' Rosa says.

It doesn't feel like it will ever be over. I stop by the little seating area outside the coffee shop. A TV screen is mounted high on the wall opposite, yellow subtitles flashing across the screen. At a table in the corner, a patient in a hospital gown fiddles with her drip stand.

'I hope it won't take long.' The internal review is standard procedure too. I knew there would be one. Always is, after unexpected patient death. I think of the London Medical Institute's near perfect surgical mortality rate, now tarnished. A panel of senior surgeons will analyse everything that happened. Everything that went wrong.

'They have to prevent it happening again,' I say hollowly.

'No one could have prevented it,' she says firmly. 'You were unlucky to be there. Don't blame yourself. If it was any other surgeon, the same thing would still have happened.'

She's trying really hard to be nice so I smile, though I don't believe her.

'Thanks. I appreciate that. It's my treat today.' Ignoring her protests, I go inside to order our coffees.

*

When I come out, Rosa turns quickly, shoves her phone in her pocket with a strange expression. She grabs her coffee quickly, takes a sip, then makes a face.

'I got yours,' she says, handing it back to me. The sticker on the lid reads *decaf*, same as I almost always get. I watch her as she swaps it for her latte. Maybe it was an easy mistake to make, but Rosa is usually very observant of small details. It's one of the things that make her a great surgeon. The error, combined with the guilty look on her face when she put her phone away, makes me wonder if there's more to it. Or am I being paranoid?

She takes a deep drink of her coffee.

'Let's get to handover.' She power-walks to the lift and jabs the button repeatedly.

We get in, the doors close.

Rosa turns to me. 'This will all blow over, Anika.'

'You think so?'

A flash of that guilty expression again.

'Yes. Once the review is done,' she says, not looking at me. 'We're late for handover.' She takes us up to the surgical ward like she's on a mission. Even though my watch tells me handover doesn't start for another five minutes.

The team sit around the wide table in the small meeting room, talking quietly. The registrar Malachi and the nurse in charge for the night both have dark shadows under their eyes. It must have been a busy night. Next to them are two junior doctors, the nurse in charge for the day, and the consultant for the day, Sara.

In the doorway, I pause. The circumstances under which I saw the team last loom large and I want to run away.

They all look up, stop talking. I can't run from this. Like Rosa said. Time to rip the plaster off. Then it will all blow over.

'Hi,' I say.

Sara nods. 'It's good to see you, Anika.'

A strange silence follows, as the eyes of the other staff members linger on me a little longer than necessary.

'Thanks. It's good to be back,' I say. I head for the last empty seat at the table, next to Rosa. 'Good' is vastly overselling it. 'Better' would be more accurate. Better than being exhausted because, when night falls, I'm scared to sleep. Scared of falling seamlessly into the nightmares. The bleeding that's even worse in the dreams than it was in theatre. The lifeless patient on the table. The guilt that has me waking up in tears. Better than stewing on it all day with nothing to distract me.

'Are we ready?' Sara says. I think she's addressing the table, then I realise they're all looking at me. I'm standing between the table and the wall, frozen. *Shit.* I sit quickly in the vacant chair. Someone passes the freshly printed pile of lists around the table and I take one. *Act normal.*

'We had three new patients overnight,' Malachi says. I find the corresponding row on the table as he runs through the first patient's history. The patient needs a CT scan with a possible procedure today, depending on the results.

'Rosa, you'll be in theatre later, so it might come your way,' Malachi says. Then a look of surprise crosses his face. 'No, it says you're operating today, Anika.'

Sure enough, there's my name heading the list of today's staff on the first page of the document. *Operating surgeon: Anika Amarasinghe.* The corners of the paper dampen under my sweaty fingers.

'Anika is covering the ward today,' Sara says quickly. 'This must be from the old rota. Rosa will be in theatre today.'

So they changed it based on what happened. I'm not ready to be in theatre again. But I can't let them think I can't do my job.

'I can operate,' I say quickly.

The two junior doctors across from me are looking not at their lists, but at something under the table. One glances at me briefly.

'Today it's best you work on the ward, Anika,' says Sara. 'Come to my office later, we'll work out the rota for the rest of the week.' Her tone tells me her decision is made. I'm relieved.

Handover carries on. Everyone is being weirdly formal. There's no levity, no complaints, no nothing. The atmosphere is strained. I wish, again, that I could run away. But I have to stick it out. It's only my first day back. It was bound to be like this. If I keep my head down, keep going, it will blow over. It will be okay.

The morning passes in a blur. There's more staring, looks of surprise from staff when I arrive, but I decide to throw myself into a ward round of all the patients, chasing blood results and scans, dealing with minor medical issues that crop up. It's past two when Eliza messages me to join them in the mess for lunch. I tell the nurses I'm popping out, then take the stairs up to the doctors' mess. This feels mundane. Going to the mess for lunch is part of a daily routine from before. If I keep going through the motions, it will be okay. It has to be.

The doctors' mess is busy, the tables that line the square room and the little kitchenette full. The big TV at the back of the room is on, playing *News 24*. Rosa and her fiancé Ravi are sitting at a round table in the corner. With them are Flora and Yemi, two of the anaesthetists, and Isaac, one of the orthopaedic surgeons. Rosa sees me, waves.

Everyone on the table stops talking as I approach. This is getting annoying.

'Hi, guys.'

After a beat, the others return my greeting, tell me they're happy I'm back. Something is still off, though. After what happened, it's not surprising. The surgery is like a huge elephant in the room. Even though we're not talking about it, we're all thinking about it.

Ravi starts talking about a drama with some missing equipment on his ward this morning. As he talks, I notice Isaac looking at me. Isaac and I were up for the same job at the beginning of our surgical training. I got it, Isaac was allocated to some decrepit district general hospital instead. He seems to have held me personally responsible, because he's been passive-aggressive ever since we've been working in the same hospital. Either that, or he's still sore about the time I rejected his drunken advances. I don't like the way he's looking at me now. Like he has one up on me.

Ravi says he's going to make a coffee. Flora and Yemi go with him to the kitchenette. Leaving me, Rosa and Isaac at the table.

'Okay, what is it, Isaac?' I say. 'Spit it out.'

He sits back in his chair, folds his arms behind his head.

'What do you mean?'

'You obviously have something to say.'

Isaac grins.

'I don't. I'm just surprised to see you back.'

'Why? I work here.'

He mutters something under his breath.

'Leave it, Isaac,' says Rosa.

'But now that—'

'Shut up, Isaac,' says Rosa. She pushes a salad over to me. 'I got you your usual.'

Isaac's attention shifts to something on the other side of the room and he marches off.

'Thanks,' I say. 'For that, and lunch. Beats the mess toast I was going to have.'

Rosa glances at the door.

'I figured. So, how was your morning?'

'Apart from all the weird staring, fine.'

'They'll take you off ward duties soon,' Rosa says.

'I'll see what Sara says later. I have to meet her after lunch. But I don't mind the ward. I'm not ready to pick up a scalpel again yet.'

'It will take some time,' Rosa says. She seems distracted.

'Have you heard from Eliza this morning?' I ask.

Rosa pauses, her fork midway to her mouth.

'Her surgical list overran.' She looks at the doorway again. 'She'll be here soon.'

Isaac returns, holding the remote for the TV.

Then he turns up the volume.

The news is still playing. A grey-haired man in a suit is being interviewed. He looks familiar.

'Isn't that the head of the Royal College of—' I can't get the rest of the sentence out, because the words on the scrolling banner at the bottom of the screen stop me short. *Father of patient who died during surgery at the London Medical Institute calls for an inquiry.* A cold sweat breaks out on my back.

'Of surgeons? Yes,' says Isaac. Around us, conversations have ceased. The voice of the patient's father – the head of the Royal College of Surgeons – blares into the silence.

'Our family want justice. And for this not to happen again. My brother Oliver Hoxton, the health minister, is supporting us in calling for a full review.'

The segment cuts to an interview with Oliver Hoxton. My heart pounds, uncomfortably hard. A kind of buzzing fills my head and makes it difficult to focus. I catch the words *tragic death.* And, *mission to reduce surgical mortality in UK hospitals.* The health minister is involved. The patient is his *family.*

'I didn't know. The patient—'

'Went by mum's surname,' Isaac says. 'What? It comes up later in the interview.'

'What the fuck, Isaac?' It's Eliza. I didn't hear her come in. She's still in her scrubs and her cheeks are flushed, like she's rushed here. She marches over to Isaac. 'How could you?'

Isaac leans forward. His ID card on a lanyard hits the edge of the table.

'It's been playing on a loop this morning. Anika would have found out eventually.'

'She shouldn't have found out like this,' Rosa says.

This story must have been what the juniors were looking at under the table in handover. This is why people have been weird with me all day. The cold sweat intensifies.

The patient's father is back on screen now. 'Intraoperative death is sadly always a possibility, but a rare one. Especially unlikely in procedures such as this. So we want to know, was what happened truly an unpreventable complication? Or was it surgical negligence?'

Dread creeps up my spine at his words.

Eliza grabs the remote and turns the TV off. The resulting silence in the doctors' mess is so thick I could drown in it. This is worse than I could have imagined.

'You all knew?' I ask.

'I saw it this morning,' Rosa says quietly. 'When you were getting coffee.'

'Why didn't you tell me?'

'I was going to. I was waiting for Eliza to get here. We wanted to tell you together. Alone.'

I stand.

'Because this worked out so much better.'

'I'm sorry,' she says.

Everyone is staring at us. At me. *Negligence.* I read between the lines of his statement. This could become more than an internal inquiry. I want to vomit.

My pager bleeps, breaking the silence.

I run, leaving my salad uneaten on the table, and answer the bleep via the phone on the wall outside the doctors' mess.

Sara Peele answers.

'Anika, come to my office,' she says. 'Now.'

4

Sara Peele's office door is shut. I knock twice, under the sign with her name on it. As I wait, the news item plays over and over in my mind. I wonder if she's had time in her busy morning to see it yet. I've been on track to become a consultant in the next year, via a highly competitive fellowship. Then, later, to become a surgical director. I've been so confident I would get there. But now, it feels like it all hangs in the balance.

'Come in.'

Sara is behind her desk. Next to her is Yana Abdullah. The chief executive of the hospital.

'You wanted to see me?'

'Thanks for coming,' Yana says. We haven't had much to do with each other, apart from when she came down to theatre after surgery. I want to believe she just happened to be here today to see Miss Peele. I know better. This is bad. *This is bad.*

Sara motions for me to sit, in the chair in front of the desk.

'How are you, Anika?'

Sara is known for being tough but fair. She's been supportive of me thus far. How much longer will she continue to be?

'I've been better.'

'Have you seen this?' Yana asks. She's soft-spoken and her casual tone doesn't fit with what I see when she turns her laptop round. A BBC News article fills the screen, with what looks like the same clip I just saw, linked at the top. *Fuck.*

'I – yes. I have. Just now.'

Sara puts her coffee down.

'The story broke in the early hours. I had hoped to wait until the end of the day to talk to you about it. When I had an answer as to what will happen next. But the story has dominated the news all morning, and a decision has been made.'

I grip the edge of the chair hard.

'A decision?' The coarse material is worn. I find a loose thread and pull at it.

She steeples her fingers and looks over the desk at me. I've seen junior doctors, nurses, even other consultants quail under her piercing glare. Like I do now.

'There will be a review, as is procedure. The main difference is that it will happen sooner than expected.'

'How soon?'

'Instead of the informal debrief which we postponed until you were back, we'll progress straight to the internal review and root-cause analysis. For that, we need your statement.' She holds eye contact again. I have to will myself not to look away. 'The rest of the staff involved have provided theirs. Have you completed yours yet?'

I've spent the past few days reeling, trying not to think about what happened. The last thing I wanted to do was to re-examine everything. To record it.

'I need more time.

'And the incident form?'

'I'll do it soon.'

'We need both today. Any longer is in breach of protocol,' Sara says.

'It's better we do this while things are fresh,' Yana says, more gently. 'Give you a chance to get everything down.' Her tone is light but her eyes tell me I don't have a choice.

'I need a bit more time.' I need to think. To figure out what's best to do, how to defend myself.

'That we don't have,' she says.

'We must be seen to be taking swift action. Not dragging our feet. We need your statement today,' Sara says. 'And we have our monthly morbidity and mortality meeting coming up. You'll be presenting the case there.'

'But that's in a week.'

'We need to get things moving,' Yana says. 'The family, and Oliver Hoxton, are pushing for action.'

I pull the thread out from the underside of the chair, snagging my finger on a staple that holds it to the wooden seat.

'They're wrong, about what they said. It *was* a complication. It wasn't negligence.'

'We're not saying it was. But there will still be an internal inquiry, as there always is.'

'This isn't a normal internal inquiry any more. It stopped being one when the health minister got involved.'

'Regardless, we will treat this as we would any other case in this hospital.' Sara's voice is clipped and I know I should stop pushing.

'What if they're not satisfied? They're accusing me of negligence. If they don't get the result they want, they'll escalate, won't they?'

I lean closer, resting my hands on the desk close to hers.

'I know the family are angry and they want someone to blame. I can't be their scapegoat.'

'It's not up to me, Anika. We had an emergency meeting of the hospital board this morning. After a call from the health minister himself. My hands are tied.' She stands. 'I know you're an excellent surgeon. What happened was an unprecedented complication. The inquiry will find that too. Please cooperate with the process.'

'Starting now,' says Yana. 'We need that statement, by the end of today.'

'But I'm working.'

'Not any more,' says Sara. 'We're moving you to night shifts.'

'With the story circulating in the press, the hospital board think it best we help you keep a low profile for now,' Yana adds. *Help me.* Like they're doing me a favour, consigning me to the graveyard shift.

'Ward nights?'

She nods. 'It's for the best.'

Their plan makes sense. I know now that they can't let me carry on as normal while this inquiry goes on. And keeping a low profile is appealing. But at what cost?

'For how long?'

Yana checks her computer. 'We're drawn up a temporary rota. You're on nights for the next week, followed by post-night days off—'

'A whole week at a time?'

'—and that pattern will continue for the next three weeks after which we can reassess where best to place you.'

'I'll be doing seven nights in a row?'

'Yes,' Sara says. 'Will that be a problem?'

I mentioned my medical condition on the occupational health form when I started at this hospital. Though one word gives away nothing of how severe mine was. I didn't tell them about the consequences. My condition is poorly understood. Cases like mine are rare. So people don't expect it. They don't ask. I had one occupational health interview and the doctor asked if I still suffered from it. I said no. She asked if I felt able to do night shifts. I said yes and that was it. No further questions.

'I can't be on nights indefinitely.'

They look at me in unison, like I've said something out of turn.

'It's not indefinite. It's for the next three weeks and you'll get breaks and post-night days off as per a normal rota,' Sara says.

'It's just until the inquiry is done, then we can assess what to do next,' says Yana.

I've recovered. The sleep specialist said so, sixteen years ago. The experimental treatment he gave me had worked. I've done night shifts many times in the years since I've been working as a doctor. And I've never had a problem. So he must be right. But, four night shifts in a row is the most I've ever had to do. Could more prolonged periods of sleep disruption make a relapse likely? I should ask Sara and Yana now, if they know about my medical history. But then they might wonder why I didn't mention it before. They could misunderstand. I can't have them think I'm untrustworthy, especially not now.

'Okay.'

They both look relieved.

'Let's get your statement now, then. Speed things up,' says Yana. 'Get you off nights quicker.'

'I – okay.'

All I can do is state events as they happened and hope the conclusion they draw is the right one.

'I'll get the paperwork from my office.' Yana leaves, and Sara turns to me.

'Anika, I'm sorry this is happening.'

'So am I.' Something occurs to me then. 'Did you know who the patient was related to?'

She looks at me. Then she shakes her head.

'No one knew. If I had, I never would have let you operate. I would have done it.'

Most likely, she means she would never let a post-night-shift doctor stay for the procedure. And she wouldn't have let anyone less than a consultant do it. For a close family member of the president of the Royal College of Surgeons and the health minister, there would have been special treatment. One or even two consultants doing the surgery. They would have prepared for it. Sent updates to the family, both before and after. The patient would never have been on a routine list, subject to the whims of the rota. It wouldn't have fallen to me. I know all this but in the wake of everything else today, her answer feels like proof that she thinks I'm a subpar surgeon. Equals *Negligent*.

But if I had known who the patient was related to, I wouldn't have done the procedure either.

The nurses' station is empty. It's 5 a.m. and the patients are sleeping silently, apart from the occasional shout from the one on the other side of the ward. The cubicles are darkened. I find a computer and look up the results of the blood tests I ordered earlier. It's nearly the end of my first week of night shifts. With nightmares continuing to plague me, I haven't been sleeping properly during the day. So I've started taking a tablet to help me sleep before shift. This is probably not a great idea but I can't take the sleep deprivation any more.

My bleep has been quiet the past half an hour. I should use the opportunity to work on my presentation for the morbidity and mortality meeting. The surgical department has one every month, to discuss patients with less than optimal outcomes. In two days, I'll be up.

Sara has been emailing me repeatedly asking for my slides for the presentation. I checked the patient's paper notes out of medical records but I haven't had the courage to open them. They've stayed in my work locker all week. I can't put it off any more. I crack open the file.

It opens onto a page of name stickers. These will never be used again. Then a consent form, filled out by another surgeon at the pre-op clinic. Tables of observations, all normal. Nothing to even hint at what came next.

Then there's the op record, written in my own shaking hand right after the surgery. My eyes hover between the words *unexpected complication, bleeding*. The tiny bloodsplatters on the top. I slam the file shut.

The nurse in charge looks up briefly, then back at her phone.

Anxiety wells up, swirls around in my gut like it always does when I think about the investigation. The inquiry. Again, I wish I could leave all this behind. The dream of escape, browsing travel sites, has become a compulsion the last two weeks. The further flung the destination, the better. As always, the one I keep coming back to is Sri Lanka. I used to visit with my parents every summer, when I was younger. But I haven't been back in sixteen years. I've longed to, but I couldn't. It was deemed to be for the best. My parents don't live there any more. Most relatives have emigrated. There's nothing there for me now. But it also means there's nobody to stop me going back.

I take out my phone. The wallpaper is now the photo of the beach in Sri Lanka, near where we used to stay when we visited. I close my eyes for a moment and I can almost feel the hot sand spilling over my flip-flops, the smell of frying kottu roti from the beach food stalls nearby. The way the palms used to rustle when it rained. My bleep sounds, pulling me into the present. I can't take a holiday now. Not when my patient has just died in surgery. Not only do I not deserve it, but I have to be here, to defend myself now. The image dissolves, the memory too. That part of my life is done.

The nurse in charge looks irritated.

'You'll wake the patients.'

'Not much I can do about my bleep,' I say.

The ward door opens with a slam. Isaac walks in, bleep in hand going off.

'Hello, doctor,' the nurse says with a smile, and not a flash of the irritation I just got.

An unfortunate rota match has put me on with Isaac tonight. I haven't seen him since the day in the mess. I've managed to avoid him tonight, but I can't ignore him when he leans over to me.

'I hear you've been banished to permanent night shifts.'

I grit my teeth.

'It's only for a few weeks. Anyway, what's it to you?'

'They had to park you where you can do least damage, right?'

I try to focus on the images on the screen. I can't let him get to me.

Isaac looks over my shoulder.

'Preparing for the meeting? Good idea, though you haven't got much time.'

I close down the scans and turn to him.

'That was a really shit thing you did the other day.'

'I was doing you a favour, letting you know sooner rather than later.'

I clench my fists under the table. I want to slap the smirk off his face.

Another nurse, Alison her name tag says, sits across from us at the nursing station. Agatha too.

'So how is the inquiry going?' Isaac asks.

'It's none of your business.'

'Your case was on the news again today,' says Alison.

'Excuse me?'

On the computer next to me, she navigates to a news site. 'Here.'

In my peripheral vision, I can see that Isaac is watching me. So I force myself to look at the screen.

It's the patient's father. He's been coming out with a new interview almost every day. In a few he's been with the health minister. I've forced myself to watch them all, so I'm not the last to know again. And it's always bad, but the worst are the ones like today's. When he's flanked by his wife. Her eyes are red-rimmed, her posture bowed. Seeing her, it hits me like a sucker punch all over again. *This is my fault.* Tears prick my eyes and I look up. I can't cry here. Not with Isaac and the nurses watching me.

'Is there something wrong with the way we train surgeons now?' he says. 'As a junior doctor I did hundreds of minor procedures supervised, and when you do that volume of work, you encounter complications and learn how to manage them. That's no longer the case. The surgeon involved was woefully unprepared.' He places a hand on his wife's arm. 'And our family have paid the ultimate price.'

The video ends. My throat is dry. I can't speak. He's wrong, I wasn't unprepared for the surgery. And I'm not a trainee. I'm a month from consultancy. What I was unprepared for is this. The fallout. The mother's face. The guilt that I'll carry for the rest of my life. Silence stretches, heavy in the quiet ward.

'So what actually happened?' Alison says. 'How did the patient . . . ?'

'Die?' I ask.

She quails, then quickly recovers.

'What happened?'

'Look up haemorrhage. That should answer your question.'

'There's no need to be like that,' the nurse in charge says. 'She was only asking.'

'It's not her, or anyone's, business.'

'But it's on the news, Anika,' Isaac says. 'They might not know who you are. But we all do. So now it's everyone's business.'

I take my bleep, stethoscope and shove them into my scrubs pocket and rush for the ward door. Relief fills me as I emerge into the darkened corridor. In the week since I've been on nights, supposedly keeping a low profile, I've encountered more and more hostility from staff like the ones on Crimson ward. Only the ones I knew well before still treat me the same. How long will this go on for? I need the inquiry to be over.

'Why did you run off?' It's Isaac, walking out of the ward.

34

'Are you following me?'

'Heading to an emergency downstairs, actually. I guess you can't relate, seeing as you're off surgical duty.'

I square up to him.

'What exactly is your problem? Is this still about that training job you didn't get? Stop being such a sore loser and get over it. I'm better than you. I was then, and I will be again.'

Isaac leans over me, his arm on the wall.

'It's not that complicated. I just don't like you.'

'Really? I remember otherwise, that night at Eliza's birthday. It seemed like you liked me a lot.'

He narrows his eyes.

'Have you got a lawyer? Because if you haven't yet, you should. I'm serious.'

'Stop pushing me, Isaac.'

He leans closer. I can smell the disinfectant from when he last scrubbed in. He's in my personal space. Trying to intimidate me.

'Is it true?' he says. 'Were you unprepared?'

'Of course not. You know my op record,' I say, then hate that I'm having to defend myself to him.

'I don't keep tabs on your surgeries, Anika,' he says in a low voice. 'But it doesn't matter anyway, because you heard what he said on the interview. The head of the Royal College of Surgeons thinks you're incompetent.'

I push past him, and I'm shaking when I reach the lift. As usual, Isaac's words hit a nerve. Before this case, I'd had excellent outcomes on all the surgeries I've ever done. Now I have an intra-operative death on my record.

My bleary-eyed reflection stares back at me from the mirror inside the lift. Is he right about getting a lawyer? I don't even know what's happening with the inquiry. I can't think clearly about it now anyway, I'm barely functioning at the end of a shift. It's nearly time for handover. I have to make it through another half an hour. It's the last of my set of nights today. After this, I'll have a few days' break. I can sleep, with the help of the tablets. And then I can figure out what to do.

Handover passes quickly. Relief washes over me as I give my bleep to the day doctor. In the changing room, I strip off my scrubs and quickly put my jeans and sweater back on. Cool morning air bathes my cheeks as I hit the back entrance of the hospital. I'm so tired it feels like my head is underwater as I walk to my car. The car park is nearly empty, it's still early. Only departing night workers and a few people on the early shift are here. My car beeps as I unlock it.

'Going already?' Isaac stands nearby, unlocking his Saab.

'Oh for fuck's sake. Stop following me.'

He laughs.

'So, I just got out of the emergency. A good outcome. The patient is recovering in ITU.'

'Congratulations.'

He leans back against his car.

'Does that make you feel bad? Knowing that you don't get to do that any more?'

I walk closer to him. 'You know, I've had enough of you tonight.'

'Well, we won't have to put up with each other for long.'

'Meaning?'

'Come on, Anika. You're not going to be working here for much longer. It's been two weeks and your case is still all over the news. The hospital won't want this hanging over their head. They won't want you. Like that last guy of yours didn't want you,' he adds, in a low voice. 'The one you followed home from the club at Eliza's birthday.'

Isaac has been needling me ever since that day in the mess. Pushing me. I bite my lip hard. Suddenly, I want to hurt him. And not with words.

'No comeback?' he says.

Before I can stop myself, my fist flies out. Connects with his jaw. Isaac recoils in surprise. Then clutches his face. I stare at my curled fist. I didn't mean to do that. But I can't suppress the satisfaction I feel when I note the blood beading on his lip.

'You're going to regret this,' he says.

'No, Isaac. You're going to regret messing with me.'

I get into my car and drive out of the car park. My fingers sting from the punch and I take my hand off the steering wheel to flex them. Did I really just punch a colleague? I don't know what happened. It was like something took over me. I try to calm my racing heart. Tell myself it's okay. At least the car park was empty. I have bigger things to worry about now. Isaac said I won't be working here for long. Is he right?

5

A jangling noise, muffled, comes from within the twisted sheets. It's my phone. The alarm is going off and it's labelled, *M and M meeting*. Oh no. I fling the sheets off me and sit up. The clock tells me I've woken up late. I was supposed to be up before two, to reset my body clock. My throat is dry and I drain the bottle of water on my bedside table. Something isn't right. I was supposed to be up before two. *Yesterday.*

I should be able to make it to the hospital in time, just. How long have I been asleep? The last thing I remember was getting back from my night shift, on Monday morning. The monthly M and M meetings are always during Tuesday lunchtimes. Have I been out cold since yesterday morning? I can't have slept for more than twenty-four hours, surely. There are remnants of food on my bedside table. A plate with toast crusts, a mug of tea, half full. I examine the crumbs on the plate. I don't remember making this. The TV is on, playing a daytime movie channel. I don't remember turning it on.

I jump to my feet. There's no time to prepare mentally for the meeting, to get a coffee with Eliza and Rosa or even eat. I brush my teeth, splash water on my face. My hair is rumpled from sleep. Was I really asleep so long? I can't think about that now. I change hurriedly in the darkened bathroom, into a blouse and black trousers I find on the towel rail. Then I grab my phone and keys and run down to my car. As I turn out of my street a call comes in from Eliza. I haven't got time to stop and answer. I'll see her soon anyway. I let it go to voicemail.

When I get to the hospital, I head straight up to the surgical wing auditorium. The semicircular rows of seats are filled with colleagues in blue scrubs. A table near the front is stocked with platters of sandwiches and fruit. The obligatory free lunch always boosts attendance but I haven't seen a morbidity and mortality meeting as full as this one before. There are even people sitting on the steps in the aisles. Eyes swivel in my direction as I stand inside the doorway and suddenly I feel like a fish in a tank. I spot Eliza in a row in the middle and I'm relieved. I squeeze through to her. I should get some of the lunch on the way, I haven't eaten since the dubious plate of toast I don't remember making, somewhere between yesterday afternoon and this morning. Even so, the churning feeling in my stomach makes the thought of food nauseating.

I stop at the row where Eliza and Rosa are sitting. On a parallel row, separated by an aisle and half of the trauma and ortho department, is Isaac. I look away quickly.

'I've been calling you,' Eliza says.

'I was asleep.'

'For that long?'

'I don't know.'

She gives me a funny look. Because who doesn't know how long they were asleep? Have the last few weeks caused something? A relapse? Is that possible, so many years later? No. I won't accept that. I can't go through it again.

'Since last night, I guess. I overslept this morning.'

Rosa leans over with a worried expression.

'Are you okay to be doing this? You've just been on nights.'

'I don't have a choice. I'll be fine, guys. Really.'

Only one row of chairs in the auditorium has remained empty. The ones at the front, reserved for the doctors presenting. Now, they start to fill. Sara and the heads of the orthopaedics department file in through a door at the front of the auditorium. Then Yana and three people I recognise from hospital management join them. This is weird. Non-clinical management don't usually come to these meetings. Only one seat at the front is empty now. Sara is looking around now. For me.

Eliza and Rosa wish me good luck as I rush down the steps to the front.

My head feels heavy, groggy. I don't know if I'm sleep-deprived or if I've overslept. I just have to get through the next hour.

'You're late,' Sara says as I reach the front.

I take off my jacket and hang it on the back of the vacant chair.

'I was post-nights.'

'You were sleeping?' She glances at my top with a look of irritation. Then I realise. The blouse I thought I'd picked off the towel rail in my sleep-befuddled state is actually a pyjama top. Plain black and satiny, but still unmistakably sleepwear. I put my jacket back on quickly.

'Should I go first?'

'Of course,' she says. 'I'll step in, if you need it.' Her annoyed tone tells me she doesn't want to. I walk to the lectern. An auditorium full of expectant faces look back at me. I've always enjoyed presenting at surgical conferences and meetings. Talking through papers I'd authored, feeling like I'd contributed to surgical advancement, in some small way. This is the opposite. I've only ever been a spectator at morbidity and mortality meetings before. Watching someone else present is bad enough. Each case is scrutinised, the presenters cross-questioned on how they could have done better. How the unfortunate outcomes could have been prevented. Now, with all these people waiting for me to explain myself, it's like going on trial.

'Take us through what happened,' Sara says.

'I finished my shift then the day cover didn't – where do you need me to start?'

'The start of the surgery would be fine.'

A PowerPoint presentation loads on the huge screen on the

wall behind me. The first slide shows details of the case. Dry, factual ones such as age, reason for the procedure. A scan flashes up next. Ordinarily, I would have seen it multiple times before the procedure, but because of my last-minute decision to operate I only viewed the scan once, right before the surgery. It's hard to imagine being so confident. Now that I know how it ends.

'This image doesn't show the tortuous nature of the patient's vessels,' I say, trying to keep my voice steady. I don't want to sound defensive. 'When I started the procedure, there was less than the expected amount of bleeding.' I need to sound calm, in control. This is a meeting of colleagues after all. It's not like the patient's parents are here. Or the health minister.

'Anika?' Mr Chavez, the head of trauma and orthopaedics department, asks from the front. I can't freeze up here. *Focus.*

'For most of the procedure, the bleeding seemed minimal. We barely needed suction. I was ready to close the incision, and . . .' Then I hit a vessel I shouldn't have. The blood vessels, so twisted together, made it a complicated, intricate procedure. And, I was so tired. What it comes down to is this. My scalpel slipped. A tiny nick, with disastrous consequences.

'And what happened then?' Sara says. I think back to my statement for the inquiry. I tried to keep it as factual as possible, talking about the anatomy and the bleeding. That's what I have to do here, too. I have to fake a calm I don't feel, project the in-control, on-top-of-things front I always have. The version of myself which has felt so out of reach these past few weeks. She's still in there. I need to find her again. I take a deep breath.

'I first assessed the anatomy—'

That's strange. The tension in the room was thick when I started. People were silent, listening. Something has changed. A ripple of whispered conversations. People huddled to look at their neighbour's phone.

'I used a splint to hold the vessels aside—'

The murmurs in the room turn louder. People are now looking at their own phones, then at me.

'Initially this was effective, but became difficult to maintain with the viscosity of the surgical environment.' I'm not imagining it, something strange is happening. I look over at Eliza. She nods but there's something strained about her posture. I've been avoiding Isaac's side of the room since I got up here. Now, though, my eyes are drawn there. He catches my eye. The first contact we've had since the morning after shift. He looks thunderous.

'I continued to apply suction,' I say, but it's no use. I've lost them. The volume is up in here, so I have to speak louder. Part of me is relieved. It's easier if no one is really listening. I can finish up and escape back to my seat. Maybe this wasn't so bad.

Sara turns round.

'Keep it down, our speaker is not done.' But now even the department heads and Yana are looking at something, on her laptop.

I try to focus on my own phone on the lectern, with my notes from my statement.

But there's a new message flashing up, obscuring my notes, on the surgical group chat. It's from a number I don't recognise. There's a link in the message, to an article in a national newspaper. My pulse sounds louder in my ears as I open it. At the top is a video, paused on two figures which look eerily familiar. With a shaking hand, I open the clip. I watch myself punching Isaac in the face. Nausea churns in my stomach. Under the clip, within the body of the article, is a transcription of the audio. And a photo of me. Under the headline. IDENTITY OF SURGEON RESPONSIBLE FOR INTRAOPERATIVE DEATH OF HEALTH MINISTER'S CLOSE FAMILY REVEALED.

My legs feel weak. I clutch the lectern for support. Everyone knows. The public. The health minister. Conversations have stopped again. The attention is back on me.

'Anika, finish up,' Sara says. But there's no point pretending I can. I can't focus on anything but this article. And the source. Who sent that message?

'I know what you're all looking at,' I say. Silence. If it was tense before, that was nothing compared to this. This is tense, times one hundred.

'Finish up with the case,' Sara says. 'We will discuss anything else later.' She's pretending like she doesn't know.

I shouldn't have hit him. I wasn't thinking straight. Or rather, I wasn't thinking at all. Isaac knows how to push my buttons. I reacted, on autopilot. I should have controlled myself better, but I was so tired. Why do the worst things happen to me when I'm tired? *Or when I'm asleep.*

I look at Isaac again. He shakes his head at me. I didn't see anyone in the car park that day. So who filmed it? A patient or visitor somewhere, who sent it to the newspaper? But how would they know it was me? The only people who would know that are other staff at the hospital. Like, another doctor.

'This was a set-up,' I say. 'Isaac tipped off the reporter, who wrote this article.'

Sara stands.

'That's enough. This meeting is over.'

No one moves. I feel like I'm watching a car crash happening. That I'm making it happen and I can't stop myself.

Now Isaac stands.

'You really think I did this? How would I know that you'd be in the car park at that specific time?'

Voices start up, the volume in the room rises quickly.

'I said, this meeting is over,' Sara shouts.

She comes over, takes me by the elbow, directing me off the stage.

'You can discuss your personal business elsewhere,' she says. 'Although by doing this, it's become the hospital's business.' I stop at the front row of chairs, filled with senior surgeons and management. Facing them, it looks a little like the panel interviews they have for fellowship posts. But so much worse. Their expressions range from varying degrees of chilly to downright hostility. If this was an interview, I'd know I'd failed before it even started.

'This article has escalated an already bad situation,' Yana says.

'I'm sorry.'

Mr Chavez sits forward. 'Isaac is a respected member of the team. Why did you attack him?'

'I – I'm sorry. Like Sara said before, it was a personal disagreement. I thought we were alone.'

'Regardless. Your behaviour was completely out of line,' snaps Sara. 'Now your anonymity is breached. You couldn't have made this worse if you tried.'

'This is unprecedented,' says one of the women on the board. She clicks her pen. I don't even know her name, only that she's important in the scheme of the hospital. And she sure seems pissed off. She's pointing the pen at me like it's a weapon. I get the feeling, then, that I've been skating on thin ice and it's about to crack.

'Go home. We'll be in touch,' says Sara.

Around us, the room has finally started to empty. The show is over. People walk up the aisles, back to their wards.

'But I didn't finish the presentation.'

'Come back for your next shift,' she says, ignoring me. 'It goes without saying that we still need you on nights.'

'But Isaac – someone, has gone out of their way to film me. To expose me. Don't you want to find out who it was?'

'That's enough, Anika,' Sara says. I know better than to keep pushing. *But this isn't fair.*

'You should leave the back way,' Yana says. 'I've just heard from security that reporters are setting up in the street outside the front entrance.'

'Reporters?'

'Judging from the search I did, you're the top story today, since it broke an hour ago,' Yana says. 'So yes, of course there are.'

'I'm sorry,' I say again. 'I've never punched anyone before. And, I didn't know anyone was watching.'

'Given the high-profile nature of the case, the strain all this has already put on the hospital,' Sara says, 'you should have been extra careful how you conducted yourself. Regardless of who was or wasn't watching.'

'We need to plan our response,' Yana says. 'We'll be in touch if we need a statement from you.'

Sara turns, like she can't even bear to speak to me further. The department heads and managers gather in a kind of huddle. I'm dismissed.

I make for the door at the back of the stage. This way, I don't have to walk through the other doctors, some of whom are still here, milling around the free lunch or lingering in their seats.

The corridor outside the auditorium is empty and I'm relieved. I hug my jacket tighter around me.

'You're lucky I'm not pressing charges.'

I turn. It's Isaac, leaning against the wall by the door out of the auditorium. I must have walked right past him.

'I'm not going to. I could, but I think you've fucked yourself over enough, without my help.'

Me and Isaac have too much history. And as badly as we've needled each other before, I never thought he would do something like this. This is different. It's personal.

'You did set me up.'

'Oh please, don't start with that again. How about an apology?'

There's a faint bruise under his left eye and I find that strangely satisfying. I shouldn't, but I do.

'I'm sorry I hit you. Now how about you admit you set me up? And that you sent the message.'

'You're losing it if you think I was somehow involved. And I don't know who sent the article either.'

'You were pretty much following me by the end of the shift.'

'So you think I had a reporter tail us both? And that I wanted to be videoed, being punched?'

He does seem genuinely incredulous. I almost believe him.

'Or you got someone else to video me. One of your ortho buddies. You wanted my name out there.'

He folds his arms.

'Okay, so you think I had someone follow us in the hope of catching a conversation that – what? How would I possibly have known you'd say what you did?'

He holds up his phone, playing the video again. I can't look away. The audio is damning. I might as well have stood on the steps of the hospital and announced that I was the one who did the surgery. And then punching him like that. I look out of control. *Unhinged. Dangerous.*

'Face it, Anika, you did this. To yourself. You made your bed. Now enjoy lying in it.'

I'm left alone in the corridor as he walks away.

I manage to avoid any staff on the way to the car park. My phone keeps going off with notifications but I ignore them. Instead of going home as Sara demanded, I drive round to the front entrance. I have to see how bad things are. I put on my sunglasses, pull my jacket collar up and park at the end of the street. Like Yana said, there is a small line of reporters, opposite the main entrance. Outside are hospital security guards and two policemen in reflective jackets. This is bad. And Isaac is right. This is all my fault. A car behind me beeps. I start the engine and drive, holding my breath as my route out takes me right past the reporters. They don't notice me. I keep driving, until I'm miles from the hospital. And I keep going. It's hours before I get home.

6

To: Anika Amarasinghe

From: jj34578@gmail.com

Subject: Appalling negligence

You should never have been allowed to operate. It's a disgrace that someone like you is employed by the NHS. Innocent lives have been put at risk by your carelessness. Disgusted.

To: Anika Amarasinghe

From: nt109850u@outlook.co.uk

Subject: You should be struck off

You should be ashamed of yourself!!! People trust you with their lives every day, and this is how you repaid that trust? You shouldn't be allowed to practise. *You shouldn't even be allowed to set foot in a hospital ever again.* I hope Oliver Hoxton makes an example of you.

7

A falling sensation jerks me awake. My bedroom is shadowed. The vestiges of a dream linger. Screaming. It's all I can recall, but it's enough to know it's one of the old nightmares. The distinct, jarring horror is familiar. Now I'm wide awake. My arm aches, and when I check it, a faint bruise has blossomed on my wrist. I must have flung it out in my sleep and hit the wooden bed frame. A sick, heavy feeling sticks to me like the sweaty sheets.

I reach for my phone for distraction, reflexively. I quickly wish I hadn't. Notifications line the lock screen. When I scroll through the alerts, another and another open up. There are forty new emails and most are from addresses I don't recognise. It's worse than yesterday. My work inbox is the default email on my phone, and since the article exposing my identity broke, my inbox has been filled with hate mail from strangers. I start looking through them but after the tenth, I don't open any more. They're all the same. Saying that I'm dangerous. That I should be struck off. Unfortunately for me, it's easy enough to find out my email address, from a piece I wrote for the hospital website last year on a robotics project I was involved with, which won a surgical advancement award. It's the first result that comes up when you search my name. Or at least it used to be. I've asked IT to take it down but they're painfully slow and it's likely too late anyway, too many spiteful strangers have my email now.

A look into my social media accounts confirms it's just as bad. I haven't posted since last year, a photo of the view from the top of a black run, on the last holiday I took. Under it now are comments relating to the case, all from today. I change my profile to private and close the app.

Out of the window, night shows. Rain lashes the darkened glass. I was so tired when I came home, I tried to nap but I lost track of time again. My sleep cycle is messed up, I have to do something about it, or things could get worse.

Opening my email again, I change my default inbox from work to my personal email address. I might not be able to stop using the email completely but I can limit how much I have to see it. While I'm in the app, another two emails have popped up already. The subject line of the first says, *go to hell.* Great. I delete it unread. As I'm about to go to settings, the second email catches my eye. This one looks like one of the many travel and housesitting sites I signed up to recently. Subject: *Opportunities in Thailand, China and Sri Lanka.* The pull to escape grows so strong, it's an ache in my gut. I open the email, scroll to the end, to the ad for a job in Sri Lanka. I've seen this one before. It caught my eye, because it uses a photo of the same beach on my phone wallpaper.

Caretaker Needed for Colonial Coastal Estate (Pre-Renovation Duties)

We're seeking a reliable live-in caretaker for a historic colonial estate on Sri Lanka's scenic coast. This role includes daily upkeep of the main house, routine cleaning, and light maintenance of the indoor and outdoor areas. You'll also assist with preparing the property for upcoming restoration work. This role offers the unique opportunity to stay within the house while overseeing its upkeep during this transitional period.

If you have a passion for historic properties and the independence required for this live-in role, please send a brief overview of your background and interest.

It's a three-week assignment and the town, Coconut Cove, is near where my family's holiday home used to be. The payment is generous. I let myself dream for a moment as I flit between the photos at the bottom of the ad. From the white columned mansion surrounded by palm trees, back to the photo of the beach I remember so well. If only I could, but I have to stay at work and stick it out. I can't give up yet. I close down my email.

8

To: Anika Amarasinghe

From: bebo103@hotmail.com

Subject: This Should Never Have Happened

I am disgusted and angry about your actions, which cost an innocent life. I hope you are held fully accountable for this tragedy. The public deserves better than this.

To: Anika Amarasinghe

From: ao0924@hotmail.com

Subject: Actions Have Consequences

You make me sick. I hope you're ready to face the consequences of your actions and quit.

To: Anika Amarasinghe

From: Sara Peele

Subject: Next Steps

Hi Anika,

The surgical department and hospital board of directors have discussed how best to manage the current situation which has become far more problematic than we anticipated. You will likely have seen from the extensive media coverage recently that the patient's father is now looking to take legal action, with the support of Health Minister Oliver Hoxton. Unfortunately, with all this going on we have no choice but to suspend you from work. With the ongoing investigation, it is difficult to say how long this will be for. I strongly advise you to seek legal advice in the interim. We will be in touch with further developments if they arise.

Take care,

Sara Peele

9

'Rise and shine.'

I turn over, facing the back of the floral couch. Hideous pink and mustard petals stare back at me. I hate this couch. It came with the flat, I always meant to change it but never had time. Because I was too busy working. Now, this couch is my constant companion. I screw my eyes tightly shut.

The front door closes with a click. Light footsteps sound on the wooden floor. Eliza. Of course it is – she's the only one with a spare key. And the only one of my friends that visits any more.

The couch dips, a hand rocks my shoulder gently.

'You alive?'

I don't answer. Eliza sits on the edge of the couch, on my feet.

'Sorry, that was thoughtless. I mean, are you awake? It's nearly dark.'

'What time is it?' My throat is dry. It's been three weeks since my suspension. Without my usual routines of shifts at the hospital, sporadic and fitted around work social life, or anything that resembles a normal life, I've lost track. The past three weeks I've lived in a void, marked by the changing light outside the window. My only consolation is that without all the night shifts, I'm back to sleeping and waking at more normal intervals.

'Nearly eight. Please tell me you've been outside today.'

'I have.' My main daily venture out is to the supermarket. The Sainsbury's on the corner or the Tesco Express, two streets down. Or sometimes the Waitrose fifteen minutes' walk away. I wear sunglasses, always use the self-checkout and don't linger. I never go to the same place two days in a row and absolutely never the smaller newsagents, not any more. I learned my lesson after I went to one the week after my identity came out and the shopkeeper recognised me from the front page of the newspaper I was buying. Curious customers crowded round, shouted their opinions at me. All the same. All bad.

Eliza picks up the newspaper on the coffee table.

'Why do it to yourself?'

I know, keeping up with the stream of articles seems bizarre. Masochistic. But I need to know what they're saying about me. The headlines have become more inventive since the first one with the video. UNDER THE KNIFE, OVER HER HEAD: SURGEON SEWS UP DISASTER. CUTTING IT CLOSE. THE DOCTOR WILL SEE YOU NOW – AND YOU WON'T SURVIVE. I kept some, a collection of ripped-out newspaper pages thrown into a box file under my bed. A kind of macabre scrapbook of the past three weeks. Eliza doesn't know about that.

'I like to keep on top of things.'

'Looks like it.' Eliza doesn't bother to disguise the sarcasm in her voice. I think she's getting fed up with me wallowing. It isn't her style. Nor mine, before.

'I'm sorry for what happened. It was a horrible accident and it's not fair that you've been put through the wringer like this. And it's not fair how the hospital are treating you.'

'They think it was my fault, remember? My name only got out because I hit Isaac.'

'Even so. I mean, I get it. I've wanted to hit Isaac before. And they should have been more supportive, but management only look out for themselves at the end of the day. Regardless, you can't hide away any more. You're—' She looks around the disordered flat, dishes piling up in the sink, clothes strewn on the floor, curtains half open. 'You're imploding. You can't let them do this to you. You have to get out there.'

I shift position on the couch, facing her.

'And do what? I don't have a job.'

'You do. It's a temporary suspension. They'll lift it once the investigation is over.'

I flick through today's *Metro*. I've been relegated to page 3. That's something.

'It's not going to be over.' I show her the headline. DOCTOR HEADED FOR THE DOCKS AS FAMILY PILE ON THE PRESSURE OVER SURGICAL NEGLIGENCE.

An angry expression darkens Eliza's face.

'They need to fuck off. How's everything with the lawyer?'

On Sara's advice I panicked and found one, a university friend of Rosa's fiancé Ravi. Supposedly he's a specialist in my kind of case, although from his website it seemed most of his work is actually the opposite, *against* professionals like me in cases of medical negligence.

'I don't know. He's so far provided only vague advice and charged me a lot for it.' Embarrassingly, my bank account is almost drained. I near cleaned myself out when I bought this flat a few months ago. I thought, with the end of the frequent moves associated with my training in sight, I could settle, finally. Put down some roots, in a place of my own. I sunk all my savings into it. And most of my pay is going on the lawyer.

Eliza busies herself around the kitchenette, straightening and tidying.

'I'll do that.'

She looks up from loading the dishwasher.

'Sweetie, you're barely up to a shower these days, let alone housework. Speaking of, why don't you go ahead?'

'Are you sure?'

She shakes her head and smiles.

'Just go.'

The back and forth over the housework is part of our routine now. Eliza has been coming almost daily since everything happened. Long after the rest of my friends petered off. The first week or two after I was suspended, they tried. Phone calls, messages, offers of drinks that I refused. As the media coverage escalated, they stopped contacting me at all. Eliza has been checking on me daily, bringing me healthier food than the toast and Diet Coke that have made up most of my daily fare. She's been keeping me afloat. Sometimes I wonder if the solidarity Rosa and the others showed at the beginning was only because Eliza told them to. I don't deserve it. I don't deserve a friend like her.

Eliza holds up my phone, ringing.

'Want to get this?'

It's already gone to voicemail by the time I reach the phone. When I listen, I feel terrible for not picking up. Her voice is thinner and reedier on the recorded message than when I spoke to her last week. I feel bad for my grandmother, caught up in all this. I tried to keep it from her but thanks to the health minister's involvement, it became a minor international news item and my parents in Canada came to know about the case. Which of course meant my grandmother did too. My parents don't care that their daughter has become target practice for the British press. Or at least they haven't yet shown that they do. We barely speak, anyway. It's fallen to my eighty-year-old achiamma to pick up the pieces. Or try to, from the other side of the world. Her voicemail asks me to call her back. Under the missed call alert is a new email. The subject is *Sri Lanka Job Opportunity*. Last night, trawling through hate mail, I found the advert again and this time I replied. The email is from a Mr Fonseca. I open it quickly.

> Thanks for your email. The position is still available. As mentioned in the ad, the duties will involve some cleaning, light maintenance and generally keeping the house secure before contractors start restoration work. Please let me know if you're available and interested, and we can discuss further details.

I head to the bathroom, taking my phone with me. Shutting the door, I sit on the closed toilet and read the email again. There are more photos of the property attached. The interior with high ceilings, marble floors and an aesthetically pleasing mix of local wooden and European antique-looking furniture. A garden, with palm trees, trailing hibiscus and lush vegetation. The last photo shows a long veranda which wraps around the exterior. Beyond it is a stretch of beach, white sand extending to the azure sea in the distance. The longing to leave hits again, so hard I squeeze my phone in my hand. It's beautiful, this assignment sounds like a dream. The payment plus expenses is generous. As my finger hovers over reply, I hesitate. I want it and I don't, in equal measure. Is going back to Sri Lanka a good idea? There's a reason my family left all those years ago, why we haven't been back. That reason is me. If I go back, all the feelings, the demons I've tried to keep at bay will surely return. How will I be able to handle it?

I shiver as I climb into the little shower cubicle. A selection of expensive shower gels line the shelf inside. Lavender-scented to help me sleep after a night shift, orange blossom or ylang-ylang for after long day shifts on call. Showers at home used to be my favourite way to unwind after work. Hot water soothing muscles that ached from hunching over the operating table. Surgery is physical work. Flesh is more resistant than it looks. It takes pressure to cut through layers of skin and fat and muscle right, or to hold retractors straight. It takes practice. It takes controlled force. But the shower I took that awful day after the surgery hasn't left me. Now, whenever I shower I get flashbacks, of blood swirling down the drain. Now, I get in and out as quick as I can.

As I dry off, I catch a glimpse of myself in the mirror. My hair is tangled and wild, my balayage well overdue for a retouch. And my face looks pallid, my complexion sallow. I don't feel like myself any more and I don't look like myself either. I can't carry on like this. Sri Lanka might be a bad idea. But it might not. It could be the escape from everything that I so badly need. Taking a chance is better than letting them break me down. I can't stay and watch as they try. Standing in my towel, I open the email again. I hit reply.

When I come out of the misty bathroom the lounge is tidy, the waffle throw I was using as a blanket neatly folded on the couch. Eliza looks over from the open fridge.

'Better?' she asks.

Cleaner, yes. Better, no. Not yet. I fix a smile on my face.

'Much.'

I should call Achiamma back. And I should tell her. Nerves flutter in my stomach as I press her name.

She answers in three rings.

'*Kohomada, duwa?*' How are you, daughter? She's always called me that. My grandmother has been more of a mother than my real mother ever was. I have to get this out before she can give me another well-meaning pep talk about moving on. And before I lose the nerve.

'I have something to tell you. It's about a job.'

Eliza looks up from making tea with a questioning look. I mouth, *I'll tell you later*, then turn away.

'What is it? Another surgical post? Your father said you are banned from work.'

I didn't tell her about the suspension. I'm about to explain I'm suspended, not banned, then I realise it comes to the same thing.

'You spoke to Thātha?' I know they talk about me, but it would be nice if he showed some of this concern to my face, or at least on the phone, once in a while. Then again, it's probably for the best we don't talk. I don't have to hear his disappointment in me first hand.

'What is this job then?' she asks, like I didn't say anything.

'Looking after a house. A short-term thing. Three weeks. It will give me something to do. The assignment sounds okay and it's well paid.'

'What do you have to do?'

'A bit of cleaning, waiting for some contractors to start work on it. It should be easy.'

'*Owe, né?* It sounds good.' Wow. She must think things are bad if she's immediately okay with me taking a job that has no educational requirements. My family, like most older generation Sri Lankans I know, are nothing if not elitist. This tells me more about how worried she is than anything else. But I'm relieved not to meet with resistance. Not yet.

'Where is it?'

I steel myself.

'Remember the house in Sri Lanka?'

There's a pause.

'Yes, of course,' she says. I'm surprised at the breezy tone, the quick recovery. Like she's forgotten what happened the last time we were there. When of course she hasn't. None of us can. It was a long time ago, but something like that doesn't go away. However much you want it to.

I lean on the kitchen worktop. My dad's work was split between Sri Lanka and London so he had a second home there and we used to visit every summer holiday, sometimes Christmas too. I'd stay for weeks at a time, it felt more like home than London. Until – that time. Then we never went back. I remember the house though, like it was yesterday. The garden that wound round the side, full of fragrant bougainvillea. The balconies, the high white stone walls that hid the house from curious eyes on the busy street beyond. I pull myself back into the present with an effort.

'It's near there. A coastal town called Coconut Cove.'

She gives a sharp intake of breath.

'This job is in Sri Lanka?'

'I thought it would be good. I've wanted to go back and I thought it could, I don't know, give me some closure.'

'Do your parents know?' The breezy tone is gone, disapproval drips from her words.

'Of course not, we haven't spoken in months.'

'I don't think this is a good idea, duwa. Don't go back. Let the past be.'

I bite back tears. My grandmother has almost always supported me. But it looks like this is too much, even for her.

'I've accepted the job.'

'I see.'

'I think it would help.'

She sighs.

'Aren't things bad enough already? Don't go there and make things worse. For your own sake, please listen to me.'

I take a deep breath.

'I will be going. I wish you could support me on this, but if you can't, that's okay. I understand.'

She's quiet for a while, I'm about to ask if she's still there when she speaks.

'You're an adult now, I can't stop you. Maybe enough time has passed. At least you can speak the language. And I can come there if you need me.'

I stifle a smile. As if I would ever request my elderly grandmother get on a plane for me. It's sweet that she's willing though. And I'm relieved that she's on board, however reluctantly.

'Thank you. I'll call you before I leave.'

Eliza comes over.

'What was all that?'

My phone vibrates with an alert. A reply arrives from Mr Fonseca.

> Thank you for your email and for accepting the housesitting position. I'm thrilled to have you on board and will be sending you more details on the house and the location shortly. Please let me know when you are able to arrive. If you have any questions in the meantime, don't hesitate to contact me.

It feels like a sign. Outside, rain patters on the window, blurring the view of the street. I remember the photos of the beach by the house, the bright sky and inviting water, and a smile spreads over my face.

I turn to her.

'I'm going to Sri Lanka.'

PART TWO

The Escape
පලායාම/தப்பித்தல்

10

'We will shortly be landing in Bandaranaike International Airport.'

The plane wheels touch down with a bump that jolts my head from the headrest. Out of the small plane window, the tarmac is busy with shuttle buses. Beyond the runway, I can see dense foliage and the flat-roofed airport buildings. I'm really here. I follow the crowd of passengers to the exit. I managed to sleep most of the flight, without the sleeping pill I have stashed in my hand luggage. After I got the email from Mr Fonseca yesterday, I found the next flight out which departed late last night. He deposited the money for the flights as promised, and now, a little over twenty-four hours later, I'm here. It all happened quicker than I expected. So quickly that it didn't feel real. But it's starting to.

Ahead of the plane doors, heat shimmers in the air like a mirage. As I exit, it hits me, a thick kind of heat that surrounds me, seeps into my pores and makes me sweat immediately. This is nothing like the cold drizzle that followed me to Gatwick Airport this morning. This heat is familiar, though it's been so long. All the holidays in the years since I left, to warm climes like Thailand, Bali, the Caribbean, I felt hints of this but it was never quite the same. This diesel-choked heat with a hint of the sea is what I've been missing. I feel hopeful for the first time in over a month. I peel off the blue sweater I put on this morning and wave goodbye to the flight attendants as I head for immigration.

My tattered black Samsonite is one of the first to appear

at baggage reclaim. I'm used to packing meticulously with lists and shopping trips and capsule wardrobes. Last night I packed quicker than I've packed for anything before, throwing clothes, toiletries and flip-flops into my bag in a jumble. The only thing I took care over was my medication wallet. When I told Eliza that I was going to Sri Lanka, she said I was running away. That it was too soon, that I needed to think it through. After Achiamma's response, Eliza's lukewarm reaction kind of hurt even if it is true. I am running away but it feels like I'm doing the right thing. And when she saw me off last night, Eliza said it was for the best.

Arrivals is teeming with drivers holding placards and families having tearful reunions. There's no one waiting for me. When we used to visit, Achiamma, aunties, uncles and cousins would meet us at the airport and drive us back to the family house. But then everything changed. Achiamma and my parents are in Toronto now and, over the years, my relatives dispersed around the globe. Only a few distant ones are here, in far-flung rural provinces. I dodge a group of girls taking a selfie by the airport sign. I prefer it this way. No questions, no explanations. Just anonymity.

On my way out, I stop at the airport lockers as per the instructions from Mr Fonseca. I locate locker 33 and unlock it with the combination from the email. Inside is a kind of welcome pack he said he'd leave for me. In a large envelope is an international SIM card, preloaded with data because he said there's no Wi-Fi. There's a sheaf of papers with instructions, a little like the information booklets in hotel rooms but this is rather more brief. There's a map of the area with the directions to the town marked on it. A piece of paper typed with information such as where to find the sheets and pillows for the bed and that I can drink the tap water. There's also a bunch of keys. Several heavy ones and some small ones too. It looks like the bunches of keys ward sisters carry in the hospital, with keys for the drug cupboards and back-up ones for the doors in case the electronic ID system ever fails. As one of the more senior-ranking surgeons on the permanent ward roster, I had a set too. I handed it in with my ID badge and the rest of my work-related belongings when I was suspended. I slam the locker shut.

With no one to pick me up I navigate the stream of taxis at the airport entrance. I have no idea how much the fare is supposed to be so I summon up the little Sinhala I can from the recesses of my brain and approach the man at the head of the queue of white minivans that serve as airport taxis.

'*Keyuk the?*' How much. I can't remember the rest. My grandmother was overly optimistic when she said I speak the language. I did, my spoken Sinhala used to be passable, but after years without much exposure, I'm rusty. 'To Fort Road,' I finish, showing him the rest of the address on my phone. He frowns, probably thinking of the two hours' drive. Then he nods and quotes a figure in rupees. It's likely extortionate, it was always going to be, as soon as he heard my English accent. I don't have the energy to haggle. In pounds, it's not too bad.

'Okay.'

He loads up my luggage while I sit in the back, on cracked leather seats with thin red-and-yellow-striped seat covers. The van pulls away. From traffic-choked streets outside the airport, into a wide road lined with palm trees. Road signs zoom past, written in English, Sinhala and Tamil. Then clean highways, manicured hillocks, the shiny surface of a reservoir. It's not how I remember. Last time I made this journey, the country was less developed. The signage was poor, the city was dirtier, more raw. Now, skyscrapers, apartment buildings, scaffolding and cranes, all the hallmarks of development, line the roads.

Soon, we're out of the city. On the right, the view opens up. A thin blue belt of sea that widens to a pale turquoise expanse, kicking up waves of white foam. I lean closer to the window.

Trapped for so long in a cycle of work and survival, it's been too long since I've seen the sea. I peer through the grimy glass, drinking in the view. I've missed it. Small towns appear, full of square buildings with corrugated-tin roofs. Colourful wooden boats turned upside down on the grass between them, resting before their next catch. It looks so different to London and the contrast feels like relief.

The driver hits a pothole. The plastic Ganesha on a chain hanging from his mirror bumps up and down. I close my eyes for a second.

When I wake, near-darkness shows out of the window. Where am I? I sit up quickly. My head is woozy and my neck aches. I must have been sleeping awkwardly. If there is any other way to sleep, in this uncomfortable van.

'Where are we?'

The driver glances at me in his mirror.

'Ma'am is awake. We are nearly there. Past Galle.'

'Oh.'

That's two hours and then some that I've been asleep. A few minutes later, he comes to a stop.

'We're here.'

I count out the fare in rupee notes, fresh from the foreign exchange in London, telling him to keep the change. Then I jump out onto the pavement. A street lamp illuminates the road ahead. There's the coastline, the swathe of sand lined with hotels. But they're darkened.

'Are you sure this is it?'

The driver dumps my bag onto the pavement, then slams the door shut.

'This is the address you gave.' He points. I make out a building at the end of the road. Its shadow casts long and wide across the street. But where is everything else? Where are the seaside mansions, the restaurants and bars bustling with tourists? The huge five-star hotels that line the coast are darkened. My family's house was just a short drive away and I don't remember seeing an empty street like this there.

'I don't think this is the right place,' I say to the driver, now back in his seat, the door closed.

He shrugs.

'This is the only Fort Road in the area.' He starts the engine. 'I live in Colombo. It's late. I have to get back.' He holds his hands up. 'I can't help you. Sorry.' Then he's gone, in a cloud of exhaust.

With no other options, I walk down the street. Soon, I realise the hotels aren't just dark. They're not there at all. There's only one, the Raj, and it's little more than a building site. Half a sign that tells me I'm in the right place. It looks abandoned. There's something in the air under the heat, a kind of damp feeling, like rain is due. It's nearly monsoon. It's not high tourist season, maybe that's why things are so quiet today. But it's strange; from what I saw on the way here, the rest of the country is undergoing major development. Whereas here seems forgotten. What has happened here?

I reach the end of the street. One house stands at the end. But wait – this doesn't look right. The facade is yellowed and streaked with moss, the stone pillars flanking the entrance are cracked. The ornate scroll carvings along the edge of the roof are crumbling. My heart sinks. This isn't the white-walled mansion from the photos in the email. I drop my suitcase at my feet with a loud thud.

Footsteps sound behind me. A man, tall, wearing jeans and a white T-shirt. He looks around my age. He looks – normal, I think. Not dangerous. I keep my fingers curled around the bunch of keys in my pocket anyway.

'Excuse me,' I call.

The man comes closer.

'Can I help you?' he says, in the kind of accent that screams of elocution lessons. I decide to continue in English.

'Is this number 23, Fort Road?'

He points to the sign at the end of the road. Sinhala letters, Tamil, then English underneath. කොටුව පාර. கோட்டை வீதி. Fort Road.

'Is there another Fort Road?' I ask, even though I know it's unlikely.

The man shakes his head. Then he switches to rapid Sinhala. I try to follow but he talks so fast, and try as I might, I can't make sense of it. The only word I understand is *ayei*. Why.

'Why what?'

'*Ehey yannah eppā.*' The words sound familiar. It's there, the understanding, behind a veil I can't quite reach.

'English?'

He shakes his head, then he turns away.

'Wait,' I call, but he doesn't. He disappears round the corner. Then it's just me and a few crows, pecking in the dirt at the foot of a coconut palm. This place looks nothing like the photos. So much for the luxurious all-expenses-paid beach stay I had envisioned. It was too good to be true. After everything else that has gone wrong, why did I think this trip would be any different? I rub my temples.

There's a sound in the background, rhythmic, low and rumbling. I follow it. It leads me behind the house and when I see the source, I draw breath sharply. Behind the house is a wide sweep of beach. A moody, darkened sea beats against the rocks at the shore. This, at least, looks like the pictures. Its soothing cadence draws me like a siren song. I peel off my shoes and socks and bury my toes into the hot sand. The damp feeling in the air intensifies and the wind picks up, making the palm trees sway around me. This house isn't what I was expecting, but still, it's better than London right now. And maybe the inside is nicer.

11

Dayani

The sun hangs low on the horizon, bathing the empty beach in a reddish hue. They should have been home hours ago. It was only when the beach was nearly empty, tourists and backpackers already gone, that they realised they'd stayed out too long.

'Wait up,' Dayani calls to her two companions. The older, the boy, turns, laughs. '*Ickmung karanna.*'

'I am hurrying, Avila,' she calls back. She knows she is supposed to call him *aiya*, older brother, as is customary here with older friends. But she doesn't think of him in a brotherly way. Hasn't for a long time. So she calls him by his name.

'No you're not. Your amma is going to be so mad at us.' Emphasis on *us*. Because of course her mother will blame all of them, not just her own daughter. She hates her friends to be in trouble on her account. They'd been exploring a new bay Avila discovered today, attempting to surf on a surfboard his friends had made from driftwood, sanded smooth and painted blue. They lost track of time. Her legs are covered in cuts, her arms bruised from all the falls but she feels alive. He points to the rock face. 'Let's take the short cut back.'

It's the quickest way to the road. Of the three of them, she is the least accustomed to climbing. She never liked this rock much. With a path much easier to traverse off the beach, to go this way feels like an unnecessary risk. But they are late and needs must.

She shifts her weight forward and climbs, her feet finding footholds. Steady.

Behind them, the beach stretches for miles. Empty. The pale sand darkens under the setting sun. Palm trees line the shore, their trunks gnarled. Their fronds sway in the breeze, casting shadows that look almost like someone down there. Moving.

Her right hand slips for a second. Adrenaline fizzes in her veins as she grips the rock harder. *Don't look down.* She keeps her eyes trained on the patch of grass at the top as she takes the climb. Dayani breathes easier when she reaches the top. Pulling herself over the edge, she sits and waits for the others.

Avila clambers up the rock face, easily, like a cat. Like it's nothing, not slippery, rain-slicked rock. His sister follows, not without a disapproving glance up at Dayani first. She's noticed this recently, the disapproval. An undertone that cuts through the friendship they once had. Dayani doesn't know exactly what she's done wrong or why things have changed. Maybe she suspects some of what she feels for her brother. Even if he doesn't seem to know himself.

'Ane enna ko,' Dayani shouts down to him. *Oh come on.* 'What are you, a turtle?' She likes to rile him. She knows he likes it too. She's rewarded with his mischievous smile, one she's come to know well.

'Says the girl who was too scared to race me.'

'Hardly. I know what a sore loser you are.'

He laughs. Then he climbs faster, and he's nearly at the top. His sister is slower, near the bottom. She's not a natural climber like Avila, her movements more laboured, but still, she's making good progress, a few feet below him.

'Next time, I go first,' he says to Dayani. 'Unless you're scared?'

'Never.'

He reaches for the overhang at the top to pull himself up.

Then his right hand slips. He loses his grip. Dayani freezes as she watches him struggle, his left arm swinging, his right hand scrambling at the wet rock. His sister shouts his name. Her eyes meet Dayani's for a moment and Dayani sees fear there.

Then she moves swiftly, grabbing his left arm. Avila is bigger than her, she can't hold his weight. Her arm strains and for a moment she thinks he might pull her down too. Then he gains grip with his right hand. The weight on her arm relaxes. She falls back into a sitting position on the grass. Avila pulls himself over the edge. She breathes easier as he clambers up. At the top, he pushes sweaty hair out of his eyes, breathing hard.

'Thanks for the save.'
'No problem.'
He grins. Like nearly falling didn't even faze him.
'I had it though.'
'Sure you did.' She slaps him on the shoulder. 'Great idea to take the short cut when it's just rained.'
'You want to try another time? You do owe me a race.'
'You have got to be joking.'
He shakes his head.
'Admit you're scared.'
'Fine. You're on. Next time.'
He laughs.
'You bet. *Enna.*' Let's go.

12

Anika

Dust. The first thing I notice when I open the heavy front door. Dust on the stone floor, so thick I leave footprints. A thick layer on the low wooden table in the middle, on the teak chairs, shrouded in plastic sheets. A waterfall of motes dance in shafts of light, filtered through slats of the closed blinds. I swipe a damp lock of hair off my neck. The heat in here is oppressive. I wonder how long it's been, since anyone was in the house.

In the living room, two teak couches with rattan backs and a low coffee table. Propped in the corner are a mop and a bucket filled with household sprays and cloths. These must be my cleaning supplies. A curtain separates the living room from the next room. When I part it, I find a dining room. Cobwebs cross the ceiling fan in the centre. Underneath is a long wooden table with eight chairs. A sideboard sits under the window. The surface is dusty and when I move closer there are patterns in it, like fingers trailed through the dust. Maybe the owners, or workmen. I make a mental note to ask Mr Fonseca when someone was last in here.

In the photos attached to his email, the rooms had been light, full of colonial-style wooden furniture, bright pictures and cushions, trailing pot plants. But now, I don't see anything to identify who lived here. This place is like the skeleton of the house in the pictures. It smells musty inside. Of old, forgotten things. I wonder how many people have passed through here. What stories this house could tell.

Two sets of stone stairs lead up from the back of the house. I take the set of steps nearest me but there's nothing at the end. I couldn't tell from downstairs. An arched opening conceals it from view, but up here I can see that it's only empty wall. I touch the whitewashed stone. A dead end.

I try the second set of stairs. At the top is a dimly lit landing. The heat is so thick up here, I can practically taste it. It's getting dark now and I want more than anything to crash. There are five doors upstairs. One reveals an empty room, another is locked. I try the keys from my bunch in turn but none of them work. In this old place, perhaps the door has jammed, the wood rotted shut. I turn to the room across the landing.

The door creaks open. Tarnished brass lamps are mounted on the wall. I flick one on and a faint light illuminates a space lined with shelves, all crammed with books. This must be a library. The ceiling moulding is carved with intricate patterns and crossed with cobwebs. The air smells of old paper and faintly of mildew. In the centre of the room sits an oak desk, its surface littered with pages, like someone has just left. When I examine them I find architectural plans. Mr Fonseca must have been planning for the contractors. He said there would be restoration work. He could have told me more, so I would know better how to prepare. Then again he didn't mention the house was a near wreck, so he seems to have a flexible relationship with the truth.

I inspect the titles on the shelves, most in Sinhala and Tamil. When I take one out the cover nearly comes off in my hand. I put it back hastily. Some English books on a middle shelf look newer, the coating of dust on these is less thick. There are books on the spice trade, colonialism in Ceylon, one on ghosts and legends of Sri Lanka. Artefacts are displayed in a glass case on the wall. A vase, a stuffed bird of paradise, its feathers streaked with grime.

I avoid its beady eyes as I turn to the object next to it, an antique knife with a gold hilt, shiny like someone has recently polished it. Not like the other objects in this room. It's strange, the rest of the house is devoid of personal possessions but this room is crammed with them. I glance again at the architectural drawings on the desk. Maybe Mr Fonseca, or whoever lived here, needed something from this room that they didn't want to move out. The books, plans or something else relevant to the work due to happen on the place. Did Mr Fonseca live here? His email said he was the owner so I assumed he did, but looking around the dusty room, I wonder. As I bend to look closer at the shelves, something makes me stop short. In the shadows by the wall, eyes glint.

My heart rate ratchets up. But as I move closer I realise it's a mask. A wooden *yakkā* mask, mounted on the wall. This isn't like the brightly coloured ones my relatives have in their houses as good-luck charms. This is unpainted, old and weathered. There's something primeval about its bulging eyes, the carved serpents curving upwards, either side of its face. These kinds of masks were used for exorcisms or to ward off evil spirits. In some areas they still are. I back out of the room, shutting the door.

I'm relieved to find a bed frame with a straw mattress in the next room. Not exactly comfortable, but at least I can sleep here. I was starting to worry I'd have to camp out on one of the lounge couches. The final room contains a wooden cabinet, white paint chipping off the sides. Faded newspaper lines the surface of a dressing table. I make out a date on one, two years ago. I move the newspaper closer and a silverfish slithers out, making me jump.

Who am I kidding? I can't make a go of this. This place is a dump. A lot of things are starting to make sense. Why Mr Fonseca advertised on an international email blast for this job, instead of getting a local. No local person, having seen this place, would willingly do it. I should have asked more questions. But I was so desperate for an escape that I didn't question anything. I know barely anything about Mr Fonseca, or this place. He's duped me. The mirror on the dressing table is misted. My blurred reflection looks back, long wavy hair in disarray, make-up running in the heat. How have things got so bad that taking this assignment felt like my only option? For most of my life I wanted to be a surgeon. That's the problem with defining yourself by your career. Without it, you don't know who you are.

I smack the cabinet with my palm. It shakes. A door at the base bursts open and a large cardboard box drops out. White material spills from it onto the floor. I examine it and realise it's the pillows and bedsheets the owner mentioned. A little rough but they're clean and they'll make the straw mattress more comfortable. This isn't over yet. I gather the sheets in my arms. As I do, the box upturns and something falls out with a loud crack. It's a silver frame, tarnished with age. In it is a picture of three children standing on a pier, with their backs to the camera, facing a stormy sea. The photo is grainy, it must be years old. Who are they? I search the cupboard but there's nothing else there. Nothing that will give me any answers. I put it on the dressing table.

Taking the sheets into the room with the bed, I spread them out, tucking them tight around the mattress. Then I push the bed over the stone floor, up into the corner under the window. I'm sweating even more when I finish. There are ceiling fans in every room but with all the dust, I don't want to take my chances turning them on. I'll opt for what little natural air con I can get instead. There's a very basic bathroom with a cracked sink and toilet, a tap on the wall that looks like the closest I'll get to a shower in here. I wash there, change into my PJs and sit on the bed, my back against the wall. I check my phone. Eliza has replied with a thumbs-up emoji, and *send pics*. Yeah, right. My current reality is far short of her far-flung tourist expectations. I have one bar of reception, enough for me to reply with *okay, later*. I text Achiamma too, that I've arrived and settled in. Telling either of them the truth, worrying them more, is out of the question. Tomorrow, I'll explore the area. See if there's anywhere else I can stay if need be.

In a reflex move, I almost open my social media apps. I had to delete my old accounts, because of the abuse I was getting when the story broke. But I made another, *ao9789*, so I could keep track of the stories about me. I hover over the app, then close it down. I'm here now. It's time to stop checking. I delete the app.

Cracking open the window, I pull the black steel rod onto the casing to keep it ajar. Outside, it's dark now. The beach is deserted. The sea is choppier, the waves loud. It's not like the manicured hotel beaches that I remember. This is wild, untamed. Better. I open the window wider.

Cicadas chirp, seagulls call. The salty breeze is refreshing. A memory comes out of nowhere and blossoms. Being a child, playing on the beach with the local children. I haven't thought of it in years but now I examine the memory, cling to it. A reminder of a time, a version of myself that existed before. Maybe coming here wasn't such a bad idea after all. I let the roar of the ocean lull me to sleep.

A patient lies on the stretcher before me, covered in sterile drapes. Around the table are people in scrubs. I don't recognise them. But they're watching, waiting for me to start. I'm holding a scalpel but my hands don't feel right. They shake, visibly. Why? I've done this hundreds of times before. I look down at my gloves and – they're spotted with red. Blood. Blood on the white-tiled floor, on my white clogs. Blood soaking the legs of my scrubs, turning the pale blue to murky brown.

Suddenly, the operating theatre shifts and is gone, water in its place. A wave crashes over my head. Water slips between my fingers, fills my mouth and nose. I try to breathe but I can't. I try to call for help but no words come out.

Then I hear shouting. A refrain, over and over. *Ehey yannah eppā.* I've heard the words before but I don't know what they mean. The waves splash harder, pull closer to me. I can't fight it. I don't want to. I let the water pull me under.

My heart is racing. I open my eyes. And when I do, I suddenly feel dizzy. I'm standing, a foot on the ledge of the open window. Directly under my bare foot is a drop, two floors, though it looks much further. A group of rocks, jagged and treacherous at the bottom, and the sea, churning angrily at their base. My breath hitches; I clutch the frame tighter and haul myself back in, falling hard onto the bed. Hot sweat prickles on my back; my hair is stuck to my neck. Bright sunlight streams in through the open window, disorientating me. In the dream it was night. It felt so real. But now, I can barely remember anything else. Except the words. They repeat in my head like a refrain. *Ehey yannah eppā.* I pull myself up, gather the twisted sheets and fold them with shaking hands. I tried to deny it the past few weeks, but my worst fears have come true. It's happening. Again.

Parasomnia. That's what the doctors called it. A sleep disorder, which for me resulted in waking up in strange places, with no recollection of how I got there. Last time, the worst time, was when I was here, in Sri Lanka. I fold the sheets haphazardly. I started medication and the parasomnias stopped. I haven't had one since I was seventeen. The sleep specialist said it was over. I believed him.

I have to get out of here. Clear my head. I rush to the room with the dressing table, where I left my suitcase. The photo frame on the dressing table catches my eye. Now, in daylight, I can see it better. As I examine it, the pier, the sea behind, trigger something.

The dream rushes back to me. Water. Screaming. Something clicks into place. Snatches of words I'd heard years ago, mixed with words from the dream. The same ones the man said, last night. Now I know what they mean. He was talking about the house. *Ehey yannah eppā*. It means, don't go in there.

13

Anika

Then

'One more drink.' Eliza gestures at Anika with her glass. Vodka splashes out with the movement. The dance floor is packed with their friends dancing around them. The tables in their section of the bar are littered with empty glasses and bottles.

'I don't think that's a good idea.'

Rosa comes over.

'So the surprise party is going down well.'

'A little too well.' Anika nods towards Eliza, who is now standing on a chair.

'We need to get her home.'

Rosa follows her eye.

'It's going to be tough. It's barely midnight.'

'I know, but she's wasted. I'm going to get her some water. And then a cab.'

'I heard that. No water,' Eliza says. 'Shots.' She tosses her birthday crown in the air, tries to catch it and stumbles. Anika puts an arm out to stop her falling.

'One water. Not optional.'

'Fine. Then shots.'

Ravi bangs on the table.

'Tequila for the birthday girl!'

Their friends gathered around them take up the chant of *shots*.

Eliza tries to climb down from the chair and falls into a sitting position.

'Thanks for organising such an awesome birthday for me.'

'You're welcome. I'll be back in a bit.'

'Don't worry, I'll keep her away from the shots until you're back,' Rosa says in a low voice. She turns to Ravi. 'Hold off on the drinks. Seriously.'

Anika picks her way through the packed space. A group of men in expensive-looking suits is blocking her way to the bar. One of them is facing her. His blond hair is messy, his stocky physique suggests rugby player. Is it her imagination, or is he looking at her? The man smiles. Anika looks away quickly.

'Excuse me.' She keeps heading straight and they move aside. He's not her type. He looks like a typical banker. Not that surgeons are much better. Anika reaches the bar. She sneaks another look at the man as they wait. He says something and his friends laugh, he does too. There's something boyish and endearing about his smile. She turns away.

'Two waters,' she says to the barman.

'You on an early tomorrow too?'

It's Isaac. Eliza likes Isaac so Anika invited him. Even though she would rather not have.

'I am, but it's not just for me. Eliza needs to sober up or she'll end up blacking out at her own party.'

'You're a good friend.'

Anika studies him. Hmm, no hint of sarcasm.

'You're not usually nice to me.'

He smiles slightly.

'You're not so nice to me either.'

'It takes two, I suppose.'

He leans back, resting his elbows on the bar.

'I was thinking. Could it be that we rub each other up the wrong way because we're too alike?'

'It's not like you to get all analytical either. What's in your beer?'

'So I'm right?'

'You mean in surgical terms? Yes. We're both super ambitious. I know you still haven't got over me getting the training number you wanted.'

'It's water under the bridge. I'm happier doing ortho anyway.'

He seems serious. Anika won't relax her guard though. She has a feeling Isaac is up to something. He usually is.

'Makes sense – you are a stereotypical orthopod.'

'Meaning?'

'You know. You want me to sum it up?'

'Please.'

'Single-minded, brash, cocky. Kind of a dick.'

He takes a sip from his beer.

'What a flattering assessment.'

'I guess that was harsh. But true.'

'You described yourself too. And add *workaholic* to the list. You've turned into even more of one than usual this year. Which I'm guessing is in aid of boosting your chances with the fellowship?'

Anika's had her eye on a competitive fellowship post for next year. Which has meant even more hours than usual, conducting research for her consultant's papers, doing extra surgical lists on her days off. Anything to distinguish herself to the consultants who will determine her fate.

The barman places two glasses of water on the bar and Anika takes a sip of hers.

'What's it to you? We're not even in the same specialty any more.'

'If you get it, I'll be pleased for you. I just think you should lighten up. The post is now under consideration. There's nothing more you can do, until the results. So isn't it time you live a little? How long has it been since you dated anyone?'

Anika tries not to spit out the water she's drinking.

'Has there been anyone since you and the professor broke up?'

'It's none of your business. And he's not a professor. Not yet.'

'No, because you outed the fact that he published your research under his name.' Isaac laughs. 'Nice one.'

'Thanks.' Anika tries not to think about how much it hurt at the time. She still can't believe she didn't realise his true intentions, using her work to further his own career, for a whole year. She should really have known better.

'How long ago was that? Three months? Four?'

'More like a year.'

'That's a long time.' He puts his beer down on the bar and faces her. 'I know he was a piece of work, but not everyone is like that. You can't just work all the time. Doesn't it feel empty to you?'

'Where are you going with this, Isaac?'

'I appreciate you extending an olive branch and inviting me tonight. I think we might finally be getting onto the same page.'

'Which is what?'

'I think we could be good together.'

Anika laughs. The idea of her and Isaac is too ridiculous.

'You're hilarious.' But Isaac isn't laughing. She knew he was up to something but she would never have guessed at this.

'Oh. Shit. You aren't joking.'

'Dead serious.' He leans closer to her. There's a strange gleam in his green eyes. In the panning strobe lights of the bar, he looks predatory.

'What do you think?' He reaches out, strokes her buttocks.

Anika freezes for a second. Then she slaps his hand away.

'Don't touch me.'

'Ow.' He rubs his arm. 'No need to attack me.'

'I invited you tonight because it's Eliza's party and she likes you. You've got the wrong idea completely about me and you. Don't try anything like that again.'

'Everything okay here?' The man from earlier is standing behind her.

'I'm fine. Isaac was—' She's about to say *leaving*, but when she turns to him, Isaac has gone.

'All good here.'

'You seem like you can handle yourself.'

'You were watching me?'

'I wanted to make sure you were okay.'

'Do you often try to play the knight in shining armour to strangers in bars?'

He holds up his hands.

'Listen, I was only trying to help. I'll leave you alone, no problem.'

The bartender is juggling bottles as she mixes cocktails, her movements in time to the music. Anika needs to get Eliza home. And she'd be happy to go home too, wake up for the early list, do it all again. But suddenly, it does feel empty.

'It's okay. If you really were trying to help, then I appreciate it.'

'No worries.'

'Have a nice night. I have to go and get my friend out of here.'

'Oh yeah?'

'She's drunk but it's her birthday so it's going to be difficult.'

'Well, I can relate to wanting to leave,' he says. 'I have a 5 a.m. flight tomorrow. Meanwhile my friends are moving onto sambuca. Not a good mix.'

Anika glances at him. He has a nice profile with long lashes, carefully trimmed stubble. She finds herself imagining what it would feel like against her cheek. She shakes her head. *Not going to happen.*

'Where are you going?' She shouldn't prolong the conversation. But she can't help herself.

'New York. To close a deal. Hopefully.'

'I knew it,' she says under her breath.

'Knew what?'

'You're a banker, right?'

'That obvious?'

'If the suit fits.'

He laughs.

'Fine. You got me. What do you do?'

'I'm a surgeon.' She waits for his expression to change. For the look of intimidation that the answer usually gets from men in bars. She waits for him to be put off.

He smiles.

'What kind of surgeon are you?'

'General. Everything from appendix to bowel perforation.' Bowel talk should get rid of him if nothing else does.

'Wow. So you do all the emergencies?'

He doesn't seem put off. He seems interested.

'For now. I'm hoping to get into a fellowship next year. A fast track to consultancy. That's the plan. If I get in.'

'You will.'

'How can you say that? You don't even know me.'

'Because. I have great instincts for people. And I would pick you.'

He looks at her with admiration. An attractive guy looking at her like that – it's flattering, she has to admit.

'I should go,' she says. 'Try and wrestle my friend out of here.'

'How about I get a taxi for you both?'

'And then?'

'I'll walk home.'

She looks at him.

'Why would you help me? We've literally just met.'

'It would give me an excuse to leave. Then I could get at least three hours' sleep before my flight.'

'If you're sure?'

'I'll meet you outside.'

'There you are,' says Rosa as Anika approaches. Eliza is dancing around her, an unfocused look in her eyes. 'We have to get her out of here.'

'I have us a cab.' She gives Eliza the water. 'Drink this.' Eliza obediently downs it. 'Now, come with me.' Ignoring her protests, she guides Eliza out of the exit and into the cool air of the street.

Outside the club, the street is busy with taxis, the wind blowing newly fallen leaves off the pavement. She looks for the man, expecting him to have left. But there he is, standing by a waiting cab.

'As promised,' he says, gesturing to it.

She helps Eliza into the car and turns to the man.

'Thanks.'

He smiles.

'Like I said, you've done me a favour, getting me out of there.'

'Any time.'

'You going to be okay getting back?'

'Fine. Just need to get her into bed. I hope you get your flight okay.'

'Me too.'

He looks at her, his eyes searching. Suddenly, she feels like a deer in headlights.

'Look, I don't know if I'll ever see you again so . . . can I get your number at least?'

Anika hesitates.

'I'm not looking for anything,' she says. 'Not a relationship. And definitely not a hook-up.'

He raises an eyebrow.

'Who said anything about that? We could meet as friends?'
'Really?'
He shrugs.
'Why not? See where it leads?'

She considers. There's something about him. He seems different. Not like her dirtbag ex or the other guys in her past. It could be time to end the drought.

'Maybe.' She types her number into his phone.

He looks at it, smiles.

'It's good to meet you, Anika. I'm Dominic.'

14

Anika

Now

I rush out of the front door. Locking it, I stand with my back to it for a moment. I could try to write off what happened as a nightmare, but it ended with me trying to jump out of the window. *That's not just a bad dream.* I can't talk myself into believing it was.

The sun glints high, red and angry today. It's near thirty degrees and it's barely 10 a.m. Sweat builds a sheen on my upper lip, under my arms, trickling down my back. The street ahead is still quiet, empty. Much the same as last night, minus the strange man.

I study the outside of the house. In sharp daylight, the yellowing facade looks even more worn; sweeping water marks decorate the outside. It looks larger from here. There are two side wings, with boarded-up windows and no doors. I remember the empty wall at the top of the staircase. Has the owner walled off some of the house? The veranda wraps around three sides of the house. It must have been a beautiful building once. Up on the top floor is the window of the room I slept in. I remember my foot dangling out. The fuzzy, half-asleep feeling, the dregs of the bad dream, giving way to shock.

I have to get away from the house. Then I can think, without that image slamming into my brain every five seconds. Google

Maps shows me an area with a cluster of shops and restaurants, which must be the town, west of the house. It matches with the directions on the map Mr Fonseca left for me. I start walking. The road is potholed, tarmac shiny in the heat. There's no real pavement, no vehicles either but I keep to the side of the road anyway. The little blue dot on my screen wavers and spins, then settles and I follow where it points. I can't see the sea now, buildings and palm trees along the roadside shield it from view, but I can smell the salty breeze.

I pass a few more colonial-style houses, widely spaced and not in great repair either. Further down the street houses give way to small shops, a sign for a guest house. They all seem to be closed. When a car trundles past, I realise it's the first vehicle I've seen since I left the house. This area is a lot quieter than I expected. Why are the shops closed? And why are the houses here all as uncared for as the one I'm staying in? I was expecting locals, tourists, scooter taxis. Where are all the people? It hits me then, that no one knows I'm here. And there's no one to help me. I am totally alone.

I walk faster to where the road forks, taking the path that leads towards the town. Buildings intersperse the route. Here a shack, with boarded windows. On the other side of the road a series of rough brick walls, unfinished. All abandoned. All husks. What happened to this place? *Ehey yannah eppā.* This must be what that ridiculous guy meant yesterday, by telling me not to go there. This morning, when I realised what it meant, it felt like a warning of some vague and ephemeral threat. But maybe the man had been more prosaic than that. Stating the obvious. Of course I shouldn't go to the house, it's a near-wreck. Or this area, this isn't like one of the country's popular tourist spots or the pretty coastal towns where my relatives used to live. There's nothing here.

Heat seeps into my bones, slows my pace. The air even feels

thicker, my breathing is laboured. I wish I'd thought to bring a hat but in my rush to get away from the house, I only grabbed my handbag, still unpacked from the flight. My passport, my phone, a few airline tissues, a pack of chewing gum and a bottle of water are all I have on me. I didn't have a plan, beyond getting away from the house. Can I bear to sleep there again tonight? I could look for somewhere else to stay, but with my current financial situation, I can ill afford a hotel.

There is an alternative. Go home. Change my plane tickets, get the next flight back. But when I think of the last few weeks, to go back to more of the same would feel like defeat. There is no ideal outcome here.

Buildings show again in the distance. Proper ones this time, or at least, whole ones. Shops with corrugated-tin roofs, signs at the top advertising Lux soap, Bata shoes, Milo. The shops soon become more densely packed, shoulder to shoulder. It's a little busier here. Tuk-tuks and bicycles are parked by the side of the street in a row. A few shopkeepers stand in front of their stores. A group of teenagers walk on the other side of the pavement, their laughter mingling with the sound of traffic in the distance.

I stop outside a shop to look at a display of batik dresses. They're cute. Eliza would love the red-and-orange one. I make a mental note to return here before my departure, and get her one. Though I don't know when that will be I don't have a plan for after my assignment ends. My suspension is indefinite and I don't know if I want to go back to work at the hospital. I told Sara Peele that when I left. She couldn't stop me, because she and the board haven't yet decided if I'll have a job to go back to or not.

There's a tug on my handbag. I turn. A man, wiry and dressed in jeans and faded T-shirt, stands next to me. His hand is on my bag. What the hell? I grab the bag hard to my side. 'What do you think you're doing?'

He looks at me in surprise. He thought it would be easy.

Maybe it is, with unsuspecting tourists. But my reactions are lightning fast, usually. He hasn't reckoned on me.

The man tugs my bag again, he's poised to run with it. The nerve of him.

I pull harder. 'Get off my bag,' I shout.

People across the street look on now. The man pauses, then he gives a final pull, at the same time that I put all my strength into heaving in the opposite direction. The strap of the bag breaks. Belongings spill onto the pavement. My water bottle hits the ground and opens, spilling water over the pavement. I lunge for my phone and passport, grabbing them before he can.

'*Me mokada mey?*' A woman has appeared next to us, she's speaking to the man in Sinhala. I think she said what's going on? The man looks up, caught off guard. The woman takes in the bag, my fallen belongings.

'*Pallayung yannah, Nirmal,*' she shouts at the man. Get lost.

The man takes the remnants of my handbag, turns and runs down the street. The woman shouts something to a shopkeeper across the street and he half-heartedly takes off after the man. I'm not holding out hope he'll bring back my bag, but I appreciate the intervention.

'*Bohoma isthoothi,*' I say, turning to the woman. Thank you. I can already feel the remnants of language coming back. The awful dream seems to have dislodged something in my brain.

'I'm sorry about that,' the woman says, in English. 'I hope he didn't take anything valuable.' She's about my age, with long wavy hair, like mine used to be before I spent my teens flat-ironing the texture out of it. She has a friendly kind of face, open and warm.

'All he's got is some tissues and chewing gum. And the bag of course.'

'That's a shame.'

'It's okay. I've been meaning to replace it.' The handle was fraying. One of the other things I didn't get time for in my former life. My passport is wet from my water spilling on it. I wipe it on my dress. 'I still have my passport. It could be worse.'

'Would you like some water?' she asks.

'Thanks but I'll be okay,' I say. I don't want to put her out, after she's been so helpful already.

'Please. Come with me. My shop is over there.' She points to a store a few metres away.

'I – okay.' As I follow her, I notice we have an audience. Locals have gathered across the road, watching us.

'Ignore them,' she says. 'They're desperate for some drama. As you might have noticed, there's not a lot happening around here.'

She stops outside a wooden storefront. A large sign decorated with hand-painted waves bears the name Kavya's Boutique.

The woman unlocks the door and leads us in.

Inside, bikinis and swim shorts are neatly arranged on shelves, lightweight sarongs on a rack sway gently in the breeze from a ceiling fan. There's a rail of wetsuits and modest swimwear.

'I'm really sorry about that guy,' she says. 'There's still a problem with pickpockets. They only target foreigners.'

I remember that she called him by his name.

'Do you know him?'

'A little. We all know him around here.' She sighs. 'He hasn't always been a thief. He—' She starts straightening price tags on a nearby shelf. 'Never mind. It's a long story.'

'Thanks again for helping me.'

She laughs. 'Not that you needed it. He'll think twice about doing that to someone else.'

'Let's hope so.' The whirr of the fan beckons me and I stand under it, revelling in its gentle breeze as I explore the shop. 'Hey, this is nice.' I examine a mint-coloured one-piece with a chevron print. 'And this.' I turn to her. 'These designs are amazing.'

'Thanks,' she says with a coy smile.

'They're yours?'

She nods.

'So you're Kavya.'

'Right. I didn't get your name.'

'Anika.'

'So, that drink, Anika. *Enna.* Come.'

She takes me behind a curtain at the back of the shop, into a seating area with four metal tables. Little pots of plastic pink flowers sit on each.

'Would you like water, or something else?'

'What do you have?'

'Thambili,' she says, pointing to a display of orange king coconuts.

'Yes please.'

She cracks the end, puts in a straw and hands it to me. I take a deep drink of the sweet, refreshing coconut water inside, only now realising how thirsty I am.

'Good?'

'The best. It's been years since I had one.' A real one, not a plasticky imported one like street stalls in London sell. I drain the rest.

'*Lankave the?*' she asks. You're Sri Lankan? I know where this is going.

'Yes,' I say.

'*Ehenung, kohengthe, Miss Anika?*' Then where are you from? Bingo, the question I'm all too familiar with. I'd get it sometimes in London because I don't look English and I've had it here too, because I don't quite look like a local. I was once told that I looked Sri Lankan but spoke and dressed like a foreigner. Even now, the question reminds me how I don't fit in, in either place.

'London,' I say.

She looks at me curiously.

'Are you on holiday?'

'Not exactly.'

She seems nice but I don't want to explain, because one line of explanation leads to another. To things I don't even want to think about let alone share with a stranger.

'Where are you staying while you're here?' she asks.

'Not far. Fort Road.'

'Oh, I know it.'

Of course she does.

'How much do I owe you?' I ask.

She waves my money away.

'On the house. It's a small recompense for your stress.'

'Well, thanks.' I stand. 'In that case, I'm going to check out your shop.'

My bank balance can barely take it but I pick out a turquoise one-piece with cutaway sides. It's cute and not too revealing. I wouldn't dare wear a bikini here. Whether they think I fit in here or not, to the locals I still look Sri Lankan and a bikini is not considered appropriate wear here for Sri Lankan women. It's been a long time since I was here but I know that hasn't changed. I imagine the bikinis on the shelf are designed with tourists in mind. The rules for what is considered acceptable here are different, depending how you look. I add a wide-brimmed sun hat and pay in crumpled rupee notes from my pocket, telling her to keep the change. At least the man didn't get to those.

'Nice choices,' she says as she rings them up at the till.

'I'd wear any of your designs.'

It's strange, this shop is like the ones in chic surf towns like Mirissa or Arugam Bay, but without the crowds. And the town, the area where the house is, they have potential, but both seem to have fallen into disrepair.

'This area – do you get many visitors?'

'Tourism is seriously down since . . . well, some things have happened.'

'What kind of things?'

She hesitates.

'Nothing good.' She hands me my purchases in a plastic bag. Her closed-off expression, so different from moments ago, tells me it's time to go. What could have happened here, to get this reaction?

'Oh. Well, thanks for the drink. And the save.'

'Any time.'

As I reach the door, she says, 'When you head back, take the path behind the shops.'

'Why? What's there?'

She smiles. 'Trust me. You'll see.'

'Okay.'

I stop at a bakery to buy some *malu paan*, a triangular baked bread with a fish and potato filling that I remember from my childhood, for lunch. While they're packing them, I email Mr Fonseca. I tell him the house isn't what I expected, the condition is barely habitable. I ask when someone was last here, and what kind of restoration work the contractors will do.

The wide road ahead shimmers with the height of the afternoon sun. Remembering Kavya's advice, I find the path behind the shops instead. It leads to some rail tracks and I follow them for a while. It's completely unshaded and not particularly scenic; I'm wondering why she told me to go this way when I see it. The sea appears suddenly in the distance, waves lapping at the wide-open sweep of beach in front. The sand is white gold, the crystal waves inviting. I slip off my flip-flops and walk to the shore. The water is clear, I can see my feet and, around them, swim tiny striped fish, their deep blue shade bright in the water. I watch them dart around my toes. Smudges of pink and dark green colour the water ahead. Coral. I should come back another day with snorkelling gear. The water is perfect, cool and refreshing. My hem of my dress is wet now, but it will dry in no time.

The horrible dream from this morning, the pickpocket, my lost bag, feel miles away. So does London and everything I left there. I could make a go of clearing up the house, and afterwards, with the money, I could travel. Here on this beach, even the pending investigation doesn't seem so overwhelming. Coming to Sri Lanka was what I needed.

15

Dayani

'How did you get this again?' Avila asks. He sets the heavy brown glass bottle between them, on the roof.

Dayani scoots closer to him. The roof is her favourite thing about the house. And the only place where they can get any privacy.

'My dad's supply.'

Avila laughs.

'Thātha didn't mind? You rich people are funny. *Uppeh Thāthanung hondata gāhanawa.*' My dad would beat us.

Dayani glances at the embossed gold-and-yellow label on the bottle and wonders if taking it was a mistake. What if her father notices it's missing? Then again, she took it from the back of the cupboard, and there were at least five more like it.

'So would mine. I didn't tell him, obviously. He has so many bottles, he won't notice.'

She takes a swig. The arrack is bitter, burning her throat on the way down. She's had it a few times before, in similar circumstances. Her friends taking a bottle from their parents' cupboards, just like she did. She's never liked it but she knows Avila appreciates the gesture. And it gives them an excuse to be alone. Which was the entire point. She passes the bottle back to him.

'Good for us, then.' He dangles his legs over the edge. The

third-floor roof juts out over the road below. Avila isn't scared of heights. As far as she knows, he's not scared of anything.

Avila is silhouetted in the light of the street lamps below. She leans back on her hands and watches him for a moment, as he takes another drink then holds the bottle between his knees. Admires his enviable cheekbones, the way his white T-shirt stretches across his broad shoulders.

'What?' he asks with a half-smile.

She smiles back.

'Nothing.'

'You going to let me drink all of it?'

'Never.'

She grabs the bottle from him and gulps some more down, grimacing. She needs more. For courage.

'We won't be able to do this next year,' he says.

'Do what?'

'Hang out like this. You'll be going to some fancy university abroad. I'll be working for my dad.'

'You don't have to.' She knows how he feels about it. It seems so unfair. All that potential, wasted, doing the same job his father does now. Working for her father. She's heard the rumours. Her father's shady business practices. Bribery, corruption. Worse. She hopes it's all just vicious gossip. But if the rumours are true, then her father would never get his hands dirty. So the man doing the dirty work is Avila's father. She can't let Avila go the same way.

'I don't have a choice.'

'Of course you do. Why don't you tell him what you really want?'

She passes him the bottle and he takes another swig.

'You don't think I've tried? What else am I going to do anyway? It's not like I have other plans.'

'Yes you do. Engineering at Colombo Uni – don't act like you haven't been preparing for the entrance exams. That I haven't been helping you. You could do that, Avila. You really could.'

'It's just a pipe dream. I'm not like you.'

Dayani sighs. This is not going how she wanted it to. She checks her phone. It's nearly nine. Her parents will be back soon. Which means Avila needs to go. Her parents don't approve of her friendship with their worker's son, but they tolerate it. All hell would break loose if they suspected it was anything more. If she doesn't do it now, she'll lose her nerve and who knows when they'll have another chance to be alone like this.

She takes a big gulp of arrack. It goes to her head and she feels dizzy, then suddenly carefree. Like she could do anything. She's known him for nearly half her life now. And at least the last year she's liked him. She's had boyfriends before but no one she liked like this. She knows it from the way her heart beats so fast as she moves closer to him. She touches his knee, briefly. Enough to say, he's more than a friend. But not so much that she can't backtrack if he doesn't reciprocate.

'Let's not talk about that now.'

He's glances at her hand with a tentative smile.

'Fine with me.'

She looks into his light brown eyes. Takes a deep breath, steels herself. If he's not going to make the first move, she will. She moves in, brushes her lips against his. He kisses her back, for a moment. Then pulls away.

'What are you doing?'

'What does it look like?'

He half smiles again and she's relieved. Then he moves in, kisses her properly this time. She pulls herself closer until their legs are entwined as they sit, on the edge of the roof. She doesn't want it to stop.

There's a loud clatter. She springs away from him quickly. The door to the roof is open. His sister stands there. How much did she see?

'It's time to go. Thātha is ready to leave,' Ayomi says. 'He's wondering where you are.'

She has her lips pressed tightly together, her face inscrutable. Dayani realises with a sinking feeling that she saw it all.

Avila frowns.

'*Aiyo, oya mokada keweh?*' What did you tell him?

'That you're on your way,' Ayomi says.

Avila places a hand on her back, ever so brief, but it warms Dayani. It feels like a wordless promise of continuation. He dips his head and goes inside. Ayomi turns to go inside too.

'Wait,' Dayani says. She hates to let down her guard, to ask something of his sister, but she has to. She takes a deep breath and faces her. 'You won't tell?'

Ayomi regards her coldly.

'Of course not.' Then she stops. 'Only because of my brother,' she says. 'Not for you.'

Dayani bites back a retort. It doesn't matter if Ayomi hates her, as long as she keeps things to herself. As long as her parents don't find out. Her parents found out she had a boyfriend last year. The son of one her father's friends, who she'd met at some boring family function or other. But the beating she got then would be nothing compared to the potential repercussions of a relationship with the caretaker's son. And he'd broken up with her anyway.

'Why are you being like this? We used to be friends – what happened?'

'You happened. You got your claws into my brother.'

Dayani frowns. She expected Ayomi to deny things but she isn't even trying to disguise her hostility.

'You're upset I didn't tell you? I didn't know if he felt the same way, I wanted to be sure—'

'I don't care. Wise up. Do you really have no idea what you're doing?'

'I – I don't.'

'I know you're just using him. What is he, entertainment to you?'

She resents having to explain herself when they only kissed for the first time, moments ago. She hasn't even had time to process it.

'No.' She almost says, I love him. Because she's sure she does. But that's too vulnerable a detail to share even with Avila, yet. She would never tell his sister.

'I care about him.'

Ayomi laughs.

'Sure you do. You're from different worlds, we both know the two of you have no future. Your parents would never approve. Neither would mine. The only reason you're trying this is because you think you can pick him up and put him down whenever you want. Like your Barbies we used to share. You never even cared if I gave them back, because they were disposable to you, with your rich father. Avila isn't like you.'

Dayani is stung, she knows their parents' backward attitudes but never expected Ayomi to share them.

'But I don't care about any of that rich and poor stuff. Neither should you.'

'So when Avila goes to work with Thātha, and you leave for your fancy university, how do you expect your relationship to work?'

Dayani thinks of her plan. If he gets into Colombo University, she'll go there too. But that's her secret. She says nothing.

'Exactly.' Ayomi moves closer. Dayani can see the tiny red veins in the whites of her eyes. 'When you get tired of him, or your parents come between you, it will be worse for him than for you. Because he for some reason cares for you. So stop with this.

I mean it.' Her eyes are cold still but there's a glint of something else there. Something dangerous.

Dayani straightens. She won't be intimidated by the girl. Not when she's finally getting what she wanted. Like she's going to stop now.

'You should butt out. It's none of your business.'

Ayomi grabs Dayani's shoulder.

'Stay away from my brother.'

Dayani moves out of her reach. She won't give away that Ayomi's grip hurt. She laughs.

'Or what?'

'Or else I will tell.' Before Dayani can say another word, Ayomi goes inside.

16

Anika

Now

The house looks different in daylight. Shadows slant through the fronds of the palms next to it, making crisis-cross patterns on the exterior. It looks less like the shadowed half-broken hulk of last night. It has an air of faded elegance, more like the photos the owner sent. I feel hopeful, as I slide the keys into the lock.

It was getting dark when I arrived last night and I didn't stop to look around in my haste to leave this morning. Now, I examine the entrance way and the lounge. What is that on the floor, in between the couches? Glass. The crunch of it underfoot confirms, there are bits of broken glass scattered on the floor.

The windows in here look intact so I wonder where it came from. A broken bottle? And if so, who was drinking? I realise again how little I know about this place, how little I bothered to find out before I agreed to this job. So unlike me. There's a semicircular window on the far wall, made of five individual panels like segments of an orange. I cross towards it, avoiding the glass on the floor. Each panel is clouded with dust. Using a cloth from the bucket of cleaning supplies, I wipe the panels down. The effect is dramatic, sunlight streams in. It's less gloomy, the furniture looks less faded. Now, I can picture how the place must have been. How it will be again, when it's restored. I feel more energised all of a sudden. The owner said I'd do some *routine cleaning*, which is far from accurate. This place needs an industrial deep clean. But I'm up to the task if anyone is. I spearheaded turning around the disaster that was Surgical Ward 5 less than a year ago. When I left it was the best functioning surgical ward in the hospital. It's time to put my skills to something other than medicine.

I turn on the spot, surveying the rest of the room. The supplies Mr Fonseca left are not nearly enough. I'll need gloves to handle the broken glass. Dusters, bin liners, a broom. I start a list on my phone.

When I'm done, I walk through the main hall and up the stairs, to the room where I slept last night. The sheet is strewn across the bed, the way I left it. I peer out of the window, still slightly ajar. The sea looks back, calm now, the tide low and the rocks at the shore dry. Out in the distance, beyond the tall cliffs, is the town where my family's house used to be.

I sit on the bed and flex my feet. *Ehey yannah eppā.* The words that mysterious guy said to me. And the words as I heard them in the dream. The weird screaming refrain. I open the window wider as I try to remember the position I was in when I awoke. I hoist my foot up onto the exterior window ledge, duplicating the position of this morning. My foot juts precariously out. The beach below seems so far away. What if I hadn't woken up? What then?

There's a sudden movement, down on the beach. A man stands by the rock, looking directly at me.

I start back from the window, pulling myself into the bedroom. From inside, I watch, but the man rushes away, and moments later, he's gone. He wore a white shirt and jeans and had a slight, wiry build. He looked like the pickpocket. Was it the same guy from this morning? Was he watching me? I shake the thought out of my head. The man happened to be on the beach, that's all. Seeing someone with their foot half out of a window is attention-grabbing. Of course he stopped to look.

My breathing comes quicker. Can I sleep here again, after last night? I don't scare easily, not usually, but there's something about this place. There's an old, heavy feeling to the house. As if it's seen things. Knows things. No. I'm being irrational, because of last night. It's a house, not a person.

It's starting to get dark now. I walk onto the landing and into the room where I found the picture. Seeing the sea in the photo triggered my memory of the man's words. Perhaps more of the dream might come back if I look at it again. And if I could remember the dream maybe I would find out why I woke up half out of the window. I scan the dressing table but the picture isn't there. I turn, and there it is. The photo frame is propped on the window ledge. But I left it on the dressing table. I'm sure I did. At least, I think I'm sure.

Angry tears prick my eyes. I can't rely on myself at all any more. I remember the feeling, welling up from the past, not being able to trust my own mind. I don't know what is happening in the recesses of my subconscious. Or whatever is making my body act of its own accord when I sleepwalk. Why I wake up in precarious situations. My condition first started when I was in Sri Lanka. Most of the episodes happened here. Has coming back here somehow triggered it again?

I turn the photo away. I've spent the years since trying to maintain control over my life. To maintain control over myself. Five a.m. swims in the freezing-cold pool near my flat before work, hitting the ward at 6.30 before the day shift started. Staying late then pretending to drink my macho colleagues under the table after work to prove I'm better than them, at anything. Pretending, because I've had to control my alcohol and caffeine intake, to keep the parasomnia at bay. Waking up and doing it all again. Working hard and playing harder, not because I wanted to but because I had to, to maintain my self-image. And I succeeded. I was at the top of my profession, hitting all my life goals. Then everything went wrong. I can't control my body or my mind. Not even when I'm asleep.

I need to get a grip on myself, before I unravel completely. I turn on the light and the bare bulb hanging from the ceiling flickers into life. My phone feels warm in my pocket. I have a surge of longing for the way things were, before it all got so messed up. Of course that's impossible, but I could call. See how things are, in London. I place a FaceTime call to Eliza. It rings for so long I'm about to hang up, when she appears on the screen.

'Hey,' she says. 'What a surprise.'

She's wearing pink-checked pyjamas, her curly blonde hair pulled up in a messy bun. If she's sleeping now, she must have worked a night shift last night.

'Did I wake you?'

Eliza smiles blearily.

'Kind of but I was about to get up anyway. I'm back on tonight and it's been mental. There was a trauma call last night and . . .' She trails off. 'Never mind. How is everything there?'

'It's okay. You can still talk about it. I may not be a surgeon any more but you still are.'

Eliza's face falls.

'What do you mean? Of course you are.'

'I'm not. Check the GMC register.'

The words *doctor under investigation* now follow my name. Words usually reserved for gross negligence. It's humiliating.

'It's pending,' Eliza says. 'Everything will be okay, once the investigation is over.'

My stomach churns. I flew to the other side of the world to avoid all that and here we are talking about it anyway.

'Can we please change the subject?'

'Sorry. I just want you to realise that you'll always be a surgeon. I don't care if the GMC register says something off right now. It also says MBBS, MRCS next to your name.'

'Meaningless letters. I'm barely even a doctor any more.'

'You worked your arse off for those letters. We all did. Blood, sweat and tears. They don't just go away.'

'They do if I want them to.'

Eliza chews her bottom lip. Then she nods.

'Anyway, tell me about Sri Lanka. Make me jealous. Are the beaches as amazing as they look?'

'The beaches, yes,' I say, remembering the fish swimming around my feet. 'You would love them.' Then I tell her, in watered-down terms, that the trip is so far not going to plan.

'Wait, so it's like a shit Airbnb situation?'

'The shittiest. But he's paying me well, so.'

Eliza positions her phone on her nightstand and drinks some water.

'Hey, you can have a decent holiday after. You'll have earned it.'

'That's the plan.' I hesitate. 'Something else weird happened. I think I'm having parasomnias again.'

Eliza puts the bottle down.

'I thought you said you hadn't had one since you were a teenager.'

'I hadn't.' I tell her what happened this morning, again leaving out the more worrying details like my foot out of the window.

'You should see the sleep specialist again.'

'I haven't spoken to him in over fifteen years. He might have retired.'

'What's his name? I'll look him up. If he has retired I bet you could get a remote appointment with someone else.' There's a note of desperation in her voice. When I was first diagnosed, my parents dragged me to all sorts of people to find a cure. The very expensive sleep specialist they found back in London ran enough tests to get my parents to lay off. Brain scans, an overnight study where I slept in a sleep lab with EEG leads attached to my head. He agreed to prescribe a new experimental medication, on a clinical trial. The parasomnia stopped so he let me wean off the medication. It never came back, so he said I could permanently stay off it. But I kept refilling the prescription, for years after. Just in case. I still have one small strip of pills which I've kept even though it's expired, like a talisman against the parasomnia returning. It's in my suitcase, with my medical supplies. Eliza is a fixer; if I tell her, she'll try to arrange a new prescription. But it might not be a parasomnia episode at all. This feels like something I have to work through on my own.

'It's okay. I should let you go now. It was so good to see you.'
'Anika, wait.'
'Speak soon.'
I hang up before she can say anything else.

It's turned fully dark outside during the course of our conversation. I walk through the upper floor, putting on all the lights I can find. Then I find the room I slept in last night. The frame of the bed is heavy – I have to take the mattress off before I can get it to move. I heave it across the floor, until it's as far away from the window as I can get it. If I'm going to stay here, I'm not going to let myself be scared. I don't understand what happened last night but being too frightened to sleep is not an option. I might not be able to control myself right now, but I will. I always have, eventually. If I managed it last time, I can do it again. Nothing can be as bad as last time. It will be okay. It has to be.

17

Anika

Then

'And, open.'

Anika opens her eyes. They're on a terrace, lit with fairy lights that criss-cross in a canopy overhead. Little round tables adorned with white tablecloths and flickering candles are dotted across the stone floor. Soft jazz plays in the background.

Anika looks around.

'What is this?'

Dominic smiles.

'Call it a special opening.'

A waiter in black and white pulls out a chair for Anika. She sits, still fazed. It's their fourth date. Their first date, a 'friends' meeting to a midnight screening of *The Shining*, which he said he picked as the most unromantic movie he could think of, not knowing she loved it, ended in a definitely-not-just-friends kiss goodbye. The second date she insisted on another attempt to keep things friendly and low-key, with a rugby match but she found it increasingly hard to keep her hands off him. On date three, to a bar in the City, she stopped trying, finally feeling comfortable enough to let it go where she knew she wanted it to. Waking up the next morning in his bed, her body still remembering the night before, she had expected that to be it. She didn't expect a fourth date. Let alone this.

'A special opening of what?' The breeze rustles the flowers, sending the scent of gardenias wafting up to her.

'The hottest new place on the London restaurant scene. It's called Amiga.'

'I haven't heard of it.'

Dominic leans closer to her. She likes the way his crisp blue shirt gets delectably tight on his shoulders as he does.

'That's because it doesn't officially open until next week. My firm handle the parent company and I managed to wrangle a preview for you.'

The waiter places a chilled bottle of water on the table between them. Dominic lifts his glass. His Rolex catches the light as he does.

Anika moves her chair back a little. The scraping noise, metal on stone, is loud in the empty terrace.

'I thought we were friends.'

He laughs.

'We're really still doing that?'

'Fine, not friends. Casual. I thought that's all this was.'

He folds his arms and looks her directly in the eyes.

'And what if I don't want that? There's something about you, Anika. I don't want to be casual with you.'

'And that's why you've brought me here?'

'I thought you'd like it. We can go if you want.'

She considers. If she's honest with herself, she doesn't want casual either. He's been open from the start. The only thing stopping her are her own misgivings, born of her past. Nothing to do with Dominic.

'Let's stay. But only because I like tapas.'

He laughs.

'A good enough reason.'

Behind him, beyond a wrought-iron railing covered in climbing vines, is an unobstructed view of the skyline. She picks out the Shard, the London Eye. City lights reflected in the river.

She takes a breath. And decides, then, to let her cautions go. He's a good guy. They could be something. If she let them.

'I don't want to be casual with you either.'

He smiles and his blue eyes crinkle at the corners. He takes her hands across the table.

'Good.'

18

Anika

Now

I open my eyes. Bright sunlight streams through the window, on the other side of the room. The window I did not try to jump out of last night. My phone tells me it's nine. I did it. I lasted the night. No weird dreams. No parasomnias.

Throwing the sheet off me, I rush to the window. The sea is calm today, the tranquil blue sky dotted with puffy marshmallow clouds. My arms sting with mosquito bites and I make a mental note to add mosquito coils and nets to my list. But even the itching can't dampen my mood. Because the other night was a one-off. I'm going to be fine.

I shower in the bathroom down the hall. The high tap on the wall, the de facto shower, creaks when I run it and the water that comes out is cold. After the first shock, I become accustomed to the cool water, refreshing in the heat. I change into a short-sleeved blue sundress I bought months ago for a holiday I didn't get to go on. Today, I'm getting started on this project of caretaking this house. A high-pitched whine sounds by my ear and I swipe at the source. I must have missed because my arm pricks moments later, followed by a sting. Make that lots of mosquito coils. Reflexively, I look for my bag to put my phone and water in, then remember I don't have one any more. I add *new bag* to my list, put on my flips-flops and head out, double-locking the door.

Outside, the thirty-degree day hits me with its full force. I pull on my sunglasses and start walking. My sense of direction is good and after yesterday I remember the way, without needing my map. My limbs are sluggish and it takes me twenty minutes to reach the town. I pass a few shops which stock household supplies; one has stacks of plastic buckets arranged tidily at the entrance, another has a sign advertising Dyson. But before I get started on my list, I have a stop to make.

The door of Kavya's Boutique is open. Sinhala music plays as I enter.

'Can I help you?' Kavya appears from the recesses of the shop. She sees me, smiles. 'Anika. You're back.'

'I wanted to tell you that I loved your route back.'

'The secret beach, we call it,' she says. 'You can only get to it the back way. Local knowledge. *Lassanai, ne?*' Isn't it beautiful?

I wish I could express exactly what finding the secret beach felt like, the shift in my state of mind that I've felt since. But I can't find the words.

'*Owe. Hari lassanai,*' I say, agreeing.

'I'm glad you came back,' she says. 'I have something for you.'

'You do?'

She motions for me to sit at one of the tables behind the curtain. 'Give me a moment.'

I sit, drinking my water. This is more what I thought coming here would be like. Beaches, coconuts, freedom from the stress of the UK.

She returns with a package wrapped in tissue and places it on the table.

'What's this?'

'Have a look.'

The tissue rustles as I open it. Inside is my bag. The broken strap has been replaced with a new one, made of bright red gauzy fabric, like the sarongs hanging up in the shop.

'You did this?' I ask, touched.

'I repaired it. I hope you like it.'

'I love it. Thank you. How did you get it back?'

She sits opposite me.

'Gamini, the man who ran after Nirmal – the pickpocket – tracked him down and made him return the bag.'

'He came here?'

'He wanted me to tell you that he's very sorry. He won't be trying anything like that again. Not around here, anyway.'

Maybe it's too much to hope he'll stop completely.

'Hey, what time did he come here?'

Kavya shrugs.

'I'm not sure. It was near closing time. Around five, I think.'

Around the same time I saw the man outside my window last night.

'So it can't have been him,' I say, aloud.

'What do you mean?'

'It's just – I thought I saw the pickpocket last night, on the beach near where I'm staying. But it can't have been, if he was here.' He wouldn't have got there so fast. It must have been someone who looks like him, that's all.

'You said you're in Fort Road, didn't you? Where exactly are you staying? It's a big road.'

'Near the beach. The house at the end.'

'The Fonseca place?'

'Yes.' Well, that confirms he is the owner. I think.

'You're family?'

'No. I don't know him. I'm just working there.'

'What are you doing there?'

Kavya is kind, I find my defences reluctantly coming down.

'I'm caretaking, for a few weeks. Before contractors come to start work on restoring the place.'

'That's strange,' she says. 'The place has been empty for a long time. The Fonsecas come every so often but they've never had work done there before.'

'Do the family stay there?'

'Not really, they come occasionally, to check that everything is as they left it. A big, empty place like that, you have to be careful. Anyone can break in. Or even stay there.'

'You mean like squatters?' I think of the many rooms, the dark recesses and an unpleasant feeling comes over me. 'You think someone could be in there?'

'No. Not now. You're there and the Fonsecas were here a few weeks ago. They will have checked. Don't worry. I meant, he must be worried it could happen. That's why he's got you there.'

'I'm not much of a security guard.'

'Oh no. That's not what I mean.' She touches my hand. 'He must be finally renovating the place to prevent anything like that. He must have a plan for the house. It used to be a guest house. Maybe he wants to do that again, or turn it into a hotel. Please don't worry.'

I don't know if she believes it, or if she's just trying to make me feel better.

'Do you have family in the area?' she asks.

'I used to. They've moved abroad.'

She looks concerned.

'Do you know anyone in the area?'

'No. It's just me here.' It hits me again, how alone I am. Staying in this old place with possible squatters.

'I'll tell you what. Take my details. You know me, now. I live nearby. If you need anything, you can call me.'

'Really?'

'Of course.'

I pass over my phone and she types her number in.

'It's a big place,' she says. 'How are you going to manage working on it by yourself?'

'I have a plan.' I show her the list of supplies on my phone. 'Do you know where I can get these?'

'Sure.'

She takes me to one of the shops I earmarked as selling household supplies, and another I didn't notice. She bustles around each, picking out supplies from the list, at lightning speed and speaking in rapid Sinhala with the shopkeepers. They seem to be negotiating, there's some back and forth at the second shop, before she tells me the price. When we come back out, I have two bags filled with sponges, gloves and bleach, a broom.

'Do you need anything else?' she asks.

'No, I'm all set for now. Thank you for everything.'

She smiles.

'No problem. How are you going to get all that back to the house?'

'Walk, I guess.'

She looks at me like I just said I'm going by submarine.

'In this heat? You could get a taxi. I can call you one.'

'I'll be okay. It's not so far.'

I follow her out of the shop. I feel a little better for having at least one local contact. But her words have made me uneasy. I need to know more about what I'm dealing with in this place.

'Hey, you know yesterday, when you said something happened in this town? What did you mean?'

She shifts her weight, looks uncomfortable.

'Please, I need to know, I'll be staying here for a bit.'

She sighs.

'It used to be different here. It was very busy, a popular spot for surfers, tourists. But the sea is rough. Many people aren't careful.

There were accidents. First a tourist boat capsized in a storm. Many lives were lost. Locals working on the boat too.'

'I'm sorry.'

'Then some tourists who went swimming when the tide was too high, after the lifeguards had left. Locals tried to help them, but they it was too late. Not long after, there were more unexpected deaths. Surfers caught in a too-large wave, a tourist at a guest house who died suddenly. Then a reporter came here and we thought their article would raise the profile of the area, bring people back. But it did the opposite. The article was all about the accidents, how unsafe the area is. Tourist numbers dwindled. Eventually, they stopped coming at all. Now it's just us locals.'

That explains the lack of tourist infrastructure here. The abandoned buildings.

'*Eva ehama, ne,*' she says. 'Sometimes these things happen. An expression, to write off things we can do nothing about. I've heard it before. The feeling of powerlessness, familiar from long ago, nudges at my awareness.

'Are you okay?' she asks. 'Is it the heat?'

With an effort, I pull myself back to the present.

'Yes, yes, I'm fine.'

'I hope it all goes well at the house.'

'Thanks. I'll come by soon, let you know how I'm getting on.'

'I'd like that.' She waves and disappears.

I hoist up my bags. Take a deep breath. *Stay present.*

Maybe it is the heat. I should get a taxi. Kavya has a point, walking back with all this stuff is not the best idea. There's a line of parked vehicles down the road, three tuk-tuks and two cars. Behind is a glass-walled building, with a discreet sign that says TAXI. I try the door but it's locked. Perfect. Given the lack of visitors, maybe it's closed for good. Though that doesn't explain the cars parked outside. The bags sit heavy on me, digging into my arms. Now I've considered the possibility of a taxi, the thought of walking home with the bags makes me feel exhausted. Next to the taxi office is a little yellow-walled building with a thatched roof and a sign. Coconut Cove Coffee. A drink could energise me, enough to get home. The door tinkles as I push it open. Behind is a space filled with wooden tables and stools. At the back is a white-tiled counter on which trailing pot plants sit. A ceiling fan spins gently overhead. This looks nice.

I walk further into the cafe. There doesn't seem to be anyone in here.

'Hello?' I call.

There's no answer.

A clattering noise comes from behind the counter. An automatic door I didn't notice behind it slides open.

'How can I help?' The man's voice has a slight American intonation. It's familiar. I move closer. *Ehey yannah eppā.*

It's him. It's the man who warned me away the night I arrived.

19

The man steps towards me, a nonchalant look on his face.

'Would you like a drink?' He places a small chalkboard menu on the table. 'We have teas and coffees, all Sri Lankan-origin leaves and beans.'

'What did you say to me the other day?'

'And we have smoothies,' he says. 'I can get you the menu if you'd like.'

He's acting like he's never seen me before but it's definitely him. Same broad shoulders, same tilt of his head. Maybe he doesn't remember. Though it seems odd to forget someone you've warned away from a place.

'We met outside the Fonseca house. Remember?'

'There are also some specials. Would you like to hear them?'

His expression is unchanged, like I haven't said anything. The nerve of the man.

'No I don't want to hear the specials. This was a bad idea.'

'Why don't you have a seat, Miss?' He pulls out a stool for me.

At the same time, I turn to leave. I trip over the stool, dropping my bags. They tip, sending cleaning supplies flying over the floor. I rush to retrieve them. The sooner I can get out of this coffee shop, the better. I'm not getting anywhere with this guy.

He kneels in front of me, gathering supplies and shoving them into bags.

'Here.'

'Thanks.'

He reaches for a pack of mosquito coils from under the stool.

'Got enough mosquito repellent?' he says. There are about ten more packs strewn next to it.

'I like to stock up.'

'Here's a tip, open all the windows and run the fans on high. Those old houses are teeming with mosquitoes.'

I stand.

'So you do remember me.'

He sighs, then stands too. 'Maybe.'

'Why tell me not to go in the house? Messing with visitors, is that funny to you?'

'I wasn't messing with you. I was trying to tell you, it's not a nice place, the Fonseca house. As I'm sure you've realised by now, with all the mosquitoes.'

'Sure, that's the only reason. Here's a tip for you, don't deliver cryptic messages to strangers, in a language you don't even know if they understand.'

'But you did understand?'

'Barely.'

He hands me my bags.

'I think we got off on the wrong foot. I'm Dinesh.'

'Anika.'

'Would you like a drink, now you're here?'

'I might as well. But only because I have a long walk back. The taxi rank is closed.'

He raises an eyebrow.

'Is it?'

'The door is shut and locked, so yes.'

'Where do you need to go? Back to the Fonseca house?'

'Yes – why?'

'You said you need a ride.'

'You're a taxi driver?'

'One of the few. You may have noticed but we don't have much need for them around here, with the lack of tourists. So yeah, I do some driving, among other things. I do a lot of odd jobs.'

Of course he does. I sigh audibly.

'If you're my only choice, then fine.'

'A drink first?'

I scan the chalkboard menu. There are teas and multiple varieties of fancy-sounding cold-brew coffees, the kind of menu I'd expect to find in a hipster London cafe. My usual order is decaf, but I don't see it on the menu. And there's a tantalising smell of real coffee in the air in here.

'Do you have decaf coffee?'

'We have decaf varieties of all the beans.'

'Fine, then a decaf latte, iced.'

'Which bean variety would you like?' he asks. He looks like he's trying not to laugh.

I shove the board into his hands. 'You choose.'

'Okay, Miss Anika.'

'It's a little late to try to be polite now,' I say.

'I'll be back with your coffee,' he says, all waiterly deference though he's still hiding a smile. He disappears into the back. I glance around the cafe, at the prints on the walls, screen-printed batik designs in gold frames. It's actually a really nice place. What is his deal? Does he own it?

Dinesh returns with my coffee in a tall glass, complete with an intricate, latte-art swan. I scrutinise him as he arranges the coffee on the table and places a long silver spoon next to the glass. He's wearing a crisp white T-shirt and black jeans; unlike me he doesn't look sweaty or grubby from the heat. He has defined cheekbones and from the way the shirt falls on his shoulders, a nice physique. I'd be lying if I said he wasn't easy on the eye.

'There you go, Miss Anika,' he says. 'Hope you like it.' He speaks perfect English, with that slight US accent that suggests one of the big international schools in the city. I wonder what he's doing being a barista slash taxi driver and odd-job man in this forgotten town.

I take a sip of the latte. It's delicious, smooth but with a kick.

'This is actually good.'

'Don't sound so surprised. I chose a robusta for you, grown near to here,' he says, with a hint of pride.

'Good choice,' I say reluctantly.

He smiles.

'I'll let you in on a secret. They're all great. I chose them myself.'

'This is a cute place. Nice decor.'

'I'll let the interior designer know.'

'Is that you?'

'Maybe.'

'You really do have a lot of jobs.'

'I'm multi-talented.'

'You know, there are some nice spots in this street. Like, Kavya's shop.'

'You met her? Oh, of course, the business with the pickpocket. *Hari vaday ne.*'

'How do you know?'

'It's a small town. Word gets around fast.'

'Of course it does.' Great. I've landed in a place where everyone knows everyone's business. At least my skeletons are back in the UK. Most of them. Still, it makes me even more determined not to give too much away.

'You got your bag back okay?' he asks.

'Yes, Kavya helped.'

'She's decent,' he says.

'I suppose this place is okay too,' I add begrudgingly.

'Thanks for the review. I'll put it on Tripadvisor.'

'You're funny now?'

'I told you, I'm multi-talented.'

Something passes between us. Are we flirting?

'There are lots of other good places here,' he says. 'Like the surf shop at the end, the beach bars, the appa shop – I mean hoppers.'

My stomach growls at the mention of food.

'I know what appa are. Where is the appa shop?'

'Next door. You hungry? I can order some for you.'

'Really? Yes please.'

He smiles, takes his phone out of his pocket.

'What would you like? They have egg and plain hoppers. I mean, appa.'

'Egg. Four.'

'Four?' A normal order would be one, or two. But I haven't eaten properly since yesterday.

'What, I'm hungry. Just order.'

He laughs.

'Of course.' He makes a call, speaks rapidly, in Tamil this time. 'It's on the way,' he says, as he gets off the phone.

'Thanks. You speak three languages?'

'Most people here do. To varying degrees, of course.'

'You sound fluent. Speaking of languages. What else did you say to me the other day? You said a lot of stuff in Sinhala.'

He pulls up a stool and sits in front of me.

'Nothing important. I was just talking about the house. *Hari southoui.*'

'It's in a bad state? Yes, I noticed.'

'Right. So that's all. What did you think I said?'

He looks confused. I definitely read his warning wrong. Probably given that understanding what it meant came on the back of me trying to jump out of the window.

'I don't know.'

'So you're fixing up the house?' he asks, eyeing my cleaning supplies.

'Kind of. I'm cleaning up.' I tell him, in the barest terms, about my pseudo job here. 'Do you know if it's been in that state for long?'

He shrugs.

'A little while now. The Fonseca house used to be beautiful. The other old houses there too. That was nicest part of town, where the rich locals lived.'

'You know the people that lived there?'

'Not well. We knew of them. It was their holiday home. The Fonsecas have property all over. They live in Colombo.'

'Do they have children?'

A shadow passes over his face.

'Two,' he says.

'Most of the house is empty, but they left a few things.' I tell him about the photo and the library.

He shrugs.

'They had the place as a guest house for a while, before things went dead here. There were lots of tourists coming and going, it could be theirs too.'

'Oh,' I say, though none of the things look like they were left behind by tourists.

The door opens.

'*Enna*, auntie,' he says. *Come in.*

A tall woman in a sari enters carrying a large bag from which steam is rising. Dinesh clears the table and she unpacks the bag. I'd expected a bag of takeout but she arranges various ceramic dishes on the table in front of me. There's a stack of bowl-shaped appa on the largest plate, the glistening egg yolk in the centre of each, sprinkled with chilli flakes. She places bowls of coconut sambol and dal next to it.

'Darsha Auntie makes the best appa,' Dinesh says. I have a feeling she's not actually his auntie, he's calling her that as a term of respect.

'*Bohoma isthoothi*, auntie,' I say.

She laughs.

'Enjoy,' she says.

I break off some appa crust, dip it in dal and eat it, relishing the crunch and the comforting flavour of the dal.

'This is delicious. *Hari rassai*,' I add in Sinhala.

'*Sinhala puluwing the?*' she asks.

'*Tikuck.*' I can speak a little. 'It's coming back,' I add. I break off another piece of appa and use it to spoon up some of the coconut sambol. That's delicious too, spicy, and tangy with lime. 'Dinesh wasn't kidding about good spots. You really have some hidden gems here.'

'Of course,' she says. 'This town used to be a very popular place.'

'You wouldn't recognise it,' Dinesh says. 'This street we're on would be full of people, the beach bars stayed busy until late. This cafe was always popular, we had three more staff. Of course, I had to let them go.'

'Kavya told me what happened. It's a shame.'

Auntie sits on the stool next to me.

'*Owe.* Sorry to hear about yesterday. Your bag. *Hari vaday, ne?*'

Oh wow, Dinesh wasn't kidding about word getting around.

'Oh. Yes, I'm fine now.'

'Are you really staying at the Fonseca house alone?' She has a motherly kind of manner and right now she's looking concerned. In a country where women are often still expected to be escorted by a male relative if they're out late, a woman staying alone in a big house like that is bound to raise some eyebrows.

'Yes, I am.'

'And you're okay, in that house?'

'I'm fine, honestly.' I start on the second appa.

Auntie leans towards me.

'That's good, because the Fonsecas had a *naraka karleh*. How do you say . . . ?'

'A bad time.' A run of bad luck. I know that phrase well. I heard it a lot, the last time I was here. Relatives whispering it. My parents consulting astrologers and all manner of charlatans for advice on how to make it stop. Talking about me like I wasn't there. Because I was the one with the *naraka karleh*. I was the bad time. I was the bad luck.

I focus on the spinning ceiling fan above me, try not to let my thoughts travel back there.

'Right,' she says. 'And then last time they had guests in the Airbnb—'

'Don't scare her,' Dinesh says quickly.

Auntie replies in Tamil.

'What is it?' I ask.

They both stop talking.

'It's just gossip,' Dinesh says. 'I wouldn't worry about it.'

'Where are your family?' she asks. 'Do they live in the country?'

'They live abroad,' I say, surprised by the sudden change in subject.

'And they're okay with you being here?' *Hardly.*

'Oh yes, they're happy for me.'

'And you're not married?'

Ah, the auntie inquisition. I'm surprised it took this long. My own aunties are like this too. Zero boundaries, especially when it comes to the milestones women are expected to hit. I paste a smile on my face.

'No.'

She makes a tutting noise.

'A boyfriend, maybe?'

'No, right now I'm fine single.'

'How old are you?' she asks.

'Lay off, auntie,' Dinesh says with a laugh. 'That's none of your business.'

She'll be asking about kids next, if I don't shut her down.

'So what happened when the Fonseca house was an Airbnb?' I say.

Dinesh glances at her, as if considering whether to continue.

'Okay, you asked for it. The house has a strange history. It was built in the colonial times by a *suddha*.' A white man.

'Okay, so?'

'He had an affair with a local woman, and it didn't end well for them. Have you heard of Lovers' Leap? In the upcountry tea-growing regions?'

'The cliff where they have a lot of suicides?'

'That's the one. And that's what they did. Committed suicide. Soon after, the Fonseca family bought the place from the *suddha*'s grieving widow. Some say the elder Mr Fonseca took advantage of her state and bought it for next to nothing. And the house has been cursed ever since. Karma, locals would say.'

Karma. Another word that was bandied around a lot last time I was here. About me. All the trips to the temple to try to atone for what I must have done in a past life, to deserve what happened. Or, about how much bad karma I must have accumulated in this life, for what I did. Because people were conflicted on which of those it was.

They're both looking at me.

'You know what that is?' auntie asks.

I shake myself.

'Of course,' I say. 'How were they cursed?'

'Lots of things. Near when they bought it, there was huge fire. They had to rebuild some of the house.'

I remember the stairs leading nowhere. The wings of the house with no entrance.

'That could explain the extra sections.' I tell them about it.

Dinesh nods.

'They boarded up some of the fire-damaged areas. Before they turned it into a guest house, there was a lot of building work to seal up the house from the inside.'

'But why didn't they demolish the extra bits?' I ask.

He shrugs.

'Something to do with the structure. These old places are fragile. Tearing down a section could have resulted in more damage. Whatever Mr Fonseca did to salvage it was a huge undertaking. They had builders in for months.'

'Then, later on, after they recovered from that, there was that business with the daughter,' auntie says.

'What business?'

'Something not far from the story of the original *suddha* and his woman,' she says.

Dinesh sighs.

'And that brings us to the ghost.'

I remember how superstitious my relatives are. Folk tales, ghost stories, are part of the very fibre of the psyche here. If you believe in that kind of thing.

'Ghost? What a load of rubbish.'

Auntie clucks her tongue.

'We mustn't make light of this. Not after what happened.' She looks visibly agitated now, fixing her sari with nervous fingers.

What is she referring to? It might be nonsense but I need to know if I'm staying there. I push my plate away.

'Tell me about the ghost.'

'Another time.' Auntie stands. '*Khannah.*' Eat. 'I must go. Nice to meet you.'

She leaves, her sari pallu swishing behind her.

'What was that about?' I ask as the door shuts.

'She gets a little sensitive about this stuff. Most locals do. Shall I pack that up for you?'

'Please.' It might be nonsense but something about her manner rubbed off on me.

Dinesh boxes up the appa and hands it to me.

'I'm sorry about her questions,' he says.

'It's okay, I've had it enough from my own relatives. I'm used to it.' It's annoying but it didn't used to be such an issue, because even if I wasn't hitting the expected life milestones, I was exceeding my career ones. I don't want to admit it but now, on the back of everything, her words hit a nerve. My career is going up in flames and on top of that my relationships have all been a total bust. And now I'm here. What have I achieved? Now, I'm a failure by all standards.

'It's not okay,' he says. 'I get it, Sri Lankan aunties are always going to meddle but I know it's worse for women.'

'So she doesn't ask you when you're getting married,' I say.

'She knows there's nothing to say about that. You still want that ride?'

Hmm, so he sounds single. *Not that it should make a difference to me.*

'Yes,' I say.

'Let's go.'

The sun is at its zenith; sweat immediately starts to trickle down my neck as we go outside.

Dinesh unlocks the first car in the line, a VW Polo. The paintwork is faded, it might have been navy before the sun got to it. Now it's a murky greyish-blue. He loads my bags in the boot and opens the door for me. 'Shall we?'

We lock eyes for a second. Yes, I think he's flirting with me.

The plastic seat cover is hot on my bare legs. I pull my dress down to try and stop as much of my legs touching it as possible.

'Can you crank a window in here?'

'I can do better than that,' he says from the driver seat.

Moments later the air con kicks in, filling the small space with cool air.

'So, the Fonseca place? Tell me the rest of the story. Even if the ghost stuff is made-up nonsense.'

He drives along the coast. With no other vehicles on the road, the view of the ocean is uninterrupted. The sea glitters under the blazing midday sun. A few fishing boats lie upturned on the beach.

'You're a foreigner, that's why you say that.'

'I'm not a foreigner. I'm Sri Lankan.'

'Are you? How long have you been away? Sri Lankans are terrified of this stuff.'

I meet his eyes in the rear-view mirror.

'Are they? You're not scared.'

He laughs.

'Not any more. So, after the business with the daughter, the Fonsecas moved out. It was empty for a time, then they turned it into a guest house. It was always busy, though the Fonsecas didn't manage it themselves. Anyway, the last time they had guests, one of them died.'

'Of what?'

'Do you want the real answer or the locals' interpretation?'

'Both.'

He slows down to make way for a truck coming in the opposite direction.

'Real answer, one of the guests had a heart attack while he was out in the back garden. Locals' answer, depends who you speak to. Some would say something happened in the house. That he saw the ghost.'

'What, it scared the man to death?'

'Right. And other people would tell you that something, or someone, caused it. That someone killed the man. But coupled with all the other unexpected deaths around here over the past couple of years? We didn't expect any of it. And the town hasn't recovered. So you can understand why the locals have come up with their own interpretation.'

It was the same for me. My family wanted a reason for what happened. *Yakkās*. Bad karma. Anything was better than the truth. That there was something wrong with me.

'Maybe it was just a series of unconnected tragedies,' I say quietly.

'*Hari*. You're right. But it helps them to have an explanation. Even something as crazy as ghosts.' He stops the car. 'We're here.'

I unbuckle and open the door. The heat hits again, as soon as I do, battling against the air con.

Dinesh gets out, hands me my bags.

'You need help getting them in?' The flirtatious manner of before is gone.

'I'll be okay.'

'Are you sure?'

'You're worried about me? I thought you didn't believe the gossip.'

'I don't.' He looks over his shoulder. 'Be careful of the mosquitoes,' he says. His smile is back.

'Will do.'

'See you around, Miss Anika.'

'You don't have to call me Miss,' I say. 'Anika is fine.'

'That's not the custom here. First names are only for couples.'

Before I can respond, he gets in. I watch him drive away. Balancing the bags with one arm, I unlock the door. I get a prickle of apprehension as it creaks open, revealing the darkened interior. *It's just silly gossip.* There's nothing to be scared of here, I tell myself. I go inside.

20

Dayani

The old fort is emptying out, the last of today's visitors ushered to the exit. It officially closed ten minutes ago. Which is why they're here. Dayani takes Avila's hand and leads him along the top of the high outer edge. It's wide enough to walk on comfortably. Dusk is falling and shadows play through gaps in the large stone walls. The beach spreads out below, golden sand sweeping to the horizon. It's the beginning of a spectacular sunset, oranges, reds and pinks stripe the sky.

'Isn't it beautiful?' she says.

He looks at her.

'I think you're beautiful.'

'You want the rest of this ice cream, don't you?' She holds aloft the vanilla cone she bought from a vendor outside the fort.

'Yes, but that's not why I said it.'

'If you want it, you'll have to catch me.'

She runs across the open ground, into an area where the wall wraps in on itself, creating a sheltered alcove.

Avila chases her to the entrance. She laughs and swerves away, accidentally dropping the ice cream. Ice cream drips a trail down her neck as it falls, cone up on the ground.

'Damn. How are you going to make it up to me?'

'Like this.' He kisses her jaw. Then he traces the trail of melted ice cream along her neck with his tongue.

Warmth pools in her extremities. She leans into him.

A shadow passes across the gap between the rocks, breaking the glare of sunlight. What was that? Was someone there? A roaming security guard? Dayani looks but there's no one, only the horizon beyond. She pulls away.

'This wasn't a good idea. We should go.'

'Too soon? I'm sorry. I don't want to rush you.'

'It's not that.'

She wishes they could have more than these snatched moments together. But there's always a risk. Prying eyes, of strangers or people who know her family.

'I want to be alone with you, without worrying about who is around,' she says.

'I want that too.'

'Let's go,' she says.

They walk back out of the alcove, past weather-beaten, moss-covered walls, towards the clock tower. It's far from the security guard's post, they can exit there unseen. Below them, waves crash against stone. They don't talk, but Dayani is acutely aware of his presence. His hand swinging by his side, close to hers. She wants to take his hand but the brief moment in the alcove has spooked her. Even though there is no one around, she doesn't risk touching. It's been two weeks since their arrack-fuelled kiss. She's seen him nearly every day, hanging out in a group of friends, like they usually do. His sister is always present during these gatherings and Dayani is getting sick of it. They haven't spoken about the confrontation on the roof. Dayani hasn't told Avila, either. His loyalties are always split when it comes to his sister. Dayani doesn't want to make him take sides. So she pretends when they're with the group that she and Avila are just friends, like they always were.

There are times when she can be alone with him. She's been helping him prepare for university entrance exams, and since they got together, it's been the perfect excuse.

'How are you feeling about next week?' she asks as they approach the clock tower. Below is the town, red-tiled roofs of the houses packed close. Avila's home is there, her own is in the other direction, in the nicest part of town full of palatial, colonial-style mansions.

Avila shrugs.

'Okay, I guess.'

'What about the physics questions I gave you? Have you memorised them?'

'Sure.' He avoids her eye.

Behind the clock tower, concealed by bushes, is a set of stairs. At the end is a gate, rickety and low enough that they can climb over it, into the street beyond. Dayani follows him. That feeling of being watched hasn't left her. Now that they're back on the street, no longer trespassing after hours, among crowds of locals, she can breathe easier.

'So you're ready?'

'As much as I'll ever be.'

The whole time she's been helping him, Avila has been keen, almost desperate to pass. To get into university in the capital. This new offhand manner jars.

'What's going on?'

He stops too.

'I appreciate what you've been doing helping me but – *vadak na.*'

'Why is there no point?'

'Because I'm not going anywhere. Thātha won't allow it. I wish you hadn't talked me into thinking it was possible.'

'So this is my fault now?'

He shakes his head.

'I didn't mean it like that. It's just, university, a future is for people like you. In my family, only one of us gets that chance and my brother took ours already. Plus his course abroad costs a bomb. There's no way I can go. Thātha needs someone to take over. It will be me, you know it.'

He turns away, walking a little ahead.

Dayani catches up to him.

'Don't do that. You've worked so hard for this. You can get in, I know you can. You can't be—' She almost says, my father's lackey. Or worse. His hit man.

'You don't have to be like your father. Don't give up now. It's just a week. You can have this freakout after the exams are done.'

Avila looks at her. Then he laughs.

'Fine.'

'You can do it. I promise you can.'

'Thanks.'

It's nearly 6 p.m. and traffic is heavy. Car horns blast, the air is full of diesel fumes and the smells of frying vadai and kottu roti from street vendors setting up their wares at the roadside stalls.

'I need to get back. My parents will ask too many questions if I'm late.'

'Want me to walk you?'

She wants to prolong their encounter but it's too risky.

'No need. I'll call Thātha's driver to get me.' It's still early, she could easily walk, but a seventeen-year-old girl walking alone in the evening isn't a common sight here.

'I'll see you tomorrow?'

He smiles, dimples showing. She wants to kiss him more than anything but she settles for returning his smile.

'See you tomorrow.'

He turns for his house and Dayani calls her father's chauffeur. She waits by the side of the busy street. Her stomach growls, the smell of vadai tantalising her. Amma will give her a hard time about bringing greasy food home, spoiling dinner. She buys one anyway, wrapped in a white paper bag. She nibbles it by the roadside as she waits. Her amma would be scandalised by her eating in the street too but Dayani doesn't care. As she bites into the hot, crunchy, fried lentil ball, there's a flash of movement across the road.

Dayani looks up. On the other side of the street, locals walk and chat, tourists stop at restaurant windows, looking for a place for dinner. Nothing out of the ordinary. That feeling prickles her neck again. Like she's being watched.

Her father's silver Mercedes arrives and Dayani climbs in. She scans the street as the driver pulls away. She can't see anything to explain it, but the feeling stays with her all the way home.

21

Anika

Now

I set down my bags. Taking Dinesh's advice, I open all the windows. I wipe grime and dust off the blades of the ceiling fans, then turn them on, one by one.

From the entryway and front room, I move into the kitchen. Another area I didn't get a good look at when I arrived. An earthenware firepit dominates one wall. Clay and metal pots are stacked upside down on the floor underneath, waiting for someone to use them. There is even the remains of a fire in the oven. I prod the pile of sticks and they disintegrate. My finger comes away covered in ash.

I fill my bucket with water from the kitchen tap. The water runs murky at first, then clear. There are more arched windows in the dining room, reaching from the floor almost up to the ceiling. Slatted shutters cover them. I pull a chair away from the dining table to stand on, so I can clean to the tops of them. As I do, I notice patterns in the dust on one of the chairs, four long lines, like fingers trailed over the surface. Like the patterns on the table.

They look fresh, they haven't been there long enough for dust to settle. Who made them? The strange stories Dinesh told me about the house come into my mind. I shake my head. It must have been the owner. Kavya said Mr Fonseca came a few weeks ago. He hasn't replied to my email, so I don't know for sure. I need to ask him again.

I wash the shutters, wipe down the table and sideboard, scrubbing extra hard over the bits with the finger trails. As I sweep, then mop the floor, dirt shifts and the surface emerges – white marble with threads of pale pink. It's unexpected. Beautiful.

The room looks so much better when I'm done, surfaces shining, windows open to the palm trees outside, that I wish I'd taken a picture of how it looked before. It's a total 180-degree change. I take an 'after' photo anyway.

I clean the bedroom where I've been sleeping, and hang mosquito nets around the frame. Lighting one of the mosquito coils, I place it in the corner. Its lemony citronella tang fills the air. Sweat runs in rivulets down my back and my arms ache but it's worth it. Just like the dining room, I've effected a transformation. I take another photo.

It's dusk now. As I clean the final set of windows downstairs, facing out to behind the house, I find a door which opens outwards onto the veranda. I kick off my flip-flops and walk, off the cool tiles of the veranda onto the sand beyond. With the fall of dusk, the temperature has dropped a little, so that I can walk barefoot now. This is the view I saw on my first night. The back garden of this house is the beach.

I walk to the water's edge. The sea is calm still, but there's a ripple on the tide, which makes me think it could turn choppy fast. I don't have much time. I have the swimsuit I bought at Kavya's Boutique on under my dress. I pull my dress off and wade in. When my feet leave the bottom, I start to swim.

The water is cool, I give in to the weightlessness as I tread water, facing back towards the shore. The house looks smaller from here, and with all the lights on, it doesn't look as desolate as the day I arrived. Upstairs is a room with a balcony. That must be the one with the jammed door, because none of the other rooms I've been in have balconies.

Dark is closing in now. The nights here aren't like those in the UK. Especially in an area like this, with few buildings and no street lights. After sunset it turns pitch-black, the kind of night where you can barely see your feet. The house is the only spot of light now. But wait – what's that? A flash of movement on the balcony draws my eye. Something white. I squint into the darkness and the blurry shape takes on a form. Is that a person? Is someone on the balcony?

My breathing comes faster now. I swim, as quickly as I can, to shore, keeping my eye on the balcony. I only look away to make sure I'm swimming straight. But when I reach the shore, the balcony is empty. There's no one there.

I have to know, is someone in the house? I've explored all the rooms, except the one with the door I couldn't open. If someone was on the balcony of that room, that door would be the way in. The door is closed, locked, like it was yesterday. I try all the keys again but again they don't work. I throw my weight against the door again and again, until my shoulder is scratched but the door doesn't move. The damp sea air must have jammed the door shut. I breathe easier. I can't have seen anyone on the balcony. Because this room is the only access to the balcony and there's no other way to get in.

Still, I go back outside to be sure, and look up at the balcony. The arches of the canopy are shadowed. I walk up and down and inspect it from all angles. Until I can satisfy myself that there is nobody hiding there.

What exactly did I see earlier? A distant white shape. Which could have been a person wearing white, or a trick of the light. A beam from a passing boat perhaps, causing flickers in the gloom that I mistook for something else. I'm tired, jet-lagged and it's making my imagination run wild. I should get some sleep. But inside, as I lock the door, I hesitate.

I haven't had a response from Mr Fonseca yet, about when someone was last here. There is one place I might find answers. The one room with anything in it, that could tell me about who lived here. The library. It's the only room I haven't cleaned properly yet.

The wrought-iron lamps on the wall cast a dim glow over the dusty shelves. I'm too tired to clean in here now. I just want some answers. Outside, the sea churns, waves crashing angrily now. I remember Kavya's story about the boat that capsized. The tourists who drowned. This sea can be unforgiving. I'm glad I got out when I did. Even if it was because I was imagining an intruder on the balcony.

I use my phone torch to examine the books. From the spines they look like textbooks and novels. I don't know what I was expecting. Family photo albums? There's nothing like that here. I shine my torch over the back wall. The gold handle of the knife in the glass case glints as the torch beam passes over it. Above it, the *yakkā* mask leers. I want to avoid its eyes but I can't, the mask draws me and I move closer. The sharp angles of the jaw, the hollows of the eyes seem to eat the shadows around them. I wonder how old it is. The rituals, the exorcisms it was used for over the years. I wonder how many. There was a mask like this on the wall of the house where my family took me after my parasomnia got worse. After the last, worst time. I didn't know whose house it was. The lounge furniture had been cleared and replaced with a long table at which sat Buddhist monks in saffron robes. I was sat on the floor in front of them as they chanted pirith for what seemed like hours. Then I was taken to a church to see a priest. Different religion, same intention. To exorcise the demons that supposedly made me do what I did. Because they didn't want to accept the truth. The truth is worse. There were no demons. It was all my fault.

I need to get out of here. I turn abruptly, my phone torch beam panning wildly across the dusty floor. That's when I notice it. Next to the prints left by my flips-flops, over by the wall, is another footprint. I can make out the outline of the heel, the toes. The footprint is less dusty than the floor around it. How long has it been there? Like the fingermarks on the table downstairs, it looks new. I run out of the room, shutting the door firmly behind me.

Whose footprint was in the library? I tell myself it's the owner's, or one of his family, or a contractor. But I can't shift the feeling of unease that's settled on me. I've never scared easily, but all the weird stories I've heard today must have got in my head, because I'm imagining things on the balcony. Jumping at footprints that probably have a reasonable explanation.

Finally, I pull out my phone. I compose a new email to Mr Fonseca. Tell him that I need an answer to my previous email. I don't tell him about the finger trails or the footprint. I'll see what he comes back with first. Then I settle my phone on the floor by the bed and close my eyes. With the windows open, the sounds of the whirring fan and the crashing of the waves beyond create a soothing melody. The unease of before begins to shift. There's nothing to be scared of, I tell myself. Still, I leave all the lights on when I go to sleep.

22

Anika

Then

'Better?' Dominic asks.

Anika shifts position on the couch, leaning her head back as he massages her shoulders.

'Exactly what a girl needs after a long day in theatre.'

He kisses the top of her head and flicks a button on the remote, navigating to his Netflix list.

'So, *The Ring* or *The Grudge*?' he asks.

Anika smiles up at him. They're at his place, a top-floor warehouse conversion near London Bridge. His lounge is the size of her entire flat, the L-shaped Ligne Roset couch they're lying on the stuff of Anika's interiors dreams. But it's Dominic in his home that she likes best. He's in casual clothes, a T-shirt and joggers, not his usual work suits. And he's relaxed here, fully himself with her, in a way he isn't anywhere else. More than the fancy dinners, being here with him feels real.

'*The Grudge*,' she says. 'I'm in the mood for a laugh.'

He shakes his head.

'You're the only person I know who finds that movie funny. If I didn't like you so much, I'd be very scared of you.'

Like. His voice falters slightly on the word. As if he knows what she wants him to say. Love. But he hasn't said it. Anika won't say it first. Even though she feels it.

Dominic stands.

'I should get dinner started.'

In the open-plan kitchen he bustles about with pans and plates, as if nothing is amiss.

She takes a seat on the bar stool at the worktop in front of him and watches him peel greaseproof paper off a cut of meat.

'We're having steak?'

The hob glows bright as he starts it up.

'Your favourite, right?'

It was an offhand comment she'd made one day. He remembered. She smiles.

'You're good.'

The clock on his oven behind him says it's 8 p.m. She's been worrying about her last patient of the day, a complicated procedure that required a laparotomy instead of the expected keyhole surgery.

'I should check in with work. See how my last patient is doing.'

'Do you ever switch off?'

'Rarely.'

'And I like that about you. Go for it.' That word again. Like.

Anika crosses the hall to his bedroom. Her jacket hangs with some of Dominic's items on a hook on the back of the door. As she rummages for her phone she thinks, she could see herself here. Her things next to his. Moving in. The thought scares her, makes her breath hitch. Six months is too early for her to think like this. It's too early for love. Isn't it? But she knows what she feels.

Her hand hits on something in the jacket pocket. A box. She pulls it out and realises two things. One, that this isn't her jacket. She looked in his black jacket by mistake. Two, his jacket contains a piece of jewellery. She opens the long blue Tiffany box. On the cushion inside sits a thin silver chain. A pendant made of two interlocking circles shines at the centre.

'Everything okay?' Dominic calls.

Anika shoves the necklace back into the coat. 'All good.'

'Dinner is nearly ready.'

'I'll be right out.'

She slips the box out again. With shaking hands she examines it. She wants to tell herself it's for a relative. His mother. He doesn't have a sister. But the two interlocking circles, no the *rings*, look back at her. This is a gift for a partner. For someone he loves. It's not Anika's birthday, Christmas isn't for three months. This necklace is not for her.

'You hear about the patient?'

Dominic is standing in the hallway.

Anika starts. She remembers what she went into his bedroom for. With fumbling hands she retrieves her phone from her own jacket. Her face is flushed as she comes out, holding it.

'I - not yet.' She walks past him, back into the kitchen. Sitting at the breakfast bar, she types a message to one of the ward doctors on shift, to let her know how the patient is doing overnight.

Dominic comes back, gets two plates out of a cupboard.

'Are you okay?'

Should she challenge him outright? Or wait and see if he tells her? Dominic is like no boyfriend she's known. He's understanding of her long hours, maybe because he does them too. He sends her good morning texts when he goes to New York for work. He listens to her worries when she's had a hard day. *Too good to be true.* She hasn't quite been able to believe her luck. Now she knows she was right.

'I'm fine.'

'Are you?'

She takes a deep breath.

'I need to tell you something.'

'Me too,' he says.

Her throat goes dry. She can't bring herself to ask him. She doesn't want to hear him lie.

'You go first,' she says.

He smiles and reaches under the worktop.

'I wanted to give you this.' He places the blue Tiffany box on the worktop, next to the plate he's set for her.

Anika's heart races as she opens it. Inside is the necklace. Tiny diamonds on the rings glint under the kitchen lights.

'Is this for me?' she asks.

'Of course.'

His blue eyes hold hers. She can't look away.

'What's the occasion?'

'Does there have to be one?'

She's relieved her worst fears were wrong. The gift is for her. *I love you.* The words bubble up, but they don't come out.

'This whole thing between us. You. It doesn't feel real,' she says. She hates that she's ruining the moment. But she can't help herself.

He raises an eyebrow.

'Should I pinch you? Because it feels real to me.'

'Seriously. Be honest with me. You said you love me. Did you mean it?'

'Why would you ask me that?' There's genuine hurt in his eyes. She was wrong. Taking out her issues on him like she has since they first met.

'I'm sorry,' she says. 'I'm a little guarded, when it comes to relationships.'

He smiles wryly.

'I hadn't noticed.' He touches her shoulder. 'You've been hurt before.' A statement, not a question.

'My previous boyfriend. It turns out he was using me to climb the career ladder the whole time.' That's not even the half of it. She doesn't tell him about before. She doesn't talk about that.

'Then he's a total loser.'

'I know.'

'I'm not like that,' he says.

'You're not.' As she says it, she knows it to be true. 'I'm sorry. I don't know what's got into me.' She takes a breath. 'This necklace is gorgeous. Thank you.'

He kisses her and she feels herself melting.

Then he takes the necklace out of the box. She moves her hair aside for him to drape it round her neck and fasten the clasp.

She touches the pendant, slipping her little finger into the rings.

The steak in the pan sizzles as he fries it, filling the space with its aroma. He slices it and plates it. It's rare, oozing blood. Just the way she likes it. He passes her cutlery. He's not fazed by her strange reaction to his gift. Anika realises she's been overthinking this from the beginning. Doubting his intentions when they first met. Resisting when he tried to make them more than a hook-up. Assuming he bought the gift for someone else. It's time to let her guard down, finally.

When he sits next to her, Anika turns to him.

'I love you,' she says.

Silence lies between them, weighted.

Then he covers her wrist with his hand.

'I love you too,' he says.

23

Anika

Now

A new email shows when I wake up. It's from Mr Fonseca.

> I apologise for your inconvenience so far, and that the condition of the house was below expectations. I appreciate that the work is a lot more than you were expecting, and that I was not clear about this from the outset. I can double your payment as a recompense, if you are willing to continue.

I sit up. Double payment. And his offer was already generous. I jump out of bed. The mosquito coil has burned out overnight into a spiral-shaped pattern of ash on the floor. I step over it and to the window. A fresh sea breeze blows in, ruffling my hair. It's a hot, clear day. I slept through again last night. In fact, since I've been here, I've had two of the longest nights of sleep I've had in years.

The email ends with an answer to my question. He says he was last here with his contractor two weeks ago. That explains the footprint, the marks on the dining-room furniture. He hasn't answered my question about who else has lived here, but I will ask again.

I imagine what this place would look like after three weeks.

And then again, after the restoration work is complete. Having a part in returning this place to its former glory will be satisfying. And, if I'm receiving double payment, I can go travelling after this assignment is complete. I can afford a few things to make my stay here more comfortable too, like new bedsheets. I reply, accepting his offer. Then I change and start the walk into town.

With the hat I bought from Kavya's on, the sun is less defeating, the walk feels easier. Or maybe I'm getting used to the heat. I take a different path today, stopping at the secret beach and walking down to the shore. I wade through the shallows with my flip-flops held in my hands. I can see my feet all the way, my navy-blue painted toenails shine in the clear water. The footprint in the library was so similar to the prints my bare feet make now, in the sand of the seabed. I can remember the rounded outlines, of the heel and the individual toes. I bend to trail my fingers through the water. Mr Fonseca's email said he'd been in with his contractors two weeks ago. One of them could have made the footprint. *But why would they have been barefoot?* Why do I keep thinking about the footprint? I need to let it go. I'm getting paid double for my work now and anyway this gig will be done soon. I can travel after that. Do whatever I want. At least until the verdict on what's happening in London, what's happening with my career, is decided.

I climb some steps carved into the rock at the edge of the secret beach. At the end is a path flanked by palm trees on either side, making a canopy overhead. I'm getting used to this area. My family's house was in an area that was manicured and neat, the houses immaculately painted and fenced off. There were beaches like the secret beach in my family's town but they belonged to the big five-star hotels with their infinity pools and you'd need to show a room key or day pass before you could set foot on them.

I liked visiting but such rarefied, elitist places would make me feel uncomfortable and somehow guilty about being there. I wasn't a local, but I wasn't a tourist either. I didn't know how I was supposed to act and it didn't sit right with me. This is different. Egalitarian and wilder. I like the rough-around-the-edges charm of this place too.

A market is in progress, on the main street in town. Stalls with fabric canopies take up the road between shops. There are stalls with textiles and spices in plastic bags. The aroma of frying drifts from the stalls further away. I stop at a stall with mangoes, dragon fruit and rambutan hanging from the awning. It seems to be selling smoothies, though I can't read the menu, in Sinhala. Even when we visited here regularly, my written Sinhala wasn't great. Now, I can barely make out a word.

'Try the mango and passionfruit juice.' It's Kavya.

'It does sound delicious.' I catch the vendor's attention and ask for that. The man takes fruit from a bucket full of ice behind him, peels the mango, cracks open the passionfruit and blends it all with lime juice, crushed ice and something he adds from a bottle.

'What is that – *eh mokada?*' I add, remembering my Sinhala.

The man winks.

'*Eka kiyunna baa.*'

Kavya laughs.

'It's a – how do you say? A secret ingredient.'

The man puts the bright yellow smoothie in a plastic cup on the table, condensation already dripping down the sides and I pay. I take a sip. It's sweet and rich with lime and something else I can't place. The flavours are vibrant and delicious.

'*Harima rasai,*' I say to the man and he smiles.

'This might be the best mango drink I've ever had,' I say to Kavya as we walk away.

'I look forward to one every time the market comes around.'

'How often does it happen?'

'Once a month,' she says, taking me through the stalls. 'We have some traders from neighbouring towns as well as our own, of course.'

'I'm glad I caught it then.'

Around us, people browse, haggle. Vendors call their wares, I make out the chant of *marloo, marloo*. Fresh fish. I stop at a display of saris, admiring the jewel-bright colours. One catches my eye in particular. It's a deep forest green with silver threads shot through. The stallholder sees me looking.

'*Balanna owena the?*' You want to see? Without waiting for an answer he removes a section of fabric from the spool, gesturing for me to touch. I run my fingers over the soft, gauzy material. I haven't worn a sari in years. I used to play dress-up with my cousins as a child, raiding our mothers' cupboards and being shouted at afterwards for messing up the fabrics. When I became old enough to start wearing them myself was around the time we stopped visiting. I never wore one in the UK. There were too many bad memories. And missing ones.

'*Lassanai*,' Kavya says, appraising it. 'It would suit your complexion.'

I hold the fabric up to the light. The sun catches the silver threads, making them shimmer and dance. I'm back, after so long. Maybe I could wear one again.

'I'm going to get it,' I say, on impulse.

I reach for my wallet.

'Hold on.'

Kavya speaks to the vendor, haggling a better price and he folds the material into a neat square, packing it into a plastic bag. I take it, thanking him. He's thrown in the top free of charge, a sleeveless silvery crop that contrasts perfectly with the bold green.

'Thanks, that was some bargain,' I say as we walk away.

'Always got to haggle here,' she says. 'You know how to wear a sari?'

'Draping six feet of fabric isn't the easiest thing when you don't know what you're doing, but I'll try to remember.'

'You want me to show you?'

'Yes please. This market is great,' I say as we walk between stalls.

'It used to be bigger, before. Visitors would come from the surrounding towns and there were stalls up and down the whole street with queues at all of them. This is only a little of what it was.'

I watch a group of children play in the shade of a banyan tree. Their laughter mixes with the sounds of chatter from the market, the crows cawing overhead. The distant sound of the sea. This feels like the Sri Lanka I used to know and love.

'It's a shame. You think the town will recover?'

'I hope so.'

Some of the shopkeepers stand under the shade of a store-front nearby, chatting. Auntie Darsha is there, and a man I don't recognise.

'*Kohomada?*' auntie asks as we approach. How are you? I thank her for the appa yesterday and she smiles and says she's happy I enjoyed it. She has a warm manner, like my grandmother. It reminds me that I need to tell her how I'm doing. I'd put it off, not wanting to lie or worry her with the reality, but now things are looking up. The house looks better and I'm getting paid double. I should call her tonight.

'*Miss lankawe the?*' asks the man. Are you Sri Lankan? Kavya says his name is Ziman. He's wiry and lean, wearing a blue sarong and shirt. I explain that I haven't been here for some time.

'What do you do in the UK?' auntie asks. The auntie nosiness again. I consider telling her the truth, that I'm a doctor. Up there with the holy grail of careers in the South Asian auntie world. But that will invite more questions and every answer will feel like a lie. I decide then and there to let the identity go. Feel it puff away on the breeze, like a piece of candyfloss. I won't define myself by it any more.

'I'm in between jobs.'

Her face falls. No doubt now writing me off as a drifter with no career plans.

'Anika is doing some work on the house,' Kavya says.

I smile at her gratefully.

'And after that, we'll see.'

A man comes out of the household goods shop behind us. He's burly and middle-aged, wearing a striped shirt and sarong. Kavya introduces him as Gamini. He's the one who chased the pickpocket.

'Thanks for your help the other day,' I say.

'*Kohomada ah the?*' he asks.

'I'm fine today, uncle.'

'Nirmal's sorry for his actions. He's had a lot of bad luck, over the past year, and he hasn't had a proper job in some time. I offered him a role in my shop, until he has something else to do. He has a sick mother to support and no one else to help,' Gamini says.

'*Ehenung hondai*,' Ziman says.

Kavya pats Gamini's shoulder.

'Yes, it's good you're helping him, uncle.'

'I tried to,' Gamini says, frowning. 'Nirmal was meant to start his job yesterday, but he didn't come.'

Ziman shakes his head. 'He probably wasn't going to. Sorry, Gamini, but I think he must be back to stealing.'

'You think so?' Gamini's frown deepens. 'He was very grateful when I offered, he seemed so happy to have a job again. Then he didn't turn up, yesterday or today either.'

'I know you want to help, Gamini,' Ziman says. 'But he's a thief, he won't change.'

'You know he wasn't always like that,' Gamini says.

'Something could have happened at home. He will come,' Kavya says. 'Give it time.'

'*Balamu*,' Gamini says. We'll see.

'So how is the Fonseca mansion?' Ziman asks, turning to me with a strange smile.

'It's old and needs work, but it's fine.'

I show them the shots on my phone. Instead of looking impressed, everyone except Kavya rears back like I've shown them photos from an autopsy.

'You've done a good job,' Kavya says.

'*Eh gedara in na eppā*,' says auntie. Don't stay there.

'*Holmung innawa ney the?*' Ziman says. There are ghosts, aren't there? He laughs, but it's a tense kind of sound.

'Of course not. The house is okay. I've started cleaning and it's looking better already.'

'Do you know the stories about the house?' Ziman asks.

'Dinesh told me some yesterday,' I say. 'About the original owner and the suicide.'

Ziman raises his eyebrows.

'Is that what he said? That's the official version. A double suicide, two lovers jumping because they couldn't be together. But that's not the real story.' He looks at the others.

'It wasn't suicide. It was murder,' Ziman says.

'She pushed him. And they both fell to their deaths,' Kavya says.

Everything looks so bright all of a sudden, it hurts my eyes. I pull my sunglasses on.

'There's a third version,' Ziman says. 'The real version. The *suddha*'s wife killed them. She wanted revenge on her husband and his lover.'

My heart is racing now. I must be getting dehydrated. I reach for my bottle.

'How do you know?' I ask.

'They found some of her things, after she died. Lenore was her name. Shortly after the place was bought by the Fonsecas, she had a breakdown. She was conveyed to an asylum in the city. And after she died there, they found her diaries. They were full of unhinged ramblings about her husband and his mistress, and about what she'd done. Like a confession,' he says. 'But she was dead, so there was no point pursuing it. One of my cousins is a nurse there. He said the staff were so convinced of her guilt, it became a local legend.'

I take a swig of water. The water is warm.

'So how does that affect the town now?' I ask.

'They say she never really left the house,' Ziman says.

'What do you mean?'

'They say she cursed the place,' auntie says. Her tone is hushed, her manner tense now. 'That because her love was unlucky, she damned everyone who lived there after her to the same fate.'

'Her restless spirit haunts the place still,' says Ziman. It's the height of the sun and the air is still. Sweat trickles down my neck, leaving dampness in its wake. I checked the balcony. *There was no one there.* I move further under the shade of the awning of the shop.

'Luckily I'm single, so the curse can't touch me.'

'How do you explain the Fonseca family?' Gamini says suddenly. 'Their daughter.'

'What happened to her?' I ask.

'She had a love affair with a local boy. The Fonsecas didn't approve. It ended badly. She was so affected, she ended up in hospital.'

A car horn sounds in the distance. I jump. What is wrong with me? I don't ask what type of hospital she ended up in, though I'm wondering. I'm not indulging this.

'That's a sad story, but it doesn't mean the curse, or the ghost stuff, is true.'

'What about what happened in this town?' Gamini says. He wipes sweat from his brow with a handkerchief. 'Nothing has been the same since the boat accident.'

'Don't tell her all this,' Kavya says. 'Just silly gossip,' she says to me. 'Don't pay any attention.' She's the least affected, but all four of them look varying shades of anxious. I drink from my water bottle again. I should get some more, preferably chilled. And the bedsheets I came out for. I didn't expect to get trapped in such a strange conversation.

'I have to go,' I say. 'I need to get some things.'

'Do you want me to help you with the sari before you do?' Kavya says.

'That would be great.'

I follow her down the road.

'Perfect timing,' I say. 'I'm not sorry to be out of that conversation.'

'I know, people become worried whenever anyone mentions the Fonseca house.'

She takes us through the market stalls to her shop and unlocks it.

At the back there are two small changing cubicles. She opens the curtain of one and I hand her the sari.

'What does the boat accident have to do with the house and the curse?'

'The boat that capsized was the start of things going wrong in the town. The reason tourists don't come here any more. And the only one of the crew who survived told us what happened.' Kavya peels the packaging off. 'It was a stormy night so the boat stayed close to shore. The Fonseca house faces the beach, and when the boat passed the house, the captain saw something.'

'What?'

She hands me the end of the sari.

'The guy that survived was with the captain in the wheelhouse.

He saw it too. On the balcony. A woman pacing, wearing white, her long hair loose.'

A strange prickle of apprehension travels up my back.

'The balcony?'

'Her bedroom was there.'

My hands slip on the fabric and it falls to the floor, puddling around my feet.

Just like I saw last night.

'Lenore?'

She leans to help me pick it up.

'That's what they think. She was in a white dress, or a sari, they couldn't be sure. Then the storm picked up. The captain lost control of the boat.'

As I kneel to help her pick up the fabric, my arms prickle with goosebumps. Dinesh said the tourist who stayed in the guest house was found dead in the garden of the house. That something happened there. I thought he meant inside the house. But the garden faces the balcony. What if the man saw her too? *Lenore.*

No. That's ridiculous. I heard a lot of ghost stories when I visited here as a child. My relatives loved telling them. And there was always one that involved a woman in a white dress, or a white wedding sari, or a nightgown. They must have got into my head.

'I'm sorry that happened. But what are they saying? That a ghost appeared and caused the accident?'

She hands me the excess fabric to hold, keeping the rest hung over her arm as she drapes it around me.

'The guy who survived said he'd never seen a night like it. The sky darkened, suddenly. The rain came down harder than he'd ever experienced. They couldn't see anything. The captain lost control of the boat. They were pulled out to sea. Nearly everyone on the boat drowned.'

'How do we know any of this is true? Who is this guy who survived?'

She hesitates, the pallu of the sari in her hand.

'You've met him already.'

'Who?'

'Nirmal. The pickpocket.'

So that's why Gamini and others got so funny about Nirmal. But the fact that the story had come from a real person, doesn't prove anything.

'He could have imagined it,' I say, though my voice has less conviction than it did a moment ago.

'I hope you're right, Miss Anika.' She throws the pallu over my shoulder and steps back. 'What do you think?'

I push thoughts of the ghost out of my head as I look in the mirror. The bright material wraps around my hips in a flattering way and the gauzy fabric feels so feminine.

'You've done a great job.' I turn around, admiring the way she's created a fanlike shape out of the fabric at the front. 'I won't be able to do it as nicely as you have.'

And I would have focused better if I wasn't distracted by the crazy story.

I start to unwrap it from my body. 'So is there anywhere more lively around here?'

'There are some nice towns nearby. Mirissa, Hatton Bay, Galhena.'

She doesn't notice me freeze when she mentions it. Hatton Bay. The town where my family's house used to be.

'They sound good.' I fold the sari, put it back in the bag. 'Thanks for this.'

She smiles.

'Any time. Oh, and Miss Anika. I'm sorry about the stories. We shouldn't have told you.'

'It's okay,' I say. 'I asked.'

'Well, don't take any notice. It's silly local gossip.' But she looks troubled as I say my goodbyes and emerge onto the street, where the market stalls are starting to pack up.

As I buy bedsheets in the household goods store, I keep thinking about what I thought I saw last night. Even though I know the stories don't make sense. I tell the shopkeeper to keep the change and put the sheets in a hemp bag I brought with me from London. I picked it from a pile in a hurry, but I realise now that it's from the conference where I presented the findings of the surgical robotics project. Back when life made sense. I run my fingers over the smooth surface of the logo – it's shiny and warm, like it's melting. It reminds me of another life. And who I was then. Someone who loved horror movies, the only one of my friends at the Halloween graveyard screening of *Psycho* who didn't lose it. I was unfazed. And that's how I should be by these stories. They have no logical or scientific basis and I refuse to pay attention to them. I jam my hat harder on my head as I return into the heat. I have one more stop to make.

Coconut Cove Coffee is blissfully cool with a breeze from the powerful ceiling fan. Removing my hat, I run my hands through my sweaty hair. Dinesh is cleaning the coffee machine with his back to me. He seemed sensible, yesterday. I could do with some rational conversation.

'Hey.'

He turns, smiles.

'You're back.'

'I wanted to try more of your beans.'

He laughs as he puts down the silver strainer in his hands.

'Then have a seat.'

'Us decaf drinkers don't usually get much of a choice. But you said they're all great so hit me up.'

He pulls out a stool at the counter nearest the coffee machine.

I rest my bag at my feet and sit, trying not to notice how his shirt moves over his upper back muscles as he makes my coffee. I just came in to say hello. Though can it hurt to look?

'Here,' he says, setting a glass in front of me. The latte art is a rose this time.

'You're good at this,' I say, examining it.

'Told you. I'm a multi-talented.' He places a napkin next to it. 'This is a Sri Lankan peaberry. You're in luck, it's a rare variety and we're nearly out. You're getting one of the last ones of the season. Maybe the last one.'

'Lucky me.' I take a sip. It's even nicer than yesterday's.

'Good?' he asks.

'The best decaf I've had. Ever.'

He smiles.

'That's a better review.'

'I'll add it to my Tripadvisor rating.'

'Now imagine if you had the real thing.'

'No,' I say quickly, and louder than I'd intended.

He looks taken aback. He must think I'm really strange, getting so agitated about coffee.

'I have a thing. Med—' I stop before I say, *medical*. Apart from Eliza and Rosa, I haven't even told my friends about it. I don't need to explain it to a stranger.

'Never mind. Can I just have my decaf?'

He pulls out the stool next to me and sits.

'How is the house?'

'I took your advice and the mosquitoes have run in fear. I have fewer bites anyway.'

'Having one hundred mosquito coils per room would do that.'

I put the coffee down.

'Something else happened.'

'Something good, or . . . ?'

'I'm getting a pay rise.'

'Definitely good. How did you manage that?'

'I have my ways.'

'Must have,' he says. 'Mr Fonseca isn't known for being generous. He's like his father. And I told you the story of how his father bought the house, didn't I?'

'You didn't tell me the whole story. At least, not according to the locals. The boat story. They all seemed to believe it.'

He starts stacking glasses by the counter, not looking at me.

'But you don't?'

'Of course not.'

'I don't either.' His expression is completely unchanged. It confirms my suspicions, that the stories are utter rubbish.

'Great. So, I'd kind of like to celebrate my pay rise, preferably somewhere with less talk of ghosts and curses. How could I get to Galhena?' I don't say Hatton Bay. Instead I name one of the other spots Kavya mentioned. It's close enough that I could go to Hatton Bay from there easily. If I get the courage.

He gives me a lopsided smile. There's that energy between us again. I didn't imagine it yesterday, I don't think.

'That's a cool spot. It's not far. Fifteen minutes, twenty, tops. You'd need to drive, though.'

'So can I borrow one of those cars out there? Hire them. Do you do that?'

He shrugs.

'They're not my cars. I'm just the driver.'

'So drive me then. That's your job, right? One of them?'

'The taxi office shuts at eight.'

'That's very early.'

'There's not a lot happening in this town.' There's something in his eyes. A flirtatiousness to his manner. I wasn't imagining it. My romantic relationships are part of the wreckage of my former life. The most damaged, twisted, still smoking parts of it. I thought I was done with all that. But here, in a new environment, would meeting a cute guy be such a bad thing? No strings this time. No expectations. Which means, no disappointment.

'Is there another taxi rank somewhere? A three-wheeler? Even a bus?'

He laughs.

'You don't want to get a bus here. They come twice a day and hit all the potholes.'

'So can't you open the taxi office late for once? Or let me borrow a car. I won't tell.'

'You definitely can't do that. But – I have a vehicle.'

He looks conflicted. I know what I'd like to do. I'm not meant to be this forward. This is Sri Lanka after all. Things are different. But no one knows me here. Not really. So there are no repercussions.

'Here's a crazy idea,' I say. 'Why don't we go together?'

'You want to go to Galhena together?'

Did I just ask him out? I didn't plan to but it slipped out. He's so cute, and would some sensible company be such a bad thing?

'Why not? It could be fun to hang out.'

Misgiving flashes across his face. Was I too forward?

'When did you want to go?'

'Tonight, if you're free.'

He hesitates again. Then he smiles.

'I could do that. One thing. How are you with motorbikes?'

Even better. I smile as I stand, picking up my bag.

'Great. Pick me up at eight.'

'See you later,' he calls after me.

24

Dayani

The botanical gardens are quiet today. Dayani leads Avila down a wide esplanade lined with towering fig trees. She feels so tiny and insignificant compared to these trees that have stood for hundreds of years.

'Are you sure about this?' Avila looks up. Between the fronds of the trees, the sky is dark with rain clouds. The path ahead is empty. Not many people want to be caught in the storm that is due. That's why Dayani suggested they meet here.

'Have I led you wrong yet?'

'Apart from sneaking us in without paying?'

Dayani laughs. She noticed that path in between the fig trees last time she came here. Unmanned by security guards, a clear entrance in from the street, if you knew where to look.

'I know a place where we'll be out of the rain.' At the botanical gardens on a rainy afternoon, she doesn't have to look over her shoulder every few minutes. The feeling of being watched hasn't left her since they went to the fort. A few days ago she and Avila were walking together down a street on the other side of town. As they turned into the road that led to the beach, Dayani thought she saw a shadow on the tarmac behind them. She dropped Avila's hand and turned quickly, but there was no one there. She hasn't risked holding his hand in public since.

'This way.' She follows the signs to the Orchid House. Inside, the humidity is amplified.

She stops at a display of purple and red orchids, larger than any she's seen before.

'Aren't they beautiful?'

Avila runs a hand over his head.

'*Maara rasneigh mehe.*'

'I know it's hot. We're nearly there.'

As they exit the greenhouse the storm breaks. Cold drops hit her face.

'Cooler now?' she asks.

Avila frowns.

'That's not what I meant.'

She scans the road ahead. There's the pond dotted with waterlilies and lotuses, the surface rippling with rain. There's the cafe kiosk, shuttered now. Where is it? For a moment she thinks she misremembered. Then she sees the shelter in the distance.

'There.' She runs towards the gazebo and Avila follows. She takes the stone steps up, two at a time, and sits on the bench that runs the perimeter of the interior. Rain hammers above them. Water runs in sheets from the roof, obscuring the view. But inside is warm and dry. She pats the seat next to her.

'Better?'

Avila sits next to her.

'Why did you want to come here?'

Safe from prying eyes, she threads her fingers through his.

'I wanted some alone time.' She leans in and kisses him, swings her legs over his. Avila pulls her closer to him. Dayani doesn't want it to stop, but she has to talk to him, in a way she can't when they're around other people.

'What is it?' he asks.

Dayani folds her hands on her lap. The things Ayomi said have stuck in her brain like a splinter.

'Are you serious about me?'

'Of course I am. You know that.' He tucks a strand of hair behind her ear. 'Where is this coming from?'

She doesn't know if it's the right thing to do, telling him. She doesn't want to cause tension with his family. But he should know.

'Ayomi said something.'

He makes an annoyed noise.

'We're alone for the first time this week and this is what you want to talk about?'

'She said I should leave you alone.'

'She did?'

'She thinks we're too different. You know, because of our families. So we don't have a future.'

He leans back against the wall of the gazebo. His T-shirt clings to his chest, soaked through from just a few minutes in the tropical downpour.

'She said so to me too,' he says. He sighs. 'She's not wrong. You know what our parents are like. Neither mine nor yours are going to go for it. That's why we agreed to keep it a secret.'

'For now. What about later? One day we'll be free of their expectations.' She walks to the edge of the gazebo. The rain is letting up now, the pink bougainvillea trailing around the outside no longer a blur. She turns back to him. 'I want to fast-forward the next year, until we can be together.'

He comes closer.

'What do you mean?'

Her plan hinges on him getting into Colombo University. If he doesn't, she won't go there either. She doesn't want to put more pressure on him, so she won't tell him. Not yet.

'I mean, in the future.'

'This is all kind of heavy. Can we talk about it later?' He leans in and nuzzles her neck. Something nags at her, about his reaction. Of all people he should see things her way. She knows she should push the conversation, but finds it increasingly difficult to think straight as he kisses her, pressing her against the wall of the gazebo. Then, the drumming rain stops abruptly. The rainstorm is over as quickly as it began.

'We should go.' She jogs down the gazebo steps, slippery with rainwater.

'Are you upset?' Avila asks.

'I just want to know that you don't think like them. I don't believe in that rich and poor divide like our parents do. That kind of thinking belongs in the last century. If we want to be together, that should be enough.' They haven't been a couple for that long, but she's known him for years, she knows who he is. That he's the one she sees a future with.

He runs a hand over his head.

'You say that because you're on the right side of it. Your father is wealthy. You don't know how it is not to have money. So you don't understand how far people will go to make a living.'

'I know I can't truly understand that. But I don't know why that should keep us apart.'

'I can't give you what you want.'

'I only want you.' Why doesn't he understand? She moves closer. 'I need to know that you believe in us.'

'Of course I do.'

'Then what about Ayomi?'

'Let's not worry about my family unless they become a problem,' he says.

The path ahead steams as the rainwater evaporates. Dayani can feel her dress is drier already, too. In the distance, people arrive, strolling between the neatly tended flower beds. The brief privacy the rain afforded them is over.

'Okay,' she says. 'I should go. Amma will freak if I'm late home again.'

He sighs.

'I should go too. Thātha is expecting me to help him with a job tonight.'

Dayani looks at him.

'What kind of job?'

'I don't know,' he says, but from his expression, she knows he has some idea.

'Really?'

'The jobs Thātha has me doing have changed since I turned eighteen.'

'What do you mean?' She grabs his arm, forgetting about not touching out here in the open. 'What do you have to do?'

'I don't want to talk about this. You've heard the rumours about your thātha's work.'

'So they're true?'

Avila starts walking towards the exit.

Dayani has to run to catch up with him.

'Avila, talk to me. Please.'

'Do you get it now? Why Ayomi said those things? You have no idea how messy this is. You're a rich girl and I'm not just a poor guy, my father does some bad stuff. For your father, mostly. I could never be the guy you need.' He backs into a clearing between bushes of frangipani. Dayani loves their sweet scent but today they smell somehow rotten.

'You are what I need.'

'You should be with someone like you. With an education, money and a normal job.'

'You'll have all that one day,' she says quietly. She hasn't seen him like this before.

He walks to the exit. They're outside the gate when he speaks again.

'You really think so?'

'I do,' she says. 'Of course I do.'

Dayani wishes she could kiss him goodbye, or even hug

him, but she can't. Even if their relationship wasn't a secret she couldn't do that. That's not the way here.

'I'll call you,' he says.

Dayani waves as he leaves. She tries not to think about what he might be doing tonight. He has to get into Colombo University. He has to. Not just for their future, but for himself. He can pass the entrance exams, but his total lack of self-belief won't let him see that. She resolves to try even harder to help him. Dayani hails a scooter taxi. She's not in the mood to see her father's driver right now. The taxi pulls away. Dayani doesn't see the shadow of the gate blur, as another shadow crosses it. Or the other scooter that tails her, all the way home.

Later that night, she gets a message from Avila.
I'm sorry about earlier. I do believe in us.
Dayani smiles as she replies.
Good.

25

Anika

Now

It's getting dark when I return. Before I unlock the front door I walk round the house, checking the wings at the sides. I can't locate a door, but when I examine the windows, I find they're not boarded up as I'd assumed. The wooden shutters open outwards, and when I prise them apart I discover they're not really windows at all. Beyond is solid wall. Was this part of the reconstruction after the fire? Another of the many things Mr Fonseca neglected to tell me.

The locals' stories play on my mind as I stand on the veranda, and look up at the house. The arched stone barrier of the balcony casts shadows over the lower floor of the house. Could a person prone to superstition misinterpret it, take the play of light to be a person, pacing up and down? I squint. Even in this poor light it's just an empty balcony. Nothing more.

Upstairs, I shower. Then, heading to the bedroom to change, I pause. There's a chink of light on the floor down the corridor that I didn't notice before. As I approach it, I realise. The balcony bedroom door is ajar. Anxiety churns in my stomach. I didn't open that door. It was shut last time. Unmovable.

I open the door fully. A teak four-poster bed is in the centre of the room. The mosquito netting hanging off the frame is faded grey and torn in places. A rug by the foot of the bed is worn from use with frayed edges. I touch a threadbare patch. It's seen a lot of footfall. On a dressing table is an assortment of objects. A comb with an ornate wooden handle carved with flowers. A small hand mirror, the surface misty. An empty perfume bottle. I open the stopper but I can't smell anything. It must have been here a long time. In a small ceramic dish, now covered in a film of dust, is a single earring. It's a little silver drop with a setting for a stone, but the stone must have fallen out. The clasp is broken too. The locals said this was Lenore's room. The ghost. The idea is laughable. Or at least it was, before I was in the room, surrounded by possessions that strongly suggest a woman slept here. I shake myself. There must have been lots of others sleeping here since Lenore, if indeed she was ever really here. Maybe this was more recently Mr Fonseca's wife's room. Or his daughter's. These things could even have been left by an Airbnb guest. But it doesn't seem likely. The things in this room look old. I'll ask Mr Fonseca. There must be a simple explanation.

I move towards the window. Thin net curtains cover it, as moth-eaten as the old mosquito net around the bed. Beyond is the balcony. I try the door but it doesn't move. It must have jammed, the wood swollen from the sea air.

I can't stop thinking about the room, and the stories the locals told me. Then I remember the book. I run downstairs to the library. It's dusty and undisturbed, the footprint is still there, unchanged. Ignoring it, I bend to find it. *Ghosts and Legends of Sri Lanka.* The book is filled with the ghost stories my relatives used to tell when I was little. The stuff of many childhood nightmares, though not for me. As I got older I found my own nightmares, based on reality, were far scarier than those stories could ever be. I flick through the book but I don't find anything on Lenore. What was I expecting? It sounds like a niche local story, not something that would make it into a book like this.

It's seven thirty. Dinesh will be here soon so I run to change. For the first time since I arrived, I empty my suitcase, arranging the contents on the bed. I haven't had reason to be concerned about my clothes the past few days, picking whatever was uppermost on the pile in my case. Now, I rifle through clothes, until I find a blush minidress I love. The sari I bought is still in the bag, on the bed. A full-length mirror would help me decide between them, but there's only one I've seen in the house. In the balcony room.

Inside, I hold both the outfits against my body and check my reflection in the dusty mirror. The sari isn't the thing to wear for a casual dinner or wherever we'll go tonight but a longing to wear it overtakes me anyway. I pull on the silvery top and slip, then try to drape the fabric as best I can. My effort isn't anywhere near as polished as Kavya's, but it's wearable. Not a bad result. I sit on the worn wooden stool and put on make-up. The sari calls for a more dramatic look than my usual minimal make-up. Fluffing my hair with my fingers, I turn to go. The comb catches my eye. It looks old, like an antique. From colonial times, maybe. I picture a woman in a long white nightdress sitting here, combing her hair with it. The empty room looks back at me. One old comb doesn't prove a thing.

I return to my room where my phone is charging via one of the rickety, electrical hazard plug sockets by the bed. I've been responding to Achiamma's missed calls with short texts and I know she'll be worried. I call her now.

She answers on the third ring.

'*Kohomada, duwa?*' she says.

'I'm good. Settled in but it needs a lot of work.'

'Is it too much for you?' I can imagine her frowning now. 'If it's too much, stop. You will find something else.'

'No,' I say quickly. 'It gives me something to do. I've made a good start already.'

'Really?'

'I'll send you a picture,' I say.

'Okay, duwa.'

'Achiamma, I'm going to a town tonight, which is near where our house was.'

'Are you?'

Her voice sounds tight now.

'Galhena. And when I'm there, I'd like to see the old house again. Do you know who lives there now?'

'No, I don't.' She pauses for so long I'm about to check if she's still there, when she speaks again. 'I don't think that's wise.'

'Being here makes me think it could be okay. It could give me some closure.'

'Closure?' she says in a brittle tone. We don't talk about our feelings in my family. We especially don't talk about this.

'And then I can move on. After so long.'

'Anika. Don't. It's a bad idea.'

I take the phone away from my ear briefly.

'I thought, of all people, you would understand. You were there.'

'Enough, Anika,' she snaps suddenly. 'We were all there. It won't do you any good to delve into the past. Don't talk about this again.'

'I – I can't just forget.'

'You must try. Please, duwa. You've been through enough recently. Leave this alone,' she says, her tone gentler now. Why did I bring it up? Now I've gone and worried her.

'Okay, Achiamma. I will. I have to go. Speak soon.'

I hang up. Tears prick my eyes. Of everyone in my family, Achiamma was the only one who supported me back then. Even though we never talk about what happened when we were all in Sri Lanka last, even though my family pretends it didn't happen. Something that big doesn't go away. I thought she would understand. I shouldn't have mentioned it. I wipe a tear away and scroll through my photos, find one to show her how well I'm doing with my strange job here. Pretend like the conversation in between me promising to send her one and her receiving it didn't happen. I find a photo of the room I'm in now, and send it to her. If there's anything my family is good at, it's denial.

I move to the window. Dinesh should be here soon. Was I doing the right thing, asking him out tonight? As well as crossing some invisible lines that exist for women here by doing so, I'm unwittingly pulling him into the mess that is my past, if I get him to take me to the old house. Pulling myself down too. Is Achiamma right, and I should leave well alone?

Movement down on the street catches my eye. There's someone there, outside the stone walls that border the house. A person in white. Then the figure turns and I realise, it's a man. He's wearing a white T-shirt and jeans. He has a slight build. Then a beam of light moves across the room. Headlights. A motorbike stops in the street outside. It's Dinesh. When I look back at the wall, the man is gone. I shove my keys and phone into my bag, and run downstairs.

Dinesh looks at me with a bemused expression when I emerge.
'What?' I ask.
'Galhena is a casual town.'
I look down at my sari.
'And?'
'Your outfit is kind of fancy.'
He's right. Locals would wear Western dress to go out in the evening, unless it's for an event like a wedding.
'So what? I felt like wearing this.'
'Okay,' he says. 'Foreigners sometimes wear saris here too. It's a – how do you say it? A novelty to them.'

He looks like he's trying not to smile and it annoys me. Not just because he's laughing at me.

'I'm not a foreigner and this is not a dress-up game for me. It's—' *A part of the heritage I feel like I lost when we stopped coming here. A small connection to my past.* 'You wouldn't understand.' I glance down the street but there's no sign of the man. 'Did you see something just now? When you parked, did you notice anyone on the street?'

He shakes his head.

'No. Were you expecting someone?'

'I thought I saw – never mind.' It couldn't have been the pickpocket. Nirmal. He didn't even turn up for the job he was offered. And if the story Kavya told me about the boat is true, if Nirmal really believed he saw a ghost here, surely he would try to avoid the place. Why would he be here, skulking around? I look back at the street, but there's no one there.

Dinesh hands me a helmet.

'Are you ready? I can't promise this is going to be comfortable.'

'I can deal with a few potholes.'

He sits and revs the engine.

'You're going to have to hold on to me, you know.'

I put the helmet on, climb on and put my arms around his waist. It feels weirdly intimate, for how little we know each other.

'Will that be a problem?'

'Only if you fall off.'

'Just go.'

The bike rumbles through open roads bordering the sea. After a few minutes, the scenery changes, from empty roads to smog-choked streets. Cars, more motorbikes, three-wheelers with bright-coloured roofs and decorations announcing their religious affiliation. Buddha statues or Ganeshas hang from rear-view mirrors, some have quotes from the Quran or the Bible emblazoned across the plastic of the roof. The pavements are filled with people, both Sri Lankans and tourists. This feels more like I remember. The pace, the manic energy of the twilight hours here.

Dinesh pulls up, parking his bike in a line of others at the roadside.

'This way.'

He takes us down a road lined with buildings with bamboo and thatch roofs. Live music emanates from some of the open-air restaurants, tables and chairs spill onto the pavement.

'Are you hungry?' he asks, as we pass shopfronts displaying freshly caught fish on ice. The aroma of grilled seafood mingles with smells of coriander, coconut and lime. My stomach growls.

'Very. You know a place?'

He smiles.

'Of course. A little further down this road.'

We pass shops with handcrafted trinkets, sarongs and surf gear adorning the window displays. I find myself thinking of Kavya's Boutique. It would be perfect here. Dinesh's coffee shop too.

'Is this how it used to be? In your town?'

'It was better,' he says. 'Imagine it even busier than this. You couldn't take a photo without a bunch of tourists in the background. The secret beach was one of the only places to escape the crowds.'

It's hard to believe that Coconut Cove was ever like this.

He stops at a building with a weathered wooden sign in front. අසංකගේ කකුළු පැල්පත. Asanka's Crab Shack.

'Best food in Galhena,' he says.

A waiter gives us menus and takes us through the restaurant to a seating area outside, on the beach. Most of the tables are occupied. Strings of lights and paper lanterns hang overhead. A little way down the beach, people wade into the sea, silhouetted against the silvery-grey sky. The salty breeze from the ocean blends with the aromas of spice and coconut, wafting from the nearby barbecue. The waiter seats us at a wooden table, the legs sunk into the sand.

'You did good,' I say. 'This is nice.'

The waiter comes back and Dinesh speaks to him in Sinhala, then hands back the menus.

'What are you doing? I didn't get to look.'

'They only have one thing.'

'Let me guess. Crab?'

'With salad and rice, or salad and potato curry.'

'I would have liked a choice.'

'I got us both.'

I smile.

'Great.' Another menu, on the wooden post by the barbecue, confirms he's right. 'It's such good value,' I say, scanning the menu. The whole meal is less than the cost of a starter in London.

He shrugs.

'Maybe, but we don't have to pay. They know me, they'll sort us out.'

'That sounds like a good deal.'

He leans forward, the light from the lantern playing over his face.

'So, I'm sorry about before,' he says. 'What I said about your outfit. I shouldn't have said anything. Obviously, you can wear whatever you want, whenever you want.'

'Obviously. But it's okay,' I say.

'And you're not a foreigner. That came out wrong. I know you're Sri Lankan. It doesn't matter how long you've been away. You still are that, if you want to be. And British too. You can be both. Or one, or neither. What I'm trying to say is that it doesn't matter what other people think. You get to choose.'

I look at him. In my line of work – my previous line of

work – I'm used to dealing with toxic males, like my ex. Not guys like this. To my surprise, my eyes prick. I blow out a breath.

'I – thank you. I'm a little sensitive about these things because it's been a while since I've been here and I feel out of touch with it all.'

He sits back in the chair and stretches out his legs.

'How long has it been?'

'Nearly sixteen years.'

'Why so long?'

I want to tell him the truth, for some reason. Being back here, I'm starting to feel like I could talk about it, maybe. And something about Dinesh makes me think he would listen. But I don't want to see him look at me the way everyone else did. Whatever this tenuous friendship or flirtation is between us, I don't want things to change.

'The family moved all over. There was no reason to come back.'

'So why now? And don't tell me you're here for the Fonseca house. That can't be all there is to the story.'

The waiter places water on the table and I take a sip.

'What makes you think there is a story?'

'There always is.'

'I needed a change.' I drink some more of my water. The couple at the next table have colourful cocktails. Green for him, red for her. Sugar bombs, full of dubious colourings, but I crave one anyway. About once a month is as often as I drink, and even then not very much. But I need something to take the edge off. To help me forget.

'My relatives used to live in Hatton Bay,' I say.

He looks surprised.

'That's a few minutes' drive away. You want to go? See how it's changed?'

It could be that easy. I could just say yes. I *should* listen to Achiamma. She's probably right – dealing with this her way has kept us all sane in the intervening years. But the possibility of closure looms large, like a neon beacon. To be this close and not even try? I can't pass up this chance.

'Yes,' I say. 'I'd like that.'

Dinner is delicious but I can't finish it, my stomach flutters with anxiety over what I just agreed to. As I count out a tip that covers the cost of dinner and more, the notes crumple in my sweaty palms. Now it seems like a terrible idea. I dread it. And I want it.

Dinesh walks us to his bike, oblivious to my mixed feelings.

'Ready?'

'Wait. Do you know anywhere good to get a drink?'

'Sure. I know a place.'

'Of course you do.'

He takes us to a hotel at the end of the street, its facade glowing warmly against the night. A door in the side opens, music streams out.

'This looks good.' I cut in front of him and walk inside.

The bar is lit in deep purple and heaving with people, stretching to the dance floor. On one side, an entire wall is glass, showcasing the seafront to spectacular effect. A band plays on a stage at the back, three guitars, a keyboard and a drummer giving a Sri Lankan twist to a drum 'n' bass track.

'This is cool,' I say. I make a beeline for the bar. That's really why I'm here. To blunt my nerves before I face my past.

A barman, pulling bottles from the bar, sees Dinesh and waves. Dinesh weaves his way over, leans across and says something to him.

'What do you want?' he asks me.

The bottles behind the bar catch the roving purple light.

Whisky, vodka, tequila, any number of ways to quiet the anxious voice in my head. I'm not supposed to drink, and in light of the other day I should play it safe and avoid alcohol completely now. But keeping to one drink once a month, or less, has been okay so far. I haven't had one in longer than that, and if ever I needed it, it's now.

'If you're not sure, Anand made a special for tonight,' Dinesh says, oblivious to my deliberations.

'Give me that,' I say quickly.

The barman shakes the drinks up in a steel tumbler. He sets two tall glasses of something red and strong-looking in front of us.

'What is it?' I ask.

'A surprise. You'll like it. I'm the best barman here.'

Dinesh hears him and laughs. 'Only because I left.'

'*Oyate pissu*,' Anand says. The words are familiar, though I can't remember what they mean.

I down the drink in one. It burns and I'm glad. That means it will work.

'I take it you like it?' Dinesh says.

I drain what's left in my glass.

'You used to work here?'

'For a time. I haven't always lived in Coconut Cove.'

'I was wondering about that. What's your story? Where did you live before?'

'Here,' he says. 'And then Coconut Cove.'

'Really? Your accent – you've been to a fancy school in the city.'

He snorts.

'My school was the opposite of fancy.'

'Or watched too much American TV.'

'Yes. That. I do love those *Die Hard* movies.'

He isn't telling me everything, that's for sure. But I'm not being honest with him either. What does it matter anyway? This is the anonymity I wanted when I came here. I put the drink down. I need to do it before I lose the moment.

'I think I'm ready to go.'

My heart races all the few minutes' drive out of town. Dinesh follows the instructions I give him when we reach the centre. I thought I would have forgotten but I remember the route as well as I did years ago.

Dinesh parks at the end of the street. I walk down the broad, well-paved road, passing white-walled mansions with high gates and railings, on one side of the street. Neatly trimmed palms and clipped foliage line the opposite side. Jasmine grows in the bushes. Memories I haven't had for years materialise, so fast they tumble over each other. Walking the Dalmatian my relatives owned down this street. Sneaking out to bars with a fake ID, that time we were busted because of course someone working there knew our parents and took us home. The garden, the balconies, the big flat roof. And how the street looked, that night.

I feel sick now. My legs are heavy. I want to turn and run, get back on Dinesh's bike and ask him to ride far away. But I'm so close. I can't stop now. I wanted this. *Closure.* I force myself to keep walking. Most of the houses are dark. It's after midnight now. Scanning numbers on the metal gates, I stop. I can't move any further. I want to sink down to the ground.

Dinesh stops next to me.

'Is this it?'

I can't answer. Because where I expected the big house to be, there's an apartment block. There's the shop I remember, the house next door with the swimming pool on the roof. But ours – it's gone. The block looks back at me. It's shiny and new. Plastic covers the windows, some of the door frames look unfinished. It confirms my worst suspicion. The house has been razed to the ground. Replaced by this impersonal luxury apartment block. A wooden sign is hammered into the earth next to the block. Under construction.

I thought you couldn't make it go away but they have. They've erased it.

Nobody told me. My family would have known. But they kept it from me. I choke back tears. Maybe it's better this way. This block is new, fresh and untainted. Ready for new people to make new, hopefully better memories than the ones I've been running from all these years.

I head towards the beach. At least they can't erase that.

Dinesh follows.

'Miss Anika?'

I whirl round.

'Stop calling me Miss.'

There it is. The beach from my phone wallpaper. The one I've longed to come back to for years. The pale sand glows in the moonlight. There's the surf shack, closed up now but it's in the same place, as if no time has passed. I'm finally back, but what I came for has gone. I still don't have the one memory I desperately need. Those few missing minutes. The last piece of the puzzle of what happened.

Along the beach is the pier I used to run along with my cousins and local kids. It's cordoned off now. The slats of the pier extend into the distance, into the dark, sludgy-looking sea. Plastic tape criss-crosses the start; a loose strand flaps in the breeze.

I stash my handbag in the compartment of Dinesh's bike. Then I walk towards it.

'Come back, Miss Anika. The wood is rotten.'

I ignore him, step under the security tape and walk on.

'I'm serious,' Dinesh calls. 'The tape is there for a reason. Come back.'

I take off my sandals.

'Have you ever just needed a distraction?' I ask.

'Of course, but not this. This pier isn't stable.'

'That's okay. I won't be on it long.'

'*Mala varthay*,' he swears. 'Come back.'

'I'll be fine.' I rush to the end of the pier. Traffic sounds recede as the crashing of the waves gets louder. Thoughts in my head whirl over each other, too fast to track any more. I don't want to think. The tide is high tonight. The sea churns and foams at the metal poles which anchor the pier into the seabed. It vibrates with the force. It's not the night for a swim. Dinesh is still shouting behind me but I tune him out. I should go back but I don't want to. I want to feel the water around me. I want to forget. I hitch my sari up, so it won't restrict my movement. Then I arch my arms, bounce on the balls of my feet and dive in.

I plunge under. The water is colder than I expected, the shock of it forces breath from my body. The current is stronger than I expected too. With all my strength I kick until I break the surface, gasping for air. I should be scared but I'm not. It's exhilarating.

Dinesh stands on the bank, looking on in shock. He waves with both hands. I can't wave back, the current is so strong I need my arms as I tread water. Dinesh is still talking, but I can't make out what he's saying. The wind swallows his words. He runs up to the edge of the pier. Then he's taking off his shoes. What is he doing? I call for him to stop but he doesn't listen. He jumps off the pier.

The water churns. I can't see him. I look for his white T-shirt in the water but I can't see it. Why did he do that? Can he even swim? Panic fizzes through my veins.

Then he emerges next to me, his hair plastered to his head, his shirt clinging to his chest.

'What the hell, Dinesh. You scared me.'

He swims close to me.

'I could say the same. I didn't even know if you could swim.'

'Ditto. And, I'm a strong swimmer.'

'So am I.' He shakes his head. '*Pissu*.'

Now the meaning comes back to me.

'I'm not crazy.'

He smiles, treads water quicker. 'So you do speak Sinhala.'

'I used to. I've forgotten most of it. I want to learn again.'

He swims closer and grabs one of the poles with his hand. 'I can teach you.'

It starts to rain, light drops pattering the surface of the water. The energy between us intensifies. I kick out until I'm underneath the pier.

'I'd like that.'

My sari has come loose, the fabric splays out around me like paint spilling into the water.

He curls the material at my shoulder around the wrist of his free hand.

'By the way, this suits you. You look beautiful.'

'Thank you.'

I lean closer. He does too. Then he kisses me.

The rain hammers down. The electricity between us crackles as we press closer together under the shelter of the pier. Soft lips, salty from seawater. A hint of his cologne, the smell of the rain. For that moment, everything else fades away.

26

'We're here.'

I look up blearily. We're parked a few feet from the house.

Dinesh kills the engine. 'Were you sleeping back there?'

I didn't mean to drift off. One moment I was fully alert – I can recall the lights whipping past as we left town – and then, nothing. No drowsiness, no struggle to keep my eyes open. A complete blackout, and on a motorbike. Talk about dangerous. That hasn't happened before.

'No. Not really.'

He grins. 'Did you not remember the part about not falling off?'

'I stayed on, didn't I?'

The rain has stopped for now, but the wind is high. My sari is still wet and the added wind chill makes me shiver. Then I laugh.

'What?' he asks.

I step off the bike.

'I'd almost forgotten what a cold wind feels like.'

'I'll let you go inside then. Get out of those clothes.'

'So should you.'

He twirls a lock of my wet hair around his finger.

'What happened back there? People don't jump off piers for no reason.'

'I used to jump off that pier all the time. It's not a big deal.'

'Do you want to talk about it?' he asks gently.

One of my favourite things about our brief acquaintance is

that Dinesh doesn't push me or ask too much. I could say no, or tell him more lies. But I don't want to.

'The house is gone.'

'And you didn't know.'

'Right.'

His face is full of understanding. 'It's hard when things change, out of the blue.'

'Yeah. And – I suppose I thought seeing it again after all this time could help me put some ghosts to rest.'

He frowns.

'More ghost stories?'

'Not like that. More like, personal ghosts. Unfinished business. The past.' I want to say more. *I thought seeing it would jog my memory. Give me back the knowledge of that night. I want to be able to trust my own mind again.* But I don't think anyone could understand.

'I know about those.'

'You do?'

'I have some personal ghosts of my own.'

The wind picks up. I hug my arms around myself. 'You want to talk about it?'

He gives me a lopsided smile. 'Maybe one day.' He glances upwards, at the palm fronds shaking and rattling. 'I should get back before the storm starts. You going to be okay in there?'

The Fonseca house casts a long shadow over the road. Untamed foliage extends gnarled branches beyond the white walls. The night accentuates its abandonment and its wildness.

'I don't believe in those kinds of ghosts, remember?'

He grins.

'Of course not. I'll see you soon.'

His motorbike roars into life, then, in a flash of lights, he's gone. Leaving me alone in the darkness. The storm breaks then.

Thunder rumbles, lightning flashes across the sky. The house stands illuminated in the stark white light.

I rush to the front door. The keys are slippery in my wet hands as I fumble for the lock. As I close the door behind me, the drumming of rain on the roof grows louder. It smells of wet earth inside, just like outside. Is there a leak somewhere? I flick on the lights and check the entryway, the living room and the dining room. A dripping noise is coming from the kitchen. A leak in the roof sends a stream of rainwater to the ground, soaking the dead kindling in the firepit. A kitchen window is open, too, rivulets of water slide down the wall. I shut the window and put a bucket under the leak. I'll have to hope the bucket holds tonight, and deal with fixing it tomorrow.

Upstairs, I peel off my wet clothes and shower. The cold of the tap jars today but I grit my teeth and let the water wash sea salt from my hair and skin. In the bedroom, I move clothes off the bed, searching for my pyjamas. Thunder rents the air again, then lightning throws the room into high relief. About to pull my pyjamas on, I hesitate. Something looks different. But when I scan the room, all is as I left it.

I climb under the sheet and reach for my phone. There's a new message from Achiamma. *Don't search for the house, duwa. Let things be. Call me tomorrow.*

Her message rankles. She must know the house is gone. That's why she's trying so hard to stop me going there. Or maybe she doesn't know, maybe my parents kept it from her too. Either way, I don't feel like replying. I'm about to put my phone away when the message before catches my eye. The photo I sent her, of this room. *That's strange.* I jump up and hold up the photo, comparing it to reality. The bed has moved. That's what looked different about the room.

I enlarge the photo, checking again and again. It wasn't so obvious that I noticed it immediately, but from the photo, the change is unmistakable. The bed is closer to the window now. Just a few steps away from it. I moved the bed away from the window, after my nightmare. Could it have shifted position when I was sleeping? No, it's a heavy frame, there's no way it could move unless someone pushed it. I try anyway, but it doesn't move.

The bedroom window casts shadows on the floor. A gust of wind rattles it. The window is ajar. I go closer, the stone floor cool against my bare feet. The hair on the back of my neck prickles. The kitchen window was open too. But I closed all the windows. Didn't I?

I think I did. A pressure builds in my head. Why are the windows open? Why has the bed moved? And why was the balcony-room door open earlier? I sit heavily on the bed. If I can't even remember something so simple, how can I ever expect to remember what happened that night? And now the house is gone. With nothing to stimulate it, any hope of recovering my lost memory is gone. Because that's what I really wanted. What I hoped would happen. I only acknowledge how much I wanted this now that the chance has been taken from me.

I shouldn't have drunk tonight. The alcohol is messing with my recollections and with my perception. I walk through the house, checking doors and windows. Making sure they're all closed.

I won't sleep in that room tonight. The balcony room is a better option. The door out onto the balcony is jammed shut. With that and the bedroom door locked, I'll be safer. I move my things into the balcony room and make up the bed. About to move the things from the dressing table to make space for my own, I hesitate. My own mind is more dangerous than any ghost story but still, I leave the things untouched.

I sit back on the bed, and close my eyes. I refuse to believe there's anything wrong with me. I can't. I have no explanation for the moved bed though. Except – I glance around the room, dark and crossed with shadows. This is Lenore's room. What if it was her that did this? It's a crazy thought, not one I believe, but I wish I did. Because if it wasn't her, then it was me. My stomach turns. There must be another explanation. There has to be. My mind is restless with uneasy thoughts when I drift off.

I wake with a start. I'm not sure how long I've been asleep. The room is still dark and – what is that noise? A faint creaking. Is it the rain? The wind. But it doesn't sound like either. It's a groaning kind of creak. It must have woken me. What is it?

I want to hide here, to not leave this room. But I have to find out what it is. I pull myself out of bed, grabbing my phone as I go. I've left all the lights on but the bulbs are dim and the hallway is thick with shadows. I turn on my phone torch, shining it in front of me as I walk. At the top of the stairs I pause. There's the noise again. It's coming from my left. In the direction of the other set of stairs. The one that leads to nowhere.

My heart pounds, my legs feel like lead as I drag myself down to the ground floor, then up the other set of stairs. Things are quiet now, apart from the rain. It's letting up but there's still a steady drip, drip of water sliding from the awnings outside. At the top of the stairs, I shine my phone beam over the wall. It's made of heavy stone. Solid. This is the bit Mr Fonseca had sealed up. There's nothing there to explain the noise. It must have come from outside. The weather, an animal, or – the creaking starts again. It's louder now and up here, I can't deny it. It's coming from inside the wall.

The solid stone wall. How can that be? Then her name pops into my head again. *Lenore.* I was sleeping in her room. Have I angered her? *There's no such thing as ghosts.* It's just a noise outside. The creaking starts again. My heart pounds so hard I think I might have a heart attack.

Then the noise stops, suddenly. I stand frozen for a long

minute or more. Then I rush down the stairs and back up to the bedroom. Lenore's room. I can't stay in the room with the moving bed, where I tried to jump out of the window. So it will have to be here. I shut the door and sit on the bed, my back to the wall, listening. The house stays quiet. There are no ghosts. I tell myself that until I fall asleep.

27

Dayani

'You going to be okay from here?' Avila asks.

Dayani surveys the darkened road. Her house is at the end. She stayed out too late with Avila tonight. They went to a cinema in an area not frequented by people either of them knows. And it was empty enough that they had some privacy. She can't remember much of the movie.

'What happened to leaving in the middle of the film?'

He raises an eyebrow.

'Hey, I said we should go halfway through, but you were very distracting.'

She moves closer to him. There's no one around and they're under the shelter of a tall palm.

'You're distracting.' It's not enough for her. She wants to be with him, in a place where she doesn't have to worry about others seeing.

'I've been thinking,' she says. 'You should come over.'

'Your parents would love that.'

'I mean, they know we're friends.'

'They only put up with it because they know you'll be away at university soon. If they knew about us?' He makes a face. '*Maava marai.*' They'd kill me.

Dayani chooses not to acknowledge his words. She doesn't

want to consider the full extent of the risk she's taking by inviting him over. 'You'll be away at university soon too.'

He runs a hand through his hair. His exam was last week and she knows he's been anxious about it.

'If I passed.'

'I really hope you did.' She threads her hand into his. She can tell him now his exams are done and the pressure is off. 'Because I applied to Colombo Uni, too.'

His eyes light up.

'You're kidding.'

'No.'

'Do your parents know?'

'Of course not.'

Avila laughs.

'You'll get in. Obviously. So, if I get in too . . .'

'We'll be together. And they can't stop us.'

He strokes her cheek.

'You're sure that's what you want?'

Dayani doesn't want to hear it, how he's not good enough for her. Away from this place where they both live, things will be different.

'I know I want you.' She pulls closer to him. A chance like this so rarely comes around. Thātha never misses the annual government charity benefit. Not with so many powerful people there to potentially further his business interests. And her amma always makes an appearance too.

'So, about coming over. My parents are going to be at this benefit in Galle next week. They'll stay overnight, at a hotel. I'll be alone.' She winds a tendril of hair around her finger.

'Apart from the servants,' he says.

'They'll be asleep,' she says.

'I don't know. This is so risky. Are you sure?'

She takes both his hands in hers.

'I told you. I want you.'

He smiles.

'If you think it will be okay.'

She releases his hands. She wants to kiss him again, but not yet. Soon.

'I'll make sure it is.'

Dayani sneaks in through a back door. The house is dark. Her mother will be asleep, her father most likely running late at work. He's been there even more than usual lately. Only the servants will be around now, and she can give them the slip. She knows this big old house better than them. All the short cuts and shadowy corners.

She slips off her shoes and tucks them into the cubbyhole by the door. The lights are off in the entryway. But there's a puddle of light coming from the living room. No one is supposed to be in there, now. She hopes it's one of the servants. She rushes towards the stairs. Her room is up there.

'Dayani.' Thātha's voice, from the living room. With growing foreboding, she turns.

Her parents are sitting in the living room. Nothing out of the ordinary so far, but she can tell from their serious expressions that they heard her come in. Her heart sinks. If she knew, she would have tried another way in. Then she rallies. They know she's late, but not why. There could be any number of reasons. It doesn't have to be about Avila.

'Amma. Thātha.'

Her father scratches his beard, like he does when he's thinking. Takes a long time to say something. She's seen him do this routine with his employees. Dragging it out, making fully grown men sweat as they wait for him to speak.

'I didn't think you would be up,' she says.

'We didn't think you would be either.' He stands. 'Where were you?' Dayani quails under the look he's giving her, but stands her ground.

'At the cinema.'

'With who?' her mother asks. Her voice is dispassionate, like she's asking what Dayani had for lunch.

'Some friends. Neela, Roshani, Zara.'

'Should we call their parents?' her father asks.

Why did she choose friends whose parents her father knows? Then again, what choice did she have? He knows everybody. Or if he doesn't, he'll know a way to get to them.

'No, don't do that,' Dayani says. 'They'll be asleep.'

'Enough.' Now her mother stands. She's nearly shaking with anger. 'We know you were with that boy.'

Dayani's throat goes dry. She should have not come back so late. She should have been more careful.

'I wasn't,' she says.

'Stop lying, Dayani. Remember, I can call Avila's father and get the truth.'

Her heart sinks further. She doesn't want Avila to be in trouble too.

'Don't do that,' she says quietly.

Her mother's fists are clenched, her face a mask of cold anger. 'Why not?'

'I wasn't with him. You're wrong.'

'We know you're lying. Our driver saw you go into the cinema together.'

Her cheeks burn.

'You had me followed?'

'The son of a *vada careya*?' Her mother shouts. 'Are you mad?'

Dayani recoils.

'I don't care if his father is a servant.'

'Don't care? You don't get a choice,' her father says.

Dayani turns to him.

'He's not just a servant, is he? I know he does your dirty work. Everything you don't want to do.' She knew it was true from what Avila said. The anger that flashes over her father's face now confirms it again.

'How dare you,' he says.

Her mother comes forward. Dayani thinks she might say something in her defence. The slap takes her by surprise. Dayani is too shocked to even feel the sting.

'Slut,' her mother shouts. That surprises Dayani more than the violence. Her mother doesn't swear, claims to hate bad language. 'We let it slide when you had that dalliance with Mr Perera's son last year. I had the boy agree to stop seeing you, that was the end of it.'

Dayani stares. She didn't think they knew about that. And she never dreamed Amma was the reason he broke it off with her.

'How long have you been spying on me?'

'Spying?' Her mother laughs harshly. 'We didn't have to spy to find out these things. Your friend told us. She doesn't want you seeing her brother either.'

Brother. So Ayomi made good on her threat. Dayani mentally kicks herself. The girl had left them alone for weeks. She thought Ayomi had got over her little outburst about Avila when she saw them on the roof. But now she has had her revenge.

'How could you stoop to this? It's beneath us,' says her mother. Another slap lands on the other side of her face. This time Dayani feels the impact. It makes her bite her lip. She tastes blood.

Her mother is looking at her with pure hatred in her eyes. Dayani thought she would be in trouble, but never like this. She always thought her mother was the less severe of her parents, but she realises now that she had it wrong. Her mother is the one driving all this. The one she should have been scared of, all along.

Her father has been watching, wordlessly. Now, he comes closer.

'One day you'll marry someone we deem fit. Someone more suitable. Until then, no more boyfriends. You go to university, you keep your head down.'

Her mother adjusts her sari where it has come loose. 'We can't have you seen as used goods,' she says, pinning the pallu back onto her shoulder like nothing happened. 'You're ruining your reputation. And our good name. You've brought shame on the family.'

Dayani touches her cheek, still smarting. Her mouth is filled with bloody saliva. She wants to spit on the marble floor next to her mother's red-painted toenails. Instead she swallows it, wincing at the metallic taste.

'I'm not marrying anyone you want. I love Avila.'

Her mother starts towards her. Her father puts a hand on her arm. Restraining her.

'Love?' he says. 'You don't know anything about it. You will marry whom we choose, when the time is right. Or you won't see a penny of my money.'

'I don't want your money,' she says.

'You say that only because you've always had it,' said her father. His eyes are like concrete. Like the blocks he sells, transfers into houses and businesses and apartment blocks on which their family fortune is built. And her mother, the slave to convention, obsessed with appearances over anything else. Over her daughter. Hot tears sting Dayani's eyes. She hates them both. And she won't end up like them.

There's a noise in the corridor. The servants must be outside, listening to the show. Her mother's eyes move to the door.

'Go now,' her father says. 'You won't be leaving this house without our say-so,' he adds. 'And you're never to see that boy again.'

PART THREE
The Body

28

Anika

Now

I rub my eyes. The room is bright. It's morning. My neck aches from the awkward position I fell asleep in, sitting up against the wall. I slept fitfully, my dreams disturbed with visions of a woman in a long white dress pacing along the balcony.

Downstairs, morning light filters through the tall, arched windows, casting golden beams across the marble floor. And it doesn't look so scary now, in the light of day. It's hard to believe what I thought I heard last night. I check at the top of the stairs again anyway, listening near the wall but there's nothing. It's all quiet. Whatever that sound was, it was coming from outside. This place is echoey – it could distort sound, make it seem like it was coming from inside. That must have been what happened.

Satisfied that everything is as normal downstairs, I go back upstairs to shower. But the light in the bathroom isn't working. I click it on and off, but it doesn't make a difference. With no windows in the bathroom and no other light source, I have no choice but to shower in the dark. I should have got some light bulbs when I bought the other supplies. Who knows when the bulbs in this old place were last changed. I'll head into town today, get some more. And while I'm there? Last night, in between disturbing dreams, I had an idea. I need to speak to someone who can give me some answers. The only one alive, who has supposedly seen the ghost. The pickpocket, Nirmal.

He's imagined it all, of course. But if I can hear his account, which is no doubt fantastical, if I can find the flaws in it, then I can reassure myself that it's all a load of nonsense. Much as I don't want to talk to someone who stole my bag. But what do I have to lose? Aside from my valuables, which I'll keep well out of sight. From the way the townspeople talked about him, other than his predilection for petty theft, Nirmal didn't sound particularly threatening. That uncle, Gamini, even gave him a job at his shop. It should be easy to talk to him there.

I dress quickly. A yearning for something close to normality overcomes me. I rush out of the house, making sure I double-lock the door. I thought I did that every time, but now I can't be sure. I head out the back, onto the veranda. The beach ahead shows no sign of the storm of the night before. Calm waves lap at the shore. The air is still, the day near thirty degrees again. I FaceTime Eliza.

It rings and rings, I'm about to hang up when she answers.

She smiles.

'Anika. Hey. How are things?'

'I've been better.'

'Oh no.' She switches her phone to her other hand. 'What's wrong?'

I want to unburden myself, tell her the honest truth. The house is creepy and the locals think it's haunted. But she looks worried already.

'Nothing major. I'm fine.'

'You're sure?'

I sink my toes into the sand. At least I have one nice thing to share with her.

'I went out last night. I kissed a guy.'

I expect her to be stoked about this but she frowns.

'You did? Already?'

'I think it could be the start of a holiday fling.'

'Oh. Cool.'

'Okay, what is it? You'd normally be pressing me for all the gory details.'

'Isn't it a bit soon? You've only been there a few days. How well do you know him?'

'Not very.'

'Well, then, is it a good idea? After everything that happened.'

It's not like Eliza to be all judgy. I don't think I've ever seen it from her before. And I don't like it.

'I don't need a lecture. I thought you wanted me to forget about everything, to have fun.'

'I did. I do. I'm just worried about you. You went through a lot.'

'I know. I don't want to talk about it.'

'As long as you're sure about this guy.'

'He seems nice,' I say, though that doesn't mean much, given my track record.

Eliza glances over her shoulder. The phone shifts, and more of the background comes into view. She's in the operating theatre changing room. Footsteps sound in the background. Eliza greets someone I can't see.

'One second,' she says. The FaceTime call ends. Then an audio call comes in.

'What's going on?' I ask. 'Who was that?'

'I should change. The afternoon op list is about to start.' She sighs. 'We should talk about the case.'

The way she says it worries me. I wonder if it's still in the papers or old news now. I don't want to know if it's anything but the latter.

'I don't want to talk about that.'

'Have you heard from Sara, or anyone at the hospital?'

'I haven't checked my NHS mail since I left.' And I've only transferred a handful of my contacts to the new SIM Mr Fonseca left for me. No one from hospital management made that list. Blocking myself off from it all has felt so freeing. 'I'm here to escape all that, remember?'

'For how long?'

I watch a gull swoop and land on the waves.

'I don't know. I should go. I'll call you later.' Before she can answer, I hang up.

Eliza suddenly acted weird when a colleague appeared in the changing room. She must be embarrassed to speak to me, with everything going on. I remember the way the staff treated me before I left. I know Eliza meant well trying to talk about the case but I don't want all that intruding here. Things have been going wrong here, but when I think of how things were for me in the UK, it is still preferable. At least here there is hope that things might get better.

As I leave the beach, I walk around the house, wondering again why Mr Fonseca chose to seal the wings from inside instead of build something new there. The storm last night has washed away some of the dirt and grime and the exterior walls look cleaner. I touch the vine of jasmine trailing down the side of the house, inhaling its sweet smell. The garden is in disarray but among the tangled foliage there are spots of beauty like these. The ruffled pink hibiscus with its curling stamens. The tall palms that border the house. With some trimming, cutting, replanting, it could be something of what it must have been. It will be, once the restoration is finished.

I press the vine back against the wall. But wait. What is that? Hidden under the trailing leaves is an irregularity in the wall. The vines concealed it well but as I move them aside, the wooden door shows clearly. It's latched shut with a slim metal catch at the top. It's more like the door of a shed than a house. I look around. The air is still. Crows caw, car horns sound in the distance. I look at the door again.

The metal catch is rusty and it seems stuck, but with some pushing it gives. Darkness yawns inside. I don't want to go in but I need to know what's there. What was making that noise. I find a rock from the garden to keep the door open. Propping it as wide as I can illuminates the few feet in front of me. I put my phone torch on and I enter.

The space opens up into a stone-walled cellar, around five by five metres. Dust hangs in the air, swirling in the sunlight. The wall on one side is lined with old wooden crates, stacked to the ceiling. A large oval mirror stands against another wall, its surface opaque with dust. The air here is cooler and heavy with the scent of mildew. A glance into the crates reveals that they are full of building materials. Tiles, bits of wood. As I move further into the room, I notice three old trunks, piled one on top of the other against the back wall. The leather straps on the topmost one feel brittle and the brass buckles are tarnished. I hesitate. Then I unfasten one. The buckle gives easily and I lift the lid. Inside are piles of material, neatly folded. I give one a shake and hold it up. A musty smell comes out. It's a dress, made of red velvet with a white lace collar. It looks old. Like something a white colonial woman would have worn. The back of my neck prickles. I know who these belong to.

I run out of the storage space and latch the door. Then I half run, half walk out of the gate and into the street beyond.

The sun blazes down and the open road provides no shelter but I keep pace anyway. I need to speak to the pickpocket, find out everything he knows about Lenore. And about the house.

My dress is stuck to my back with sweat by the time I reach the town. Some of the stores are still shuttered closed, shopkeepers sit out in front of others. About halfway down the street is Gamini's shop. The sign is faded, bleached in the sun. Household goods are set out outside. There are brooms, tablecloths, tea towels and a stack of plastic chairs.

Gamini comes out of the shop.

'*Kohomada*, Miss Anika?'

'I'm good. *Hondai.* How are you, uncle?'

'*Thambili owenada?*' He points to the bunch of orange king coconuts hanging from the low eaves near the door.

'Yes please.'

He cuts one down with a huge silver knife, slices off the top and hands it to me.

I reach for my wallet.

'How much—'

He dismisses my payment with a shake of his head.

'On the house.'

It's a nice gesture but I'm painfully aware of the lack of customers around here.

'Do you sell light bulbs?' I ask.

'*Owe.*' He motions for me to follow him inside.

While he's in the back finding them, I walk around. Gamini's shop seems to sell a bit of everything. There are shelves stacked with packets of Ceylon tea, tins of condensed milk and woven baskets full of green bananas. The aroma of spices comes from burlap sacks in the corner. Behind the counter, a radio crackles with cricket commentary. I pick up a packet of instant noodles, a papaya and some of the bananas. Then I stop at a table of souvenirs. Next to wooden elephants and key rings are *yakkā* masks. These are small and painted in blues, greens and reds. More like the ones my relatives would have in their homes to ward off bad luck. Not ancient and menacing-looking, like the one in the library. Even so, they bring back bad memories.

'*Mewa hari the?*' Gamini says, holding out the light bulbs.

'Yes, I think those will work,' I say. 'And I'll take these, too.' I add a packet of incense. Something to lift the musty odour of the Fonseca house.

'How are you getting on, Miss Anika?' he asks as he bags my purchases.

As with Eliza earlier, I resist the urge to tell the truth.

'It's going okay. Actually, I wanted to ask you something. Has Nirmal started working for you yet?'

Gamini looks solemn.

'Not yet. He is not answering my calls.'

My heart sinks a little at his words. The pickpocket is proving elusive and he's my only lead.

'If you see him, could you let me know? I want to talk to him.'

'Okay,' Gamini says curiously. He grabs a pen and I write down my number.

'*Okama hari*, uncle.' It's Dinesh, coming out of the back of the shop. He drops a box onto the floor. 'That's the last one.' His shirt is smudged with dirt, like he's been moving things.

'*Isthoothi*, Dinesh.' He adds to me, 'I have a bad shoulder. I can't lift the heavy things any more.'

Dinesh looks at me in surprise.

'Miss Anika. I didn't know you were here.'

'I was just going.' I sling the bag onto my shoulder. 'Thanks for these, uncle. I'll see you later.'

I wanted to talk to Dinesh, but I didn't know what to say. Not there, anyway. I don't want Gamini to think anything is up.

'Hold on.' Dinesh comes out of the shop, catching up to me in a few paces. 'What are you doing here?'

'Getting supplies. You?'

He stops under the shade of a palm tree by the roadside. 'Did I hear you were looking for the pickpocket?'

'You did.' I notice a grey streak of dirt on his cheek. 'You have some—' Without thinking, I reach up to wipe it away. Then drop my hand. 'There—'

'Right.' He wipes his face. 'You want a drink?'

'Sure.'

We don't talk as I follow him into Coconut Cove Coffee. You're not supposed to kiss people casually here. Not supposed to have holiday flings, if that is what this is leading up to. Not as a Sri Lankan woman, anyway. I don't know if he thinks that way too.

He pulls out a seat for me and immediately starts making coffee.

'Aren't you going to ask what I want?'

'Right. What do you want?'

'A latte, decaf.'

He laughs.

'I guessed as much.'

'I am predictable like that.'

The machine hisses as he steams the milk.

'So how are you doing?'

'You want the real answer?'

'Always the real answer.' He places a coffee in front of me, with a rose design in the foam.

'Cute.'

He sits on a stool opposite me.

'I was going to tell you about this arabica from the hill country but I'll spare you that today.'

'But I was getting used to your coffee notes.'

He half smiles. 'Maybe next time. What's going on?'

I tell him about the noises I heard. 'But they were coming from outside,' I say. To reassure myself as much as him.

'How do you know?'

'I checked where I thought they came from. The wing at the side isn't sealed up. Not all of it.' I shudder as I remember Lenore's clothes.

'Is the fan too high?'

'No. I'm fine.' I tell him about the storage area. 'There was nothing else beyond that, to explain the noises anyway. Perhaps it was something hidden.'

'Like what?'

'Like the pipes or—' If that was the plumbing I heard last night, it sounded very unhealthy. Like it was about to burst. 'I think Mr Fonseca needs to get the plumbing checked.'

'You could get a hotel,' Dinesh says.

I look at him. I thought he'd tell me it was all nothing to worry about. That I'm overreacting.

'There aren't any. And I need to be here, to finish my job at the house. And get paid, so I can stay in a hotel somewhere else afterwards.'

'You're not going straight back to London?'

I've never not had a plan before. It feels deeply uncomfortable but I know that's what I need. To give myself the space to figure out how to salvage things.

'I don't know yet. I'm focusing on my job here for now. Speaking of, I should get back to it. I was thinking the garden could do with some work.'

He starts playing with my spoon, tapping it against the side of my empty cup.

'You're really getting into this, aren't you?'

'Despite all the weird issues, it has been satisfying.'

'What weird issues?'

I haven't told him about imagining Lenore on the balcony. The photo that moved. Nearly jumping out of the window. The moving bed, which I have no explanation for. He looks worried enough from what I've told him today. If I tell him the rest, he'll think I'm crazy.

'You know, the possible plumbing stuff.'

'Hari.' *Right.* He looks distracted. 'You want a lift back?'

'Please.'

We go outside and he locks the door, not looking at me. We

haven't talked about our night, and the flirtatious manner he's had with me before is gone. Dinesh said he didn't believe the stories but superstition is part of the culture here. It's not so easy to reject it. I had to, all those years ago, because if I believed everything that my family, even strangers, said about me, then it would make it as if it were all true. And I refused to let that happen.

Dinesh is holding the other helmet for his motorbike.

'*Hari the?*' You ready?

'Let's go.'

We speed along the coastal road. The salt-scented wind whips past my face. I hold on tight to Dinesh. Every time he leans into a curve, I cling to him more, not because I'm trying to be close to him, but because I'm worried I'll tumble off if I don't. He's driving faster than last time. There's no traffic on the road and it feels like barely five minutes have passed before we approach the narrower stretch of road leading to the Fonseca mansion. Dinesh pulls up to a stop and I jump off. My legs are shaky from gripping the seat so hard.

I remove the helmet and hand it to him. 'Didn't give us much of a chance to take in the views.'

He gives me a sheepish grin.

'You're not used to it. I didn't think. You need some help with the bulbs?'

'Sure.'

I unlock the door and take us inside.

'Which light is it?' he asks.

'Upstairs.'

As I cross the floor I notice something. The marble floor which I had made sparkling clean yesterday is now streaked with grime. In a patch at the centre is what looks like dust. No, sand, I realise, as I bend to examine it. I did come through in a wet sari last night, dripping water and probably sand too. That must be it. But why didn't I notice it this morning?

'What is it?' Dinesh asks.

I won't go down that line of thinking again. There is almost always another explanation. This morning, I was distracted, thinking about the noises I heard in the night. So I didn't notice. That's all.

'Nothing. Up here.'

I take him up to the bathroom. Inside, I flick the switch, to turn off the electricity before he replaces the bulb. But to my surprise, the light comes on.

Dinesh looks at me quizzically.

'It's working.'

I flick it on and off again to test it. It's working fine.

'It wasn't this morning.'

'The electrics must be temperamental in here,' he says. 'Given how old the place is. You have some spare light bulbs now, anyway.'

Temperamental electricity, pipes that sound like they're about to explode in the night. I have a lot to say to Mr Fonseca. I only have his email. If only he'd given me a phone number.

'Hey, do you know where Mr Fonseca lives now?' I say as we come out of the front door.

Dinesh shrugs.

'He has property all over. I don't even know if he's in the country.'

'Does he travel a lot?'

His motorbike is parked by the perimeter wall. He stops by it.

'I'm not sure. Ask Darsha, or one of the others. They know more of the gossip than me.'

'You're not into that, are you?'

'Not my thing.' The corners of his lips curl up slightly. 'You know, we don't even have each other's numbers.'

I'm relieved that we're finally talking about us. Whatever that might mean. But now that he is, I don't know what to say.

Yesterday I thought I wanted a holiday fling but every relationship I've had has ended badly, in one way or another. Even Eliza was worried about me this morning.

'You think we should?'

He smiles properly. Now we're outside of the house, he seems more relaxed.

'I had fun yesterday.'

'Me too.' I have an urge, like I did yesterday, when I asked him out. To forget the rules. Live the way I want to. 'We should hang out again,' I say.

'I would like that.' He holds out his phone and I put in my number.

After he's left, I brush the sand off the floor and light the incense I bought earlier, shining it into the corners. The tip glows as sandalwood-fragranced smoke curls up into the air. It's a smell I remember well, from the temple or from my grandmother using it at home. They used to say it purifies air, and as I breathe in its warm and comforting smell, I hope it will help to dispel the ghosts. Not Lenore's, but mine.

I turn all the lights on, relieved they still work. I haven't ventured into the kitchen much at all yet, except to clean it soon after I arrived and to get water. Now, I open the cupboards and find some faded silver spoons and forks, a few clay pots and steel pans. Basic, but enough to make the noodles I bought from Gamini's shop. I get a fire going and boil the water, stirring the noodles in the clay pot. There's something soothing about it. Getting back to basics, almost like camping. When the noodles are done, I blow the fire out and take the pot onto the veranda and sit on the edge with my toes in the sand as I blow on my Maggi noodles. I haven't eaten since last night. I didn't even realise how hungry I was until now and I finish the noodles, scoop the orange flesh of the papaya with a spoon. In the distance, sailing boats bob on the waves. This beach was so treacherous not that long ago. It's hard to reconcile that with the calm sea now. I gaze at the golden glimmer at the horizon. Even harder to imagine is the supposed cause of the sinking. It was a tragic accident, most likely caused by bad weather.

I take out my phone and write another email to Mr Fonseca, outlining my concerns about the pipes and the electricity. I press send, then hesitate. I want to message Eliza. I don't like how I left things earlier. I write *I miss you*, then delete it. I do miss her, but I don't want her to worry about me any more. In the end, I send her a photo of the sea view. I send the same to Achiamma. A gentle breeze blows, tinged with salt. It gives a moment's relief from the sticky humidity.

A message arrives, from Eliza.

Jealous! PS Sorry about before. Tell me all about your fling. I smile. I wonder if there will end up being more to say about that.

One comes through from Achiamma soon after.

Enjoy, duwa. I hope you're eating properly.

Suddenly, I miss them both so much. I send them the same reply.

I'll call you soon.

I run down to the shore and into the sea, until my knees are submerged. The water is refreshing and crystal clear. The photo I sent expresses what I can't in words. Not in a way that either of them would understand. That despite everything, right now, I'm happy to be here.

29

Anika

Then

The restaurant is full with round tables of guests in suits and cocktail dresses, the air abuzz with conversations and clinking glassware. As Rosa and Ravi make a speech, as they cut into a cake with the words *Congratulations On Your Engagement* iced across the middle, Anika feels increasingly desperate. She checks her phone in her handbag. Eliza, across the table from her, catches her eye with an understanding look. She knows what Anika is checking for. Between them, the seat is empty. Dominic's seat.

Anika slides her phone back into her bag, disappointed. No new messages. Where is he? He promised he'd come to Rosa's engagement party tonight. He seemed happy when he agreed to be her date, excited to meet her friends for the first time. Things have been going well. Anika has allowed herself to relax in the relationship. Now she wonders if that was a mistake. She checks her phone again. He said he'd be here.

The speech ends and slices of cake arrive at the tables. Anika joins in the conversation, pushes the cake around her plate but she's all too aware of the unfilled chair next to her, like a visual announcement to everyone, that her boyfriend doesn't care enough to turn up. She pastes on a smile for the rest of the evening, tries to focus on her happiness for her friends and not her disappointment for herself.

Dominic has not let her down before and she tries to tell herself that there's an explanation, even though he hasn't contacted her in the past five hours, has ignored her calls and her messages. Her cheeks ache from forced smiling by the time guests start to trickle out. She stays as long as she can but it's a relief when she can leave the restaurant, escape into her waiting Uber.

Her apartment is cold, the heating takes a while to kick in. She has a long, hot shower to warm up, and to try and wash the day away. He still hasn't called. There could be an explanation but to not even message her? Is he okay? She knows he's fine. He's chosen not to be there. Chosen to ignore her. Perhaps he's ghosting her, in a particularly cruel way. In the safety of the small cubicle, she lets her tears fall.

When she comes out, the doorbell is ringing. Insistently, continuously, like whoever it is has been trying for a while. Pulling her towelling robe on, she answers the door.

It's Dominic. He's wearing jeans and a blue V-neck jumper. Not clothes to attend the engagement dinner. He's holding a bunch of pink roses.

'My flight was delayed,' he says. He makes to come in and she steps back to let him pass. 'I'm so sorry.' He tries to kiss her but she turns her face away.

'Why didn't you tell me?'

'I only just got off the flight. I really am sorry.' He hands her the flowers and she puts them on the hall table. It's sweet that he thought to bring them for her and a flight delay is a reasonable explanation but – he looks calm and his clothes are neatly pressed. He doesn't look like he's rushed off a flight. She lets him take her in his arms. As she stands there, she thinks. His flight was delayed but she's been refreshing the arrivals throughout the evening. She didn't see a single delayed flight back from New York tonight.

'How long was the delay?'

He draws back, looks at her.

'I flew back on my firm's charter.'

'But private jets aren't subject to delays like commercial ones, are they?'

'Of course they are,' he says.

'And don't they have Wi-Fi? You could have messaged.'

There's a flash of something in his eyes she hasn't seen before. Something cold.

'You don't believe me?'

'Of course I do. I just – I wanted you to be there.'

Then the expression is gone. Anika wonders if she imagined it.

'I'll make it up to you,' he says. 'I love you.'

She looks at him. He hasn't said it since the first time, when he gave her the necklace. She'd worried he hadn't meant it so she hasn't said it again since then either. Now she smiles.

'I'm glad you're here now.'

He glances at her bulletin board. At the invite pinned there.

'For the wedding, I'll be there. I promise.'

30

Anika

Now

I wake in the balcony room and it's morning. I've slept through again. No wake-ups, no strange noises. And as I enter the bathroom to shower, I find the light switches on. The tap works fine too. Mr Fonseca hasn't replied to the email I sent last night, outlining my concerns about the pipes and the electrics. But whatever the problems with those are, they seem to be erratic, because things are working today. I'll take advantage and do as much work as I can on the house today. In my last email, I told Mr Fonseca that I want to end my assignment early, if I can. So I'm hoping he'll agree and get the contractors in sooner. Then I'll be free to travel around, figure out my next move.

On the back of a full night's sleep, the balcony room seems more innocuous. I take my suitcase in and move some of the things on the dressing table aside for my own toiletries and hairbrush. I rearrange the possessions neatly at the side of the faded wooden tabletop. They belonged to someone in the Fonseca family. Or they were Lenore's things. I wish I knew more about her. The real story. Not the ones the locals have got carried away with.

My phone is charging on the floor by the bed. I check again for an email, but this time my phone won't turn on. I press the power button again and again. My improved mood of this morning dissipates as I stare at the black screen. I left it charging all night. When I check the lights in the balcony room, they don't turn on. So much for everything working in here. So there was likely no power to the charger all night. Or the dodgy electrics in this old place have fried the charger. Or my phone. *Great.* I need to get it looked at and someone in town might be able to help. Point me to the nearest phone shop. Changing into a white tee and denim shorts, I head downstairs.

At the bottom of the stairs, my foot skids. I lose balance, grabbing onto the banister for support. As I straighten up, the cause of my slip becomes evident. There's dirt on the floor again. An unmistakable patch of mud at the foot of the stairs. *I cleaned this up last night.* The floor is wet, too. I didn't hear anything last night, but there's a dripping sound inside now, like after the last time it rained. It must be another leak in the roof, to explain the watery mess on the floor. I left the broom out on the veranda last night. Opening the heavy wooden front door, I trudge round to the side of the house to retrieve it. The broom is there, propped against the wall like I left it and I'm relieved. More evidence that I did clean the floor as my memory tells me I did.

Hand on the broom, I hesitate. The door of the storage room is a metre or so away, and it's open a crack. I latched it shut yesterday. I'm sure I did. As I move to close it, I stop. The pipes stayed quiet last night, but who knows how long that will last. Although I didn't see any pipes in the storage room, the sounds did seem like they were coming from that direction. When I discovered the storage room, I was freaked out by Lenore's clothes and I didn't want to linger. Now, after an uninterrupted sleep in the house, I can more easily dismiss the worries I had yesterday. It's worth another look.

Without my phone torch for visibility, I settle for wedging the door as wide open as I can with the rock I left nearby. It gives a wide beam of daylight, enough to find my way. I enter the storage room.

The scent of damp wood surrounds me. Unlike the rest of the house, the ceiling in here is low. I scan the room, searching for the pipes amid the shelves and crates. When I don't find them, I walk the length of the walls, trailing my hands over them but there is no break in the rough stone. No exposed pipes here. They could be within the walls, but as I knock on the stone, the wall is solid, unyielding. Beyond is bricked up.

I look at the trunks. I only had a quick glance in the top one last time – what if there's something in them? Something to tell me more about Lenore. I check the trunks, they're heavy but I pull each one down and open them in turn. Sifting through the clothes I check right to the bottom but all I find are more dresses in velvet and moth-eaten white silk petticoats. These clothes were obviously of good quality, the materials rich and detailed with intricate embroidery and tiny pearl buttons. Worn by age, but still, they're the best kind of vintage. The oval mirror is propped on the floor by the crates. Shaking out a deep green ankle-length skirt, I stand in front of it, holding it against me. If the locals weren't so jumpy about Lenore, these items could be useful. They could even exhibit them in a museum. I wonder if Mr Fonseca would consider donating them.

The beam of daylight from the open door isn't enough to dispel the gloom, it's dark in here. As I squint at my reflection in the clouded glass, something looks off. The surface of the mirror is irregular. There are patterns in the dust. I peer closer. There's writing on the mirror. Trailed in the dust, as if made with a finger, is one word. *Remember.*

Suddenly, it feels cold in here. Goosebumps stand out on my arms. I shove the skirt back in the trunk and come closer to the mirror. The writing wasn't there before.

The walls seem closer now, as if they're pressing down on me.

As if the house is pressing on me. I rush out of the storage room. The door creaks as I slam it shut.

The beach outside is calm. The air warm again. I watch the waves roll in and out until my breathing settles. It's thirty-plus degrees, but, goosebumps still stand out on my arms.

I latch the storage room shut and come out onto the street. It's been a week and it feels like any progress I make here is quickly followed by a new complication. It feels like things are against me. Almost like the house is against me. *She's still here.* That's what the locals said. Ghosts can cause a change in the environment. They have in every horror movie I've seen, every story my relatives used to tell. Like cold spots. Messages written in strange places. Bad weather. Boat accidents. The one explanation for everything is Lenore. But I don't believe in ghosts.

I hurry down the street, keeping my back to the house now. I came here in search of my missing memories. The one memory in particular. And the writing in the mirror said, *Remember.* I wish I did believe in ghosts, because the other explanation is more disturbing. It was me.

The warm, humid air clings to my skin as I walk along the road. If it was me, when would I have written it? I was out cold last night. Didn't even hear the rain. Was I really asleep? Or did I get up last night, sleepwalk? I imagine myself walking around the darkened storage space, looking into the mirror, while only partially conscious. Writing a message to my waking self, in the dust. All with no memory of it. A car honks as it drives past and I rear back.

No. I always woke in the middle of my parasomnia episodes. That's the only reliable thing about them. Like when I arrived here, woke up with my foot out of the window. I did wake up. Even if the memory I most need is missing at least I know this.

At the point where the road forks, I head right. I'll take the back way again. Go via the secret beach. I need to feel its calm, its tranquillity again. Being there will make me feel better. The knowledge of what happened that night is gone. It's time I accept that. I'd rather take my chance with a ghost than whatever is going on in my subconscious. Because ghosts don't exist.

At the shore, I stop. Listen to the waves, feel the warmth of the sun. Down here, tempered by the sea breeze, the sun doesn't feel as harsh on my skin. However strange things are getting here, I won't let the house, or my own subconscious, intimidate me. I won't lose control.

I close my eyes. There's another sound, under the soft lapping of the waves. A kind of slapping noise. I open my eyes, my senses on high alert. I stand still for a few moments, listening, but there's no one around. Nothing to explain the sound. Ahead of me is a small rocky outcrop, a few metres into the water. I wade in up to my calves, and the noise is louder from here. It sounds more like a thud. It's coming from behind the rocks. I wade in further, until the bottom of my shorts is wet. There's something behind the rocks. A body.

A man lies face down, his shirt and jeans soaked through. I watch in horror as the tide pushes him in and out, against the rocks. That's the noise I heard. I feel lightheaded all of sudden. He's surely dead, by the way he's lying, motionless. But the doctor in me forces me to lean down, feel the pulse at his neck. His skin is cold, there is no pulse at all. *Fuck.* Nausea builds as I turn the man over. It takes all my strength, but I manage it. Then I see his face. It's Nirmal. The pickpocket.

31

I should do CPR. One look at the man's lifeless eyes tells me it's futile, but I try, pumping up and down on his chest. As his torso moves with the action, I notice something else. A trail of blood from his side. Moving him sets it flowing, it stains the water at my feet pink. I stand, turn towards the town, and run.

A few people are out on the street, chatting outside their shops.

'Help,' I shout. '*Oothow karanna*,' I add. More and more words have come back to me since I've been here.

The people look on in shock. Kavya is there, Gamini, and some men I haven't met before.

'Miss Anika, what is it?' Kavya says, running over.

I stop, my hands on my knees, out of breath from running full pelt.

'A man. Nirmal. On the secret beach. Dead,' I manage.

'Are you sure?'

I nod, take a ragged inhale. 'I think he drowned.' The others have converged on us. Now, they look at each other. Then the men run in the direction of the beach.

Kavya takes me by the arm.

'Miss Anika, are you all right?'

I stand. My side aches with a stitch. Then I remember the blood in the water and feel sick all over again.

'I—' Then I'm crying. It takes me by surprise.

'Come.' She leads me into the back of her shop. I'm in a numb state now. On autopilot, my limbs moving mechanically. I let her sit me down, bring me a glass of chilled water. Outside the window, a lone three-wheeler putters by. A gecko darts up the wall. I watch as it disappears behind a picture frame. There's a dead man on the beach. Tears come again.

Kavya hands me a tissue.

'Thanks. I never cry at work,' I say, almost to myself. 'This should be no different.' A dead virtual stranger. A frequent enough occurrence in all the on calls and emergencies I've attended. So why am I reacting like this?

Kavya looks at me in surprise.

'What is your work?'

'I'm a doctor. Or, I was.' It feels good to say it, finally.

Understanding passes across her face.

'This isn't work,' she says. I'm relieved she doesn't ask any more. 'You just discovered a dead man,' she says. 'It would be a shock to anyone.'

Footsteps sound from within the shop. Kavya checks beyond the curtain.

'They're back. Stay here.'

'No. I want to come.'

I follow her into the shop. Gamini and one of the other men are there. Gamini looks stricken.

'The others are with the ambulance. They're taking him away,' he says. 'But he's dead.'

Kavya touches his shoulder.

'Was it him?'

'Yes. It was Nirmal.'

She takes us into the back room, sits Gamini down the way she did with me.

'What did the paramedics say?' I ask. 'Did they think he drowned?'

'They don't know for sure yet. But they think—' Gamini sighs heavily. 'It could be murder.' I remember the blood coming from his corpse. I thought it was from the impact of the rock. I never suspected this.

'He was murdered?'

Gamini nods, his face sombre. '*Aheme vagay.*' It seems so.

'*Hari vaday,*' Kavya says. 'How terrible.' She touches his shoulder. 'That's why he didn't come to his job with you. *Uparāthé.*' What a shame.

'But that was a few days ago,' I say. 'He can't have been dead for that long.'

If he was, his corpse would have been bloated with seawater, his face unrecognisable.

'Otherwise he wouldn't have looked like that.'

They both look at me.

'Also, I think I saw him outside the house.' I tell them about what I saw the other night. Dinesh was there and he didn't see Nirmal, but I don't mention that.

They listen in silence.

'So he was alive two days ago,' Kavya says finally.

The pickpocket is dead. Murdered. Something about it doesn't feel real. 'Who could have killed him?'

'With everything he's been involved with since—' Gamini breaks off and I know he's thinking about the boat accident.

'What do you mean, uncle?' Kavya says.

'I don't know the details, but he was desperate for money, got involved in some bad business. He must have made enemies.'

'Are the police involved?' Kavya asks.

'They're here now.'

'*Ehenung hondai,*' she says. That's good.

'You asked for him when you came to my shop. Why were you searching for him?' Gamini asks.

I look at him. Now I won't ever get to speak to Nirmal. I wanted to know about Lenore. If he really saw her. But Nirmal is dead.

They're both already in shock about it. If I mention Lenore now, they'll get even more upset, thinking about the curse that's supposedly affected the town. They'll think it's connected. So I won't mention it. Even though, having found his body, a tiny part of me is starting to wonder. Is there something in the story after all?

'Nothing really. I – I don't remember,' I finish weakly.

They look at me strangely but they don't push it. Perhaps they think I'm in shock too.

'I am sorry, Miss Anika,' Kavya says. 'Things like this don't happen here, usually. Didn't used to, anyhow.'

I pick up my bag. 'I only came into town to fix my phone.'

'What's wrong with your phone?' Kavya asks.

I show her the dead screen. 'I don't know, there was a possible power outage in the bedroom so it might need a charge.'

'Let me try,' she says.

Gamini is sitting motionless at the table, staring into his glass of water.

'Are you okay, uncle?' I ask. 'I know you tried to help him.'

He smiles sadly.

'That's why I offered him the job. As a way out of all the petty crime, the people he was involved with. If he had come, maybe this could have been prevented.'

'You did all you could. The police will find who killed him.'

'I don't think they'll do much. Not for a poor thief,' Gamini says. He looks downcast. The air feels heavy. I suddenly want to get out of here.

Kavya comes back with my phone.

'*Hari*. It's working.' She shows me the screen, now on, the long charger cable winding behind it.

'Thank you,' I say. 'That's a relief.' I'll need to tell Mr Fonseca to get an electrician in. I hope he's replied to my previous email, because the thought of chasing him again makes me feel exhausted.

'I'm sorry, uncle,' I say.

'*Aheme, ne.* What can we do. The police will come tomorrow. Let's see. Do you need someone to walk you home?'

'I'm okay,' I say. 'But thank you.'

'Are you sure?' Kavya says, starting after me. 'You are still in shock.' She looks at my clothes and I notice the streaks of blood for the first time, on my denim shorts. 'You want a change of clothes?'

'Really. I'll be fine, I can change at the house.'

She squeezes my hand. 'Call me if you need anything.'

'I will.'

I leave the two of them in the shop. Despite how tough things have been since I arrived here, the townspeople are decent. I feel a little safer for knowing that. But now Nirmal is dead. And I don't know if I was really asleep last night. I can't shake the unsettled feeling. Like I can't trust my own mind. The pressure behind my eyes, like a valve about to burst.

There's a crowd outside Kavya's Boutique, buzzing with conversation. Their eyes are on me as I leave. Soon after, they start to dribble inside the shop, no doubt to get the details. I walk away from them.

Dinesh isn't in the coffee shop today. I go through to the back, but he's not there. I'm about to leave when the back door opens and he enters.

'Miss Anika.' His smile dies as he takes in my appearance, my clothes wet, bloodstains on my shorts. 'What happened?'

'You'll find out soon enough.'

'I'd rather hear it from you.'

Tears start again and I dash them away.

'The short version is, I found a dead body on the secret beach.'

I tell him about finding Nirmal. That the police think he was murdered.

Dinesh blows out a breath.

'*Mala vaday.*' Terrible. He places a hand on my shoulder, his eyes full of concern. 'Are you okay?'

'No. Not really.'

'Can I help?' he asks.

I want to feel his arms around me. For him to make this all go away, just for a short while. I think of what Eliza said. That it's too soon, that I need to be careful. Because of what happened before. Right now, I don't care about any of it. I take a step closer to him. Then I kiss him hard on the lips. He tastes like salt, his hair is wet, like he's just been for a swim in the sea. He kisses me back just as hard, for a moment. Then he draws away.

'Miss Anika, what are you doing?'

'For fuck's sake, stop calling me Miss. We're past that now, aren't we?'

There's an alcove by the back door, leading to what looks like a storeroom. Coffee tins and boxes are stacked up on the floor. It looks private. Women here would be chastised, there would be serious consequences for what I'm about to do. A feeling of shame bubbles up, a reflexive response to years of conditioning. I ignore it. Because I don't care about that any more. I push him into the alcove.

'Things are going from bad to awful since I got here. And I need to not feel any of it.' Inside the storage space, I shut the door. I push him back against the wall and kiss him again, like he's oxygen and I can't breathe. This time, he doesn't stop me. He picks me up and perches me on a chest of drawers. I wind my legs around his waist. He presses closer to me and there's something fevered in the way he kisses me, undresses me. I'm trying to escape reality. To forget. And it feels like he's trying to do the same thing.

32

Dayani

Dayani listens for the sound of her father's car pulling away. When the rumbling of the engine quiets, she slips her phone out of the box under her bed. Her parents think they've confiscated it but, unbeknown to them, she has an old phone and she's using that now instead. She hasn't been allowed to see her friends or to go out unaccompanied for the past week. She's barely been allowed to leave the house at all, since her parents found out about her and Avila. She hasn't been sleeping properly either. But tonight is the night of the charity benefit in Galle. And her phone is showing a new message from Avila.

I'm here.

She opens the window and goes out onto the roof. He's there, in the shadow of the date palm by the front gate. She waves, and motions for him to come round the back. This is the riskiest part of her plan. Getting him up to her room.

When she opens the back door, Avila is standing behind it. His face is full of apprehension.

She pulls his shirt and takes him inside. Dayani knows the servants are asleep. She made sure of it, waiting until the last servant had left for their quarters on the other side of the house before she asked Avila to come. But still her heart pounds. Together, they pad up the stairs, Avila holding his shoes in one hand.

In the safety of her room, she breathes easier. She shuts the door.

'It's good to see you,' Avila says. She goes to him, burying her face in his chest, inhaling his familiar smell.

'I missed you,' she says.

'I'm sorry your parents found out.' A strange expression flits across his face, then is gone before she can fathom it. 'Are you sure this is a good idea? I keep expecting them to come back any second.'

'They won't. They just left for a function in Galle. And they think they took my phone, so I can't contact you.' The more they oppose her, the more she wants Avila. He's everything they're not. And everything she needs. She doesn't know how this summer will end but she knows tonight is her only chance to be alone with him. She wants this one night with him.

'Hey, I have some news,' he says. 'I wanted to tell it in person.'

'What is it?'

He gives a coy smile.

'I passed my exam. I have a place at Colombo University next year.'

She wants to scream, but that would wake the servants. She settles for throwing her arms tightly around him.

'I didn't want to ask. I'm so happy. We'll be there together next year.'

That strange look crosses his face again.

'I can't wait.'

'I'm so glad you're here.' She kisses him. He pushes her gently down onto the bed, pulling the mosquito nets loose around them. She tugs his buttons undone and peels his shirt from his shoulders. He slips down the straps of her vest and kisses her shoulders. But something bothers her. There was something off about him, when he talked about his exam. She thought he would be happier.

'Is everything okay?' she asks.

'Of course. Are you sure you want this?'

She opens her eyes and he's looking at her like he always did. Like he adores her.

'Of course I do.'

'You mean it? If you want me to leave, just say the word.'

'Shh.'

'I love you,' he says.

'And I love you.' He was probably just nervous. About being here, at her house. Understandable, especially in light of everything. Maybe she asked too much of him. But as he kisses her neck, whispers her name, as she starts to forget about everything else, she thinks again. It's worth the risk.

33

Anika

Now

In the confined space of the storeroom, we put our clothes back on. We're not looking at each other. Or, I'm not looking at Dinesh. He's trying to catch my eye but I turn away as I do up my bra and pull on my shorts. I know how this kind of situation goes, and I want to minimise the awkwardness.

'I should go.'

He stops mid pulling on his T-shirt.

'Let me give you a ride back.'

'You don't have to.'

'Are we going to talk about earlier?'

'If you mean what happened on the beach, we did. The pickpocket is dead. Do you need a recap?'

'I don't mean that. Do you want to talk about how you're doing?'

'Not really.'

Dinesh perches on the edge of the chest of drawers. 'The others are right. He must have been caught up in something bad. A debt gone wrong. Something like that. The police will check into it.'

'I'm not holding out hope.' Then I remember, the townspeople said the secret beach is the only place where you used to be able to get away from the crowds. Local knowledge. Nirmal was there. So, unless he washed up there from somewhere else, which is unlikely given how recently he seemed to have died, then the murderer is from this town. Suddenly the Fonseca house, set away from the town as it is, doesn't seem so bad. I hitch up my bag and stand.

'Let me take you home. My bike is outside.'

'Okay.'

He takes a back route home, avoiding the main road through the town. He doesn't drive as fast as last time but still, the journey is quick. Before long, he pulls up outside the house.

I jump off quickly.

'Anika, wait.'

I turn back to him.

'We don't have to talk about what just happened.'

'What do you mean?'

'You're Sri Lankan, I know from the way my family, my relatives used to talk about women like me. So I know what you think of me now. You don't have to pretend. Many women are expected to wait until they're married, to do what we did. They definitely aren't supposed to—'

'Hook up in a storeroom?'

That feeling of shame comes up again, like it always does, and I push it away. I don't care what people like my family think of me, any more. Of all the things they put on me, shame was the easiest one to reject. The rest, not so much.

'Exactly. And, I'm not ashamed. So I don't care what you think.'

'I don't think anything,' he says.

'It was just a distraction. I didn't want to think any more. I needed to take my mind off everything. It doesn't have to be anything else.'

He gets off the bike.

'What if it could be?'
'You hardly know me.'
'Maybe I know enough.'
'And I hardly know you. You're not exactly forthcoming.'
He raises his eyebrows.
'Neither are you. That's why, so far, this has worked.'
'I think for it to work any longer we'd have to share something more. And neither of us is prepared to.'
He runs a hand through his hair.
'I wanted to see you home. Make sure you're okay. Can you just let me?'
His eyes hold mine. There's no judgement there. Hasn't been, since the day I met him. He's not acting at all like I expected.
'I'm sorry. You know what a monumentally fucked-up time I've had this morning, and then there's the other stuff that has been happening to me.'
'What do you mean? What else has been happening?'
I shouldn't tell him, the whole thing sounds crazy. But I'm sick of pretending I'm okay. Sick of hiding things.
'I found something this morning. There's a storage area at the house, round the back. Trunks full of clothes. I think they belonged to the woman that lived here. Lenore.'
'You found her clothes?'
'And there was a mirror.'
'A mirror?' He's looking at me oddly.
The best thing is to show him.
'Follow me.'
Without waiting for a response, I walk round the side of the house, to the storage area. I unlatch the door and turn to him.
'Are you ready?'
He looks over my head, at the door. It's open a few centimetres. Within is pitch-dark.
'How did you find this?'

'By accident. It was pretty well hidden.' Was that due to the overgrown foliage, or was it hidden on purpose? The more I find out about this house, the more it feels like it's shifting, changing. Toying with me. But it's a house. It can't do that.

I reach for my phone, to turn on the torch, but Dinesh already has his on. The light shines into the gap beyond the door.

He moves ahead of me, opening the door fully.

The beam of his torch dances over the walls. Even with the light, it takes a moment for my eyes to adjust. There are the crates. But the other side looks different

'Check over there.'

'Where?' he says, and I realise he can't see where I'm pointing in the dark.

'This way.' I take him by the arm and lead him over to the wall, where I saw the trunks. He shines the torch in that direction, and as it pans over the stone surface, I realise the trunks are gone.

I rush over, running my hands over the wall, searching the corners of the room. Dinesh follows, his torch trained over me.

'You sure this is where you found them?'

'Yes. They were here and—' I grab his phone and turn, shining it at all sides of the room, but the trunks are nowhere to be seen. Where are they?

'There was something else, the thing that freaked me out, that I wanted to show you.'

'What is it?'

I can't see his face in the dark, but his voice is full of doubt.

'Please, just look.' I guide him towards the mirror and shine it over the surface. But the mirror looks different too. The surface is dusty, grimy and uniform. Like it's always been that way. The writing is gone.

'It was there,' I say. I choke back a sob.

'What was?'

'The writing.'

Dinesh leads us out of the room, shutting the door and latching it firmly. Then he walks over to the beach, motioning for me to follow. A breeze blows and I hug my arms around myself. I'm cold again, like before. Dinesh strolls across the beach, to the veranda. It doesn't seem to affect him. He doesn't seem cold at all. Why am I?

'Here.' He motions for me to sit on the wooden swing seat.

'I saw the writing,' I say, looking at my feet. 'It said *remember*.'

'That's it?' he asks.

'You have to believe me. I saw it.'

'I do,' he says gently. 'But you've been under a lot of stress, with the house, everything this morning,'

He touches my arm cautiously, like he's worried I'll lash out. I thought showing him would prove what I was trying to tell him, but this is much worse.

'I wasn't imagining it,' I say. I don't think I was. I was worried about parasomnia but maybe it's not that. Perhaps I'm simply losing my mind. A breakdown. Like Lenore. Like Mr Fonseca's daughter. *Women who lived in this house.*

'I think you need a break,' he says.

'This was supposed to be the break.'

'What are you doing tomorrow?'

The house looms over us in the darkness. I suddenly feel so tired at the thought of working on it again. I want to be somewhere comfortable, where I don't have to worry about writing in the mirror, disappearing antique luggage or ghosts on the balcony.

'Getting some distance from here, hopefully.'

'I think I can help with that.'

'You can?'

He smiles.

'I was going to ask you this before we – before today. There's a place I think you'd like, nearby.'

'What kind of place?'

'You'll see. It's a surprise. I'll pick you up tomorrow at ten. Bring swim stuff.'

'Like a date?'

'If you want it to be.'

In spite of myself, I'm getting to really like him. Even if we both have a lot to hide, could this be more than a fling, more than just a distraction? I'd like to find out. And it seems he does too.

'I – okay. Yes. It's a date.'

'You going to be okay in there tonight?'

The Fonseca house looks back at us, weather-beaten and crumbling.

'I'll be okay.'

'Call me if you need anything.'

'I will.'

After he's left, I peel off my clothes, throw the bloodstained shorts into the bathroom sink and run the tap over them. I let it run for a few minutes, try not to remember the bloodstains on my scrubs that day after surgery.

The water is still running over the shorts but the bloodstains are there unchanged. It doesn't look like they will come out. I stuff the shorts in a plastic bag and take them downstairs to the bin. I should have done that with my scrubs that day. A symbolic gesture, to not let events define me. But I didn't, I let things happen, I let it all destroy me. Eliza is right, I was imploding in London. And now I'm letting the house get to me. Did I really imagine the writing? I can recall it so clearly. The word, *remember*. The way it made my hackles rise, seeing it written in the dust. Now the writing and clothes are gone, without a trace.

As I walk down the hallway to go back down, I notice something. The library door is ajar. I closed it but – the wind has pushed it open. I go to close the door, then notice something inside, on the big oak desk. It's the book, *Ghosts and Legends of Sri Lanka*. It's open.

I shut the book last time I was here and I put it back on the shelf. *I'm sure I did.* I look at the page, and when I read it, I start.

'Local legends: the ghost of Lenore Foster.' Fear prickles my neck as I read. It matches with the story the locals gave. The jealous wife of a British colonial settler who finds a local mistress. It says everything they told me, including the bit about the balcony prowling. I didn't see this before. I don't think I missed the page because I looked through the book carefully. As I move the book, the page falls out. It's faded, fragile, the edges torn. Like this page has been turned a lot. How did I miss it when I looked? Tears prick my eyes. Why don't I have an explanation for the strange things happening in the house? Is it the ghost or is it me?

'I'm getting tired of this,' I shout, at the empty room. Silence answers me. The *yakkā* mask leers down at me. Even the furnishings are mocking me.

But wait, what is that? Something looks different, on the wall under the mask. The glass case. The stuffed bird is still there. But there was a knife displayed next to it. A dagger with a gold hilt. It's gone. I lean closer to make sure it hasn't fallen from its casing. The glass case is empty.

Sweat runs down my back. I didn't turn on the fan when I came in, and the heat in here is stifling. Where is the knife? Did I move that too?

Dinesh is right, I have been under a lot of stress. I might be having some kind of breakdown. And the episode of waking up climbing out of the window must have been a parasomnia episode. There's no other way I can explain that. There is a possible solution to all this. My medication. Expired years ago, unlikely to work, but it's all I have. Tomorrow I'll look for a sleep specialist online, but for tonight, the medication is worth a try. I once read about a trial testing the true shelf life of a number of different medications. They found many lasted a lot longer than the manufacturer expiry dates. In some cases, years more. Even if my medication is no longer active, there's a chance I'll get a placebo effect. It can't hurt.

I head to the balcony room, where I left my luggage. When I open the suitcase, dresses and T-shirts are strewn on top of each other, my make-up hidden in the mess. I didn't leave it this way. Did I? I rummage for the little cloth bag and I know immediately that something is wrong. The bag feels flat. I unzip it, turning the bag inside out, but it's empty. My medications are gone. The other thing I kept in there too. My passport.

I sit on the bed and examine the bag. I know they were all there this morning, because I remember reaching into the bag for insect repellent. This is one memory I can trust, from the lemony tang of the spray on my arms. I should be worried, scared. But all I feel is relief. It wasn't me. Someone got into the house and stole the medication, the knife and the passport. The main things of value here. The medication is a strange thing to take but some of them aren't available over the counter here so they could have decent resale value. And a British passport definitely would. The knife looked antique, it must be worth more than my passport, if it's real gold. Maybe the intruder took the trunks, too. The vintage clothes which could be worth something too.

An intruder having been here is a scary prospect, but one I can try to manage. If I make sure the entry points are locked, if I stay alert, I might have a chance against them. But if it's me? If I have no control over my brain? I have no chance at all. The important thing, the best thing, is that it wasn't me.

The bed frame is heavy and reaches almost to the floor. There's no way someone could hide under there, but I shine my phone torch into the cracks under the bed anyway until I'm satisfied there's no one here. I check all the rooms in the same way.

I don't find any broken windows or unlocked doors. If someone did break in, how did they get in? It's late but I'm wide awake.

I get into bed and rest my head against the headboard. Being without my passport is bad, but I can get a new one. The annoyance and cost of that I can deal with. I can replace some of the medication too. Not the expired pills, but I don't need them any more anyway. It was time to let that old strip of pills go. I'm not a parasomniac. I don't need medication. There's nothing wrong with me. Is there?

34

Anika

Then

It's Anika's turn to host the annual Christmas gathering for their friends tonight. It's been their tradition ever since they left medical school. After dinner is done, Anika goes to the kitchen to plate a chocolate cheesecake for dessert. From the lounge come sounds of laughter, Rosa singing badly and loudly to 'Last Christmas'. Anika stops for a moment, savouring the sound of her five best friends and four partners, partying in her home. She doesn't host often, doesn't get time to, which made today even more special. It would have been even better if Dominic had come. But he's away, working again in New York. He gave her an early Christmas gift before he left, to make it up to her, he said. Anika's hand goes to her shoulder, to the strap of her black top. The lacy black bra set underneath. She puts down the cheesecake and bottle of red wine, and pulls out her phone. Texts Dominic.

Miss you.
He replies quickly.
Can't stop thinking about you.
I'm wearing the lingerie you got me.
His reply comes through almost immediately.

Show me.
Anika's cheeks flush.

'Okay, what are you grinning about?' It's Eliza, carrying an empty bottle. She swaps it for the full one on the table

'I'm not.' Anika puts her phone down, but not before she reads the message again. 'I'm just happy we all got tonight off to do this.'

'It's a rota miracle,' Eliza says. 'But I know that's not it. You have the kind of sappy smile that only comes from being in love.'

Anika reaches into the drawer and pulls out a corkscrew. 'Would you open this?' she says.

'We don't even know what he looks like.' Eliza hands her the open bottle.

'You saw him at your party.'

'I was in no state to remember, remember?'

'That's true.'

'I don't think I could pick him out of a line-up.'

'Luckily you won't have to.'

'Tell your guy we need to meet him.'

'You will, at the wedding.'

'He's coming?'

'I hope so.'

'Can't wait. And see if he can bring a sexy friend or two to the reception party?'

'One not enough for you?'

'I like to have options.'

Anika laughs.

'Sensible.'

'My middle name.' She stops in the doorway. 'Seriously though, anyone who has you this happy is in with me.'

'Thanks.'

*

The party wraps up around two, when the last of the guests leave. Her flat is in disarray, cups and dessert plates on the coffee table, empty bottles on the floor. Normally Anika wouldn't leave the mess but tonight she doesn't care. She makes her way to the bedroom. Her cheeks feel warm at the thought of Dominic finally seeing her in the underwear he chose for her.

In her bedroom, she peels off her dress. Sitting on her bed, she sends him a message.

You up?

Instead of a reply, there's an incoming FaceTime call. Anika hesitates. Then answers.

'Hey.'

A slow smile spreads across his face when he sees her. She's angled the camera so the top of bra and the beginning of her cleavage show.

'God, I miss you.'

'I miss you too.'

'Let me see how it looks,' he says. 'All of it.'

She bites her lip. Moves the camera down a few inches.

'All of it? Or all of me?'

His breathing is shallower now.

'Both.'

She smiles, balances the phone against the headboard.

'Fine. If you will.'

'You first.'

'Okay.'

She reaches behind her and unhooks the bra.

35

Anika

Now

Heat clings to the air, thick and heavy, even at 10 a.m. I walk around the perimeter of the house, examining it. Every window and door is a piece in the puzzle of how the intruder got in. But I can't work it out, because all the doors and windows are shut. Sunlight glances off the roof, highlighting a darker area at the side. As I move around for a closer look, I notice a patch of terracotta tiles that have fallen away, exposing the skeletal frames of the rafters beneath. It corresponds to where the roof was leaking. Could it also be an entry point?

'What are you doing?' It's Dinesh, walking through the front gate. His footsteps crunch softly on the gravel as he approaches.

I point to the hole in the roof.

'Do you think a person could fit through there?'

Dinesh laughs. 'Why? Are you planning a break-in, or just bored of using the door?'

'Not me.' I tell him about the missing medication and passport. 'And the things in the storage room, I think they were stolen too.'

His brow furrows.

'What medication was missing?'

I look at him. I was half expecting him not to believe me. 'Antimalarials, antisickness, painkillers,' I say.

He grabs my arm, his expression intense.

'What are they called?'

'Doxycycline, cyclizine, paracetamol – why?'

He blows out a breath.

'Then I think I know who took them,' he says.

'You do?'

'The police returned to the town last night. Nirmal was taken to the morgue, and when they examined his body, they found medication in his pockets. Similar things to those you described.'

The humid day feels airless now. I sit on the stone wall bordering the house.

'Are you sure?'

'The townspeople were talking about it. Some of them thought he was selling the drugs, others that he had an illness. They were looking up the names. That's why I remembered. If it's your medication, then he's the one who stole it. There was another medication too – they didn't know what it was for. I can't remember the name.'

I glance at him. My parasomnia medication.

'I don't know how much he would get for your items, but from the sounds of it, he was desperate.' Dinesh surveys the roof. 'He could have got in there. On an old place like this it wouldn't be so hard to pull the tiles off. There's no one around, he could have worked undetected for a while.'

I remember the pickpocket's wiry frame.

'The hole could accommodate someone his size.' Crows caw as they fly past, their shadows crossing the path ahead. Nirmal was the intruder.

'Hari vaday, ne?'

'Something doesn't make sense. I opened the bag the medication was in yesterday morning, used the insect repellent before I went out. The medication was all there. The only time he could have taken them was that morning. Because not long after, I found him dead.'

'You think he was watching the place?' Dinesh says. 'Waiting until you were out?'

I look at him.

'The day after I arrived, I thought I saw him down on the beach, outside the house. But Kavya said it couldn't have been, because he'd returned my bag in town at around the same time. Then the night we went to Galhena, when you picked me up, I thought I saw him outside. But then he disappeared.'

'Did you get a good look?'

'Not really. Both times he moved off before I could be sure. I remember a man with a similar frame but I didn't see his face well.'

'It's very strange.'

'And a gold knife from the library was missing. It could have been taken earlier, I didn't pay much attention to it. Maybe he's been here more than once.' Dinesh slings an arm around my shoulders, and I lean against him.

Was it all him? The strange noises. The moving bed. That was the same night we went to Galhena. Did he move it, to be nearer the window so he could get out?

'I thought I saw someone on the balcony once. I convinced myself it was my imagination, but that could have been him too.'

'Ziman said he has a list of crimes to his name, according to the police. Other breaking and entering incidents,' Dinesh says. 'And, the police thought he may not have worked alone.'

'Gamini said Nirmal was involved with some shady people,' I say. 'That one of them might have killed him.'

He sighs. 'I'm sorry this happened to you. I wish we could plug the gap in the roof somehow.'

There's a murderer on the loose and they might have been in this house. Maybe even when I was inside. And they might come back. Relief that the strange happenings weren't caused by me gives way to fear.

'You think one of his accomplices might break in?'

'I don't think anyone will come back here, you said all the things of value were taken. But I think you'd feel better if the gap was closed.'

Dinesh's words make sense but I can't wait to get out. And I already dread coming back. I stand.

'I'm so glad you suggested getting away from here. Where are we going?' I glance at the street outside the house. 'Where's your bike?'

'We don't need it today. It's just a short walk.'

I follow him as he heads towards town. Before long we're at the path that leads to the secret beach.

He touches my hand.

'Don't worry, we won't go that way.' He leads us instead along a small dirt road down the hillside. It branches at the bottom, one path follows the shoreline and he takes us that way.

'There are a lot of secret paths round here, huh?'

'I like that about it,' he says. 'It still feels undiscovered, in parts.'

'I like that too.'

'By the way,' he says, 'did you speak to the police yet?'

'The police? No.'

'You should tell them about the break-in. They wanted to interview you. They were looking for you yesterday.'

My cheeks flush as I think of why they weren't able to find me.

'What did you tell them?'

'Relax, I didn't say anything about that. That's between us,' he says, like it was a strange question to have even asked.

'I hope so.' The ground is uneven now, full of loose pebbles that get under my flip-flops. I slip a few times.

'You need a hand?'

'I'm fine.' I shift my weight back and try to keep myself steady. 'I feel bad for Gamini.'

'Me too. He was very upset. He came by yesterday evening. He'd been to see Nirmal's mother.'

'That must have been tough.'

'It sounds like it was. The police confirmed that he was stabbed.'

'That's awful.' It feels so surreal. He stole the knife, cases full of old clothes. Where are they? With his accomplices? And why did he still have my medication with him when he died? I feel like I'm missing something. But I don't know what.

Dinesh stops at a bay I haven't been to before. A few rowing boats are docked here, bobbing gently in the sea breeze. There's a wooden hut a little way down and Dinesh leads us there.

'What is this place?' I ask.

'One of our watersports rentals. Like most places here, it doesn't get a huge amount of business these days.'

'Is it closed?'

'Not any more.'

He unlocks the door. Inside, surfboards are lined up on one side, wetsuits and life jackets neatly organised by size on a rail on the other side.

'We're surfing?'

'Paddleboarding. You know how?'

A smile breaks out over my face.

'Yes.'

'I had a feeling you might.'

'And if I didn't?'

'Then I figured you'd learn quick. Shall we?'

He gauges my board size and gives me a life jacket. As I take it from him, I can't keep thoughts of the intruder from my mind. Nirmal.

'Hey, you know that story about Nirmal and the boat accident?'

Dinesh looks up from fitting the life jacket around me.

'What about it?'

'Gamini and the others think the town is cursed. And Nirmal especially. Because he saw her. Lenore.'

'And what do you think?'

'It sounds like a lot of bad things have happened to him since. So why would he come back to the Fonseca house? If that was him on the balcony, why would he go back to where he supposedly saw her? And steal Lenore's clothes?'

'The stories are nonsense. *Pissu*. You said so yourself.'

'I know.'

'He was near destitute after the boat accident. The clothes were valuable and he needed money.' He fastens the buckle with a click. 'That's all I think there is to it. You ready?'

'I – sure. Let's go.'

Dinesh packs our stuff into a waterproof bag attached to his board, finds me a paddle, then we set off.

It's a clear day, the morning sun shimmers over the turquoise water. As we move away from the shore, I feel a weight of something lift off me. It feels so good to be on the water. It feels free. The sea stays calm as we float along. The ripples of my paddle keep time with the gentle cadence of the waves. It's rhythmic, meditative. We move into deeper, crystal-blue water. Ahead, the cliffs rise high.

'Where are we going?' I call to Dinesh.

He dips his paddle in and out of the water. A smile tugs the corners of his lips.

'Can you hear it?'

Under the soft sound of the paddles slicing into the water is a faint roaring noise.

'What is that?'

He nods into the distance, to a break in the cliffs where mist rises from behind the jagged rocks. 'This way.' He glides ahead. As I follow Dinesh to shore, the roaring gets louder. Then I see it. A waterfall tumbling down from the cliffs, rushing into a pool at the base. The sun catches the mist, creating a soft halo around it.

I wade into the pool, into the water, a perfect turquoise that looks like something out of a dream. The waterfall thunders down, its noise drowning out everything else. I can feel its pull. Droplets splash against my face as I press closer, my fingertips grazing the steady stream. The waterfall is smooth at first, like silk through my fingers. Then it pushes past in a powerful cascade, cold on my palm. It's wild, untamed, and yet there's something soothing about its relentless energy.

'You like it?' Dinesh stops behind me, his arms around my waist.

'It's beautiful.'

I watch the water churn at the base of the waterfall. The rugged cliffs rise up either side, tangled with vegetation.

'Can you go up there?' I ask.

'I think there's a path. I haven't been,' he says. 'You want to go?'

Suddenly, I think of the story of Lenore's husband. The waterfall in the hill country. Lovers' Leap. The locals said she pushed him and his lover from the cliffs at the top. The water feels colder now. Why am I thinking about that here? Dinesh certainly doesn't seem to be. He's calmly surveying the top, probably looking for the path. What is wrong with me? I'm here to not think about the house. And anyway, Lovers' Leap is a huge, much more powerful waterfall. Not like this.

'No. Here is perfect.'

Dinesh breaks away, walking towards the boards.

'It's also a great spot for this.' From the backpack, he pulls out snorkel masks and fins.

'No way. I've been wanting to do that since I got here.'

He throws one to me.

We put on the snorkel gear and wade back into the sea. Before long, my feet leave the bottom. Pink and orange coral formations decorate the ocean floor. Schools of small blue and green fish dart in and out. Light filtering through the water casts dancing patterns on the seabed. It's so peaceful here. So quiet. All I can hear is the sound of my breathing and the movement of the water as Dinesh swims around me. Among the waving coral, I spot a hatched pattern. A sea turtle.

When we come out I sit on the sand, next to the waterfall.

Dinesh takes off his fins. 'You liked it?'

'That was incredible.'

'Like a different world, right?' he says.

'I've been swimming in Sri Lanka many times but never had an experience like this before.' I watch the sunlight play over the droplets of waterfall, creating hundreds of tiny rainbows. A lump forms in my throat. This has felt like exactly what I needed, after everything that happened in London, and here. But because of all that, I don't deserve to be here. I don't deserve all this.

'I think this might be the most beautiful place I've ever been.' Tears spring to my eyes. 'Thank you.'

'Hey, what is it?'

'Nothing.' I dash them away quickly but it's no good. Tears flow down my cheeks.

'Come here,' he says, pulling me to his chest, stroking my hair.

'I'm sorry. I've—'

'Had a hard time lately?'

I wind my arms around his waist, let him hold me as I cry. I may not deserve it, but I'm here. And I want to bottle this moment. Hold on to this place forever.

I wipe tears away. 'This was perfect. The best date I've ever been on.'

He raises an eyebrow.
'So it was a date?'
'Definitely.'
'And you haven't even had lunch yet.'
'There's food?'
'Obviously.'

There's a little cave cut into the rocks behind the waterfall and we shelter there, to have the food he brought. Seeni sambol paan – bread rolls filled with a jammy onion chutney – mangosteens and watermelon slices.

'You didn't have to do all this.'

He rests his hands on his knees.

'You had a horrible time yesterday. I thought this would help.'

'Then thank you. It did.'

He's kind. Understanding. I might not have the best track record with men but this I'm sure of. I trust him. And I want to open up to him.

'You know the other medication that Nirmal had on him? It's mine, too.'

'What is it?'

'I have a condition. It's called parasomnia. I sleepwalk. Or at least I used to. I thought it stopped, years ago, but since I've been here, things have been happening again.'

I tell him about waking up with my foot out of the window when I arrived.

He strokes my cheek.

'Do you remember any of it?'

'Nothing else. I still don't know if I was trying to jump out of the window, or what was going on. Some people say it's caused by a blurring of the sleep–wake cycle. But in others, they occur because the brain doesn't prevent them from acting out their dreams.'

'That must be so scary.'

'It is. Since I've been here, since things have been happening again, I've felt like I'm going crazy.' It feels good to talk about it. Openly, like I haven't with anyone before. Not even Eliza, who gets so worried and wants to fix it whenever I've mentioned it. He's the only one I've told, like this. I still don't tell him about the worst time. I never talk about that.

'I've been feeling like I can't trust my own mind. Like that time in the storage room. I know now that some of it was Nirmal.'

He looks at me thoughtfully.

'You think the writing was him too?'

I want to believe so. But why would Nirmal write a strange message, telling me to remember? If it wasn't him. If it wasn't me. Was it her? Lenore.

'I don't know.' I'm doing it again. Ruining the experience with thoughts of my condition, of local legends I don't even believe in. I nestle closer to Dinesh. 'Anyway, tell me something. You paddleboard, run a coffee shop, speak three languages and organise the best dates.'

'Where are you going with this?'

'You're very eligible.'

'Am I?'

'Why are you single?'

'There's a long and complicated answer. What about you?'

'Same,' I say. Though I suspect mine is more complicated than his. I've finally opened up to him a little but I still know virtually nothing about him and he doesn't seem to be ready to share. Despite that, I'm getting to really like him. Eliza said it's too soon but I enjoy his company. And today has been perfect. For right now, that's enough.

'So, the sun is still high,' he says. 'We could head back now, or wait it out until it's less hot.'

I scoot closer to him. The cave is cosy and the beach secluded.

Here, behind the rushing waterfall, it feels like we're the only two people in the world.

'I don't want to leave.' I guide his face towards me, kiss him.

He breaks away, laughs.

'That's not what I meant.' He brushes my hair off my shoulders. 'But if that's what you have in mind.'

'I do.'

He peels the strap of my swimsuit down and kisses my shoulder.

'Then we can wait it out as long as you want.'

36

Dayani

The beam of a vehicle headlight moves across the room, travelling over their legs, intertwined under the sheet. Dayani strokes Avila's chest. She doesn't know what to say now. This is uncharted territory between them. But good. Definitely a good development.

'Hey,' she says.

'Hey.' He props himself up on the headboard. He's doing that face again. All night, he's been tender, loving. Now, that expression again, like he's closed off to her. She hasn't seen this from him, before tonight.

'What is it?' she asks. 'Something is wrong.'

'Why would you think that? I'm here with you.' He kisses her. 'And you're amazing. Nothing could be wrong.' If she didn't know him so well, she could almost believe him.

'Come on. I've known you since we were eight years old. I can read you like a book.'

He bites his lip.

'It's nothing. I should go. We've been lucky tonight. I don't want a servant to come in now.'

He stands, starts pulling his clothes on. Dayani reaches for her silk robe, puddled on the floor. She watches him carefully, doing up his jeans, eyes trained out of the window.

'Tell me what's going on.'

He turns. Then he sighs.

'I didn't want to do this now.'

She ties her robe tightly.

'Do what?'

Silence extends between them. He looks at her, then the floor. Then finally back at her. In the split second before he speaks, Dayani realises what's coming is going to change everything. She doesn't want to know. But she feels powerless to stop him.

'I don't think we should do this,' he says.

'What do you mean?' Her voice cracks.

He sits on the bed.

'My parents know about us. Your father told mine. He wasn't happy.'

Her father. Of course he did. Ayomi wouldn't have told. She wouldn't have wanted her brother to get into trouble. Only Dayani.

'Thātha forbade me from seeing you any more,' Avila says. 'Or your father forbade it and Thātha passed on the message.'

'And what did you say?' she asks.

'What choice did I have? You know how it goes. Something I do wrong reflects on Thātha. Your father was angry. He told Thātha to stop us seeing each other. And no one says no to your father.'

'I do.'

'You don't, Dayani. He's dangerous.'

'So is yours. That's why we had a plan. To leave here.' Her voice chokes with tears. 'To be together. What about Colombo University?'

Avila looks at his hands.

'I got in. I'll go.'

'Your parents agreed?'

He blows out a breath.

'Yes. If I stop seeing you.'

She stares at him. Is she hearing this right? He exchanged her for his university place? The one she helped him to get.

'I thought you agreed to stop seeing me because you're scared of my father.'

'It's both.' Avila rests his head in his hands for a moment. 'I love you, Dayani, but I don't know what to do.'

'You sounded like you did a few minutes ago.' She sees him anew, at that moment. She was willing to risk everything for him. For them. But he's too weak to stand up to his father.

'When did this happen?'

He looks at her.

'Last night.'

'So why did you come tonight?'

'I don't know. I wanted to see you, tell you in person. But then things got carried away. I'm sorry.'

'You were using me.' In the worst way. She never expected that of him. She sees red. She thought she loved him. Now that love congeals into something like hate.

'Get out.' She wants to hurt him. She's so angry, she feels she could kill him. She reaches for the glass on her bedside table.

'I wasn't. It wasn't like that.'

'Then what was it like?'

'I'm sorry,' he says. 'Let's talk tomorrow.'

How could he think she'd want to talk to him after he did this? Dayani throws the glass at his head. Avila ducks. It smashes against the bed frame, water and fragments of glass shower over the bed. Suddenly she doesn't care about waking the servants.

'*Pissu the?*' he says, brushing glass out of his hair.

Her parents have their wish. She doesn't want to see Avila ever again.

'I'm not crazy. And I said, get out.'

She had their future planned. He was her future. She thought he was. But he had his own plans. A wave of crushing tiredness takes over her body. She's not escorting him out, not after this.

'Just get out.'

She turns away, closes her eyes.

When Dayani wakes, something is wrong. The floor feels cold. Not like her bed. A foggy feeling infuses her limbs. Her mind, too. Something in her tells her to break out of it, but she can't. Through foggy vision she sees her feet are bare. She's standing on the precipice of her window. The flat part of the roof extends ahead. Her limbs move of their own volition to the roof. She lets them.

Shouting comes from too far away for her to understand. A man's voice.

Dayani keeps walking. She doesn't know where she's going. Only that she has to keep walking.

The shouting gets louder. '*Ehey yannah eppā,*' the voice yells. It's Avila. '*Eppā ehey yannah.*'

Her mind clears, enough to understand the words. *Don't go there.* Again, something in her tries to break through the fogginess but she can't. A car whips past on the street, three floors below. The wind is high tonight, it whips her hair around her shoulders.

'Come back,' Avila shouts. He walks out after her.

But Dayani can't stop herself. She walks to the edge of the roof.

37

Anika

Now

It's dark when we get back. Dinesh walks me to the door of the house. 'You want me to see you in?' he asks.

It's the first time he's suggested it. He's only been in once, briefly, when I asked him to check the lights. And for someone who suggested going in, he looks decidedly reluctant about it.

'You sure you want to do that?'

'I don't want you to be in there alone. Not after the break-in.'

His suggestion earlier, that the intruder would be unlikely to return, made sense but he seems worried now. He looks at the house again, his gaze stopping on the balcony. Is it really intruders he's worried about, or something else?

'In that case, yes please.'

Inside the house, I hit the lights in the hallway. Nothing happens. 'Hang on.' I go through to the kitchen but that light doesn't work either.

Going upstairs, using my phone torch to guide me, I try the lights on the landing, but again they don't work. I switch them on and off a few times, but it stays inky dark. I get a very bad feeling as I head down the hall to the balcony room. I use my phone torch to illuminate the way, my shadow on the wall large and distorted. The light there is broken too.

'The lights are out,' I call. 'All of them.'

Dinesh comes out of the bathroom.

'*Aiyo*. Since when?'

'I don't know. Yesterday, the bedroom electricity was out. But everything was working this morning.'

'Were the others working last night?'

'I think so.'

'*Mala vaday*. The storm must have affected the electrics. With a hole in the roof, it's not surprising.' He sighs. 'We can use our phones for light, but do you have any candles?'

'Excuse me for not thinking that was an essential packing item.'

'There could be some around. People often have them in case of power cuts,' he says.

'I'll look.' Then, an image comes to me. A woman in colonial times, walking this hall with a candle. Wearing a long white dress. Pacing the balcony. Here in the dark, the idea seems less far-fetched.

'What's wrong?' Dinesh asks.

'Nothing. I'll go and look for the candles upstairs.'

'I'll look downstairs. Unless you need me to come with?'

Yes. 'No, I'll be fine,' I say aloud. 'I have my torch.'

Shining my phone in front of me, I walk down the hall, trying to ignore the way the shadows play on the walls either side. Making me feel like they're closing in on me.

There's nothing in the room I was sleeping in when I arrived, except the bed. And I'm not in a hurry to go in there anyway. I check the balcony room, trying to be as quick as possible. There's nothing in the drawers of the dressing table. The contents on top are as I remember. The hairbrush, the mirror. The bottle of perfume. But – as the light hits the bottle, something looks different. There's something in the bottle now. Clear liquid. It's not empty. I open it and a musty old fragrance comes out, like perfume left there a long time. But I could have sworn when I found it, it was empty.

My hackles rise. Lenore comes into my mind again. Was this hers? I shake my head. I'm here to find candles, that's all.

There's another room to check, down the corridor. The room where I found the bedsheets, the night I arrived. There were cupboards there.

I open the door to a musty smell of undisturbed air. The drawers of the cabinet creak and stick, but I manage to open them. The first one is empty, the second has unopened soaps, tarnished metal spoons and bread knives. Why are the knives stored up here, instead of in the kitchen? *Who would store knives here, next to the haunted bedroom?* I try to chalk that up to one of the many idiosyncrasies of the house. I can't go there right now.

The third drawer takes a lot of pulling to get it open, but I'm rewarded for my efforts, as there is a pack of taper candles and a box of matches. Relief floods me. Dinesh was right and now I remember my family used to have candles too, for the government-mandated power cuts that used to happen regularly. I didn't think power cuts were commonplace any more, but in this place, they're likely used to dodgy electrics. I take out the tapers. Balancing my phone on the cabinet, I strike a match.

In candlelight, the shadows dance and flicker. I try to close the drawer but it sticks again. As I do, I glance around the room. Where is the photo I found last time? There were three children, on the beach. The townspeople said the Fonsecas had a daughter. She could be in that photo.

I search the cabinet, but the photo isn't there. It's on the window ledge. I pick it up. What the hell? I clutch the frame tight. This isn't it. It's a different photo. It's a child. A girl, around nine, maybe ten years old, smiling at the camera. I've seen this photo before. The girl is me.

I drop the frame. The glass shatters at my feet. *Why is it here? Why is it here?*

'Anika.' Dinesh stands in the doorway. 'What happened?'

My hand shakes as I pick up the photo and pass it to him. Why is a photo of me here? Who put it there? How did they get it?

'The photo changed,' I say, my voice trembling. 'It was three kids, now it's me, why is there a photo of me? It wasn't me, Dinesh. It was a different photo.'

'Whoa, slow down,' he says. 'Let me see that.'

He holds the candle over the photo, then looks at me. 'You're sure this is you?'

'Of course.' I grab the candle and hold it closer to the photo. 'See? That's my hair, that's . . .' I trail off. It doesn't look as much like me as I first thought. My hair is different, my face, my features are sharper. Now, I'm not so sure.

'I – I don't know.'

Dinesh looks worried.

'It's so dark in here, I wouldn't recognise a photo of myself either.'

'But it was a different photo. Before. I found it when I arrived. There were three kids on the beach, now it's this.' This girl who may or may not be me. I can't take it. I feel like I'm going crazy.

'There could have been more than one photo in the house,' Dinesh says. 'Let's leave this here. Go to bed.'

I follow him silently out into the corridor, watch as he locks the door.

'At least you have candles,' he says.

'Can you stay tonight?' I grab his shirtsleeve. All thoughts of independence go out of my mind. 'Tomorrow, I'm going to get a hotel. But it's too late tonight. I can't stay here alone.'

He looks about as keen as if I asked him to dive through

the hole in the roof. He was happier to jump off a rickety pier than this.

'Please, Dinesh. This place, it's playing tricks on me.'

'The house is?'

'There was a perfume bottle – and my phone, and – all that weird stuff the locals were talking about? You think it's true?'

'*Holmung?*' Ghosts. 'Come on, Anika. You said you didn't believe that stuff.'

'I thought I didn't. But I feel like I'm losing my mind.'

'Okay. I'll stay,' he says.

There's another solution. That I stay at his place. But he doesn't offer, and the fact that he'd rather stay somewhere he's clearly terrified of than take me to his place tells me he has a lot to hide. But it isn't the time to get into that.

'Thank you.'

He takes me in his arms. I relax against his chest. Regardless of what he may or may not have to hide, being with him makes me feel safer. Tonight, I'll take that. The rest, I can work out later.

We take it in turns to shower by candlelight. Dinesh is already in the balcony room when I come in, moving the mosquito nets aside. I set the candle on the dressing table, using some wax to tether it in place. I slide under the bedsheet. With both our phone torches on and the candle, it's a little more bearable. The sea crashes in the distance. It's a choppy night out there. I try not to think about the boat that capsized, the tourists that drowned in the storm. The dead body on the beach. *Think nice thoughts. Don't think about any of that.*

Dinesh gets in next to me, in his T-shirt and boxers.

I turn to him. Being in bed, sleeping together, this feels somehow more intimate than earlier.

'You feeling okay?' he says.

'Fine. Excuse my freakout earlier. I don't know what got into me.'

He strokes my cheek. 'This place is scary,' he says. 'And then there are the stories.'

'You mean Len—'

'Don't say her name.'

'I thought you didn't believe in that stuff.'

'I lied.'

He slings an arm around me.

'How have you managed staying here alone? This place is creepy for anybody, but with your condition?'

'With difficulty.' I move closer to him. 'Thanks for staying.'

'It must be frightening. Not knowing for sure what happens when you're asleep.'

I blink back tears.

'It is.'

'I'll tell you what,' he says. 'I'll make sure I go to sleep after you. Then I can check on you for a bit.'

'I don't know if it will help but – I'd like that.'

'And if anything else happens,' he says, 'if you get up, I'm right here.'

I pull the sheet up and look at him gratefully. 'Thank you,' I say.

38

Anika

I toss and turn, coming out of a strange dream. It slips through my fingers, like trying to catch smoke in my hands. Vestiges of it linger. Shouting. That refrain. *Ehey yannah eppā*. What does it mean again? There's a loud crash. It feels eerily familiar. Grogginess takes over. I close my eyes.

39

Dayani

The hard edge of the roof digs into the balls of Dayani's feet. Cool air fans her face. Her limbs feel heavy. She can't control them. She wants to, but she can't. *A few more centimetres.*

'Dayani. *Mehe Enna.*' Come back. Avila is close now.

Her vision clears. And she sees, her toes over the edge. The road below. How did she get here? She turns to him. The movement sets her off balance. She spins backwards. Her body goes slack. She hovers for a split second, between ground and air. Between life and certain death.

Then there's a hand under her waist. Avila. He pulls her back. Dayani regains her footing, flat on the roof.

But then the weight on her shifts. The arm around her is gone. Avila is gone. There's a sickening crash. Then screaming.

A voice from the street below shouts Avila's name over and over. Dayani stands on the roof, frozen. She can't look over the edge. She must, but she can't.

Dayani's window bursts open.

Her parents are there. Her mother rushes over and grabs Dayani's arm.

'What's going on here?'

Dayani still can't move.

Her mother goes close to the edge of the roof and looks over.

Then she reels back. Looks at Dayani but now her face is different. She's scared.

'What happened?' she asks again, quietly. 'What did you do?'

'I don't know. I don't remember coming out here.'

Dayani looks over the edge, finally. The screaming amplifies. It takes her a while to realise it's her own.

The only thing she hears louder than her own voice is the one from the street below. Shouting, *She pushed him. She pushed him.*

40

Anika

Now

I wake with a start. The sheets are tangled and sweaty around me and I'm breathing hard. I haven't had that dream in a long time. And now, like always, all I can remember is the last part. Afterwards. I keep saying, over and over, *I don't remember. I don't remember.* My face is wet with tears. Why can't I ever remember what comes before?

A piercing noise rents the air. It's coming from outside. I peel the sweaty sheet off me. The screaming continues, louder now. A woman. It unnerves me, pulls me out of my terrible memories, makes my skin prickle. I rush towards the source. The balcony door. It's open. How can that be, when that door was jammed shut?

I go out onto the balcony. I see the woman screaming. It's Kavya. What is she doing here? She's kneeling over something on the veranda below. With a sick feeling in the pit of my stomach, I run down the stairs and out of the back door.

There she is, at the edge of the veranda, a bag at her feet as if she dropped it there. And in front of her – my knees buckle. There's a man, lying face down. The blood coming from his head puddles around his prone body. The smooth stone of the veranda is slippery with blood. Kavya looks at me, her eyes stricken.

'It's Dinesh. He's dead.'

41

Kavya looks at me in disbelief.

'He's dead,' she says again. Quietly this time, like she can't believe it. It's almost worse than the screaming. 'I came to see if you were okay. To give you this.' She points at the bag. Appa fall out of the bag. One of the yellow yolks has broken, spilling into the bag. 'Now he's dead,' she says again.

I drop to my knees in front of her.

'No. No, he can't be.'

Blood seeps into the sand ahead of the veranda, turning it a sickly dark red and I know she's right. But I scramble towards his head to check his pulse anyway.

That's when I see something around his head, splattered on the stone. It's brain matter.

Nausea roils in my stomach. I've seen intestines, brains, the inside of a man's stomach, many times in surgery, and it never fazed me. But now, I want to vomit. Heave and heave until I'm empty. I take deep breaths, in and out until the nausea subsides.

Kavya is there first. She feels for the pulse at his neck. Then she shakes her head.

'He is. He's dead.'

A sound works its way from the pit of my stomach. A howl. It doesn't sound like me. He can't be dead. Dinesh who helped me, who stayed with me last night even though he didn't want to. He said he'd make sure I fell asleep first. I didn't even hear him get up.

'How has this happened?' Kavya asks. She's still speaking in that quiet disbelieving tone.

'I don't know,' I say. 'I was asleep.'

Kavya looks at me.

'How can you not know? You were here at the house last night?'

I start to cry again. Dinesh can't be gone. He can't be dead. It feels like moments ago that I fell asleep in his arms. But his body lies just feet away from me. It can't be. I turn away to look at the wall. If I can't see him, it won't be real. He can't be dead. I squeeze my eyes shut.

'Miss Anika?' She touches my shoulder. 'Were you here?'

I flinch at the touch. I want to rewind, to being back in bed. Before this happened. To right before I went to asleep. When Dinesh was alive.

'Miss Anika.' Kavya's voice sounds as if it's coming from far away. 'I know this has been a shock but I need you to think. We have to work out what has happened here. You have to tell me, did you hear anything at all last night?'

'No.' The tears fall faster now. I'm breaking down, becoming hysterical, but I can't control myself. I hold my knees and sob. Why can't I remember anything of last night?

Kavya comes closer.

'We should call the ambulance, though I don't think there's anything they can do.' She takes a ragged inhale. 'But they'll take him away.' Tears spill; she wipes them away with her fingers and makes a call. She's shaken to her core but she's trying her best to keep it together, taking action, making plans. I used to be like that. But not now. Not today.

I listen to her speaking Sinhala to the ambulance people. There's a horrible dripping sound in the background. Blood dripping down the veranda. None of this can be real.

She hangs up, turns to me.

'They're on the way.'

She takes another shaky breath. 'Dinesh is dead . . . What could have happened?'

'I wish I knew.'

'Do you think he fell?' Her flips-flops make a dull thudding noise as she walks to and fro. 'The balcony is directly above,' she says, pointing up at it. 'He must have fallen from there. Are you sure you didn't hear anything?'

I stand, trying not to look at him but my eyes are drawn to his body anyway. Lying so still. I wish I could unsee it. Whatever happened here, I wish I could undo it.

I was out cold again, last night. I was fast asleep.

'No.'

My legs feel weak and I hold the wall for support. It's rough beneath my fingers. In the distance, crows caw. Everything still feels so unreal. And blended with the strange happenings, the feeling like I can't trust myself is amplified. It feels like I'm living in a nightmare.

I stare at the beach ahead, to anchor me here. The sea laps lazily at the shore. How can it be that, a few feet away from this beautiful beach, Dinesh lies dead?

'Did you know Dinesh was here?'

'Yes.'

'What time did you see him last?'

'I—' I take a breath. 'He stayed here last night.'

Her eyes widen.

'You were having a relationship?'

'Something like that.' Tears start again. We didn't get to define it. Now we'll never be able to.

Sirens sound, getting closer. Soon after, loud knocking comes from the front of the house.

'*Kowrooth innawa the?*' Anyone home?

'The paramedics. Shall I bring them round?'

'Please.'

I pace up and down the veranda, my back to Dinesh. Moments later, a man and woman appear bearing a stretcher. They're wearing the white uniforms and gloves of paramedics. Kavya is talking to them. I watch as they bend down near him. One of them has something grey in his hand. A body bag.

Kavya looks at them, then at the house, as if weighing up which is worse. 'We can't stay here. Let's go inside for a bit.'

She leads me into the house and shuts the door.

'They'll deal with things out there.' She wipes away tears as she sits on one of the teak sofas.

'I can't believe it. Dinesh. I've known him for years. We weren't very close friends, but we were part of each other's lives. It happens that way, in small towns like this. He'd always stop to talk if we saw each other. He was a good guy.'

Dinesh really was a good guy. He was kind, understanding, full of life. He showed me the waterfall. He made that surprise for me, just because I was having a bad time. There's movement outside. They're carrying the stretcher, the body on it bagged up. Disbelief gives way to sick reality as it hits me properly. He's dead. I try to sit, miss and slide off the chair to the floor. I don't get up. I flop down to my side, my shoulders shaking with silent sobs.

Kavya comes over, her feet stop in front of me. Her toenails are painted dark red, the polish slightly chipped.

'Miss Anika?'

My limbs feel so heavy. I don't want to move. The tears slide from my face to the marble floor. There's a patch of dust under the chair I must have missed.

Kavya crouches next to me, her hand on my shoulder.

'Miss Anika, I know it's been a shock. Here.' She grabs my arm and guides me to the chair. I let her, rather than move of my own accord. 'Would you like some water? Or some tea? I'll see what you have.' Without waiting for an answer, she walks further into the room, through the entryway that leads to the kitchen. 'I've found some tea,' she calls.

There's dust on the chair too, in the crevices of the wooden flower carvings on the armrest. The room still looks uncared for, despite the work I did in here. This whole exercise has been futile. I couldn't get back the missing memories or closure I wanted. And things have been getting worse and worse since I arrived. Now Dinesh is dead. I couldn't have imagined this.

I managed to explain away all the strange things that happened since I got here. The bed that moved, the writing in the mirror that disappeared. I thought it was all the work of the intruder, Nirmal. Because I always woke in the middle of the parasomnia episodes. I thought I could rely on that. But I never knew what came before. What happens in those moments before I regain consciousness? Last time, the worst time, I awoke in the middle of it. But I told Dinesh that parasomnia for some people means acting out their dreams. Is that what happened? Did I sleepwalk last night, and not wake up, not even after it was over?

Kavya comes back holding two mugs of tea.

I drink some, it's black tea with sugar, the traditional Sri Lankan way. How is it we're drinking tea, when the veranda is still slick with Dinesh's blood?

'Have you remembered anything yet, about last night?'

She seems to think it's a matter of time. We could sit here all day, and I wouldn't remember. Last night is a blank. From falling asleep next to Dinesh, to him dead here this morning. What happened in between? Kavya thought he fell. What if it wasn't that? Did I push Dinesh? Did I kill him?

I fumble, the cup slips from my hand. Hot tea flies out, over my leg and onto the floor. The cup bounces, somehow it doesn't break. It lies upturned, spilling tea into a puddle on the floor.

Kavya passes me tissues. I pat my leg. It should sting but I can barely feel anything.

'I'm fine.' What did I do last night? I fling the sodden tissues on the seat next to me.

Kavya eyes them.

'When did you see him last?'

'We went to sleep. I had a vivid dream.' I rack my brain for everything I can remember. All I can recollect is the dream. 'Then there was a loud noise, like a crash. It was so loud, it woke me for a few moments.'

'So you did hear something?' she says.

'I don't know. I couldn't tell if it was part of the dream. Then I went back to sleep. When I woke up, you were here. And he was there. That's all I know.'

She looks into the distance.

'That noise. Do you think that was him falling?'

My stomach turns. Why is this happening again?

'It looks like he fell, from the balcony. Did you see anything unusual upstairs?'

'Only that the door was open. Out onto the balcony. That door was jammed shut. Until this morning. Or last night. I don't know when he went out there.'

I recall the yellowed net curtain billowing in the breeze. Did he open the window? Or did I do it, while I was sleepwalking? I couldn't open it when I was awake, but in the way that people in life-threatening conditions sometimes find superhuman strength, lifting cars off loved ones, the subconscious can possess strength not known to the conscious mind. What did I do?

'The police are on the way,' she says.

'The police? Why?'

'We don't know what happened to Dinesh. So they must investigate. They want to talk to both of us.'

I feel sick all over again.

'They were looking for you the other day,' she says. 'Did you speak to them, about Nirmal?'

Dinesh said they'd call me. I haven't had any calls from them. Or any messages either, in the past day or so.

'No.'

'First you found Nirmal, and now Dinesh has died here, where you're staying. While you were in the house.'

'What are you saying?'

She looks around, at the corners of the room.

'The balcony that Dinesh fell from. That's the one, isn't it? Where Nirmal saw the ghost.'

'Yes.' I debate telling her about the strange happenings in the house. I don't know whether those were Nirmal, or the ghost. Or me. The one that scares me most is the most likely. It can't be a coincidence that this is happening again. It was me the last time. And it's me again. I did this.

Kavya is speaking, with a worried expression. Something about the ghost and the balcony.

'When the police come,' I say, cutting her off, 'I can't be here.'

Kavya frowns.

'Why not? You live here. They will want to talk to you.'

'But I don't know anything. I didn't hear anything.'

She folds her arms.

'So tell them that.'

'I don't think they will be satisfied.'

If she thinks I had something to do with Dinesh's death, she'll tell the police. I remember how they work here. Easily bought, especially if the buyer is someone with connections. Like my father. That's how it was for me, sixteen years ago. That's how he made what happened with Avila go away. Other times, when there's no incentive for them, if it's a dirty cop or a lazy one, they do the easiest thing. Pin the crime on the nearest suspect who fits, not looking for more evidence because they can't be bothered.

'Please, Kavya. I can't talk to them. If they find out that a man stayed here last night and I say I don't remember what happened, they'll suspect me.'

Kavya leans forward.

'Suspect you of what? He fell.' Her expression hardens as she connects the dots, reaches the conclusion I don't fully know is true. 'Didn't he?'

'There's—' I can't get the words out. I don't want to tell her the truth, but I might have to.

'What is it, Miss Anika? If you know something, you must tell the police.'

She's looking increasingly hostile. I have to make her understand. If the police are coming, I need her onside. Or, at least, not against me.

'I have a condition called parasomnia,' I say. 'It's a medical problem, which makes people sleepwalk. Sometimes makes them act out their dreams.'

'You act out your dreams?'

'With no conscious awareness. The night I arrived here, I woke up and I was trying to jump out of the bedroom window. I used to take medication for it.'

'Used to? So you haven't been taking it?'

'I haven't done for years. I thought it had stopped.' I close my eyes for a second. 'I thought I was better. I don't know for sure what happened last night, but if I did have something to do with Dinesh's death, I didn't do it on purpose. I can't control the parasomnia. I have no awareness when it happens. If the police come, if they suspect me, they might arrest me.'

She shakes her head slowly. She looks pale.

'But if you did it, then they must.'

'I didn't. I mean, I don't know if I did. Please, it's not something I have control over.'

'But you think you might have?'

'I don't know.' I wish for the hundredth time that my brain didn't turn on me like this.

'Help me. Please. I don't want to be arrested for something I don't even know if I did.'

She stands.

'What about Nirmal? The pickpocket. Did you kill him too?'

This is going all wrong. Instead of garnering sympathy, I've made myself sound more guilty. I step towards her.

'I had nothing to do with that.'

She steps back, towards the door.

'How do I know if you're telling the truth? You just told me you're not sure if you killed Dinesh.'

Bile builds in my throat. Dinesh is dead. Whatever the cause, this shouldn't have happened to him. A barrage of painful thoughts and mixed-up memories threatens. But I can't even process my feelings about his death now. If I really did kill him, I should let the police arrest me. I should turn myself in. It's the right thing to do. But I have to be sure. If the police come, if they arrest me, they won't bother looking for evidence, in the face of a confession. I have to think fast, to make sure that I'm not arrested for a crime I may not have committed. If it wasn't me, then how could this have happened?

'I don't know anything about Nirmal's murder. Gamini said he was involved with some shady people and the police thought one of them killed him. Dinesh found a hole in the roof of this house, which someone could have used to enter. You know how Nirmal had medication on him when he was found dead? That was my medication.' I walk towards her again and this time she doesn't move. 'I think Nirmal broke in here, stole the medication, and some other things that were missing. What if the person who killed him wanted something from this house? What if they came back here, looking for it, and found Dinesh? And killed him?'

She looks like she's thinking.

'What could they want from the house?'

Dinesh fell from the balcony of Lenore's bedroom. The trunks contained Lenore's clothes. Could all this link back to her? I'm getting desperate but I want to believe it. At the very least, I need to look into the alternatives, before I can be sure. If it was me.

'Something to do with the ghost. With Lenore.'

There's a knock on the door.

Out of the hall window, I can see two men. Gamini and Ziman. I'm relieved it's not the police, but I still have a bad feeling about this.

'Hi,' I say, keeping the door half open. '*Kohomada*, uncle?'

Gamini looks one hundred per cent less friendly than before.

'Have you seen Dinesh?' he asks. 'He hasn't opened up his coffee shop as he usually does. He wasn't at his home. And he's not answering his phone.'

I freeze. What do I say? If I tell them that he's dead, that he was here when it happened, they'll understandably have questions, like Kavya did. And when I can't answer them, they'll suspect me too. Can I lie to them? It's wrong, and if they go round the back of the house, they'll see the blood. But I need time, to think, to work out if it was me, or if there is another explanation.

'I haven't seen him for some time.' My words trip on the lie. 'Not since yesterday.'

'You're a doctor, *ne*?' says Ziman suddenly. Maybe Kavya told him. Word really does get around in this town.

'Yes, do you need medical help?'

He gives a strange smirk.

'Can you help us? You are suspended, *ne*?'

My throat goes dry. 'I—' How does he know that?

'And you didn't tell us about what happened here when you were young. A very interesting article in *The Island* this morning. So much you were hiding, Miss Anika.'

I can't formulate even a sentence.

Kavya is behind me.

'*Mokada me*, Ziman? That is Miss Anika's business. If Dinesh comes here, we will call you.'

She shuts the door.

'Thank you,' I manage.

I thought she was helping me, but she looks severe as she faces me.

'What is he talking about? What are you hiding?'

An article, Ziman said. Without responding, I rush upstairs, to the balcony room. My phone is there, on the floor. It's gone dead from the torch being on all night, I must have forgotten to plug it into the charger. I do so now and restart my phone. As soon as it boots up, it starts beeping rapidly with new messages. I ignore them, searching instead for *The Island* newspaper. And there it is.

Under a photo of me, pulled from one of the London articles, the darkest part of my past is laid bare on a whole-page spread. Like it was sixteen years ago. Only then, there was no photo. My name was missing too. My father made sure that what everyone thought I did was erased. They said it was an accidental fall that caused Avila's death, and this article says the same. Only it wasn't.

I remember before, clearly. I remember Avila coming over that night, sleeping with him. Him breaking up with me. And the next thing I remember, I was on the roof. And he was dead.

And my parents were there. They'd come back because they'd found out from his family that he was with me. They all saw it happen. His family were on the street, my parents in my room. His sister screamed that I'd pushed him. Before that, when he ended things, I hated him. I wished he was dead. So I think they were right.

They tried to take me to the police station for questioning but I became so hysterical when I saw his body that I couldn't go. Later I went, my father accompanied me, stood beside me the whole time and listened to my statement. Heard how Avila was with me in my bedroom before it happened. I lied about why, but I knew he didn't see through it. And I knew also, by the stiff, distant, suspicious way he behaved, that he wouldn't bring it up again. He thought I killed Avila. So did the police. But they knew who Thātha was. So they dropped the case against me. Everyone who was there believed I killed him. I wish I could remember the moments in between the argument and his death. The house isn't even there to trigger it. I'll never get that gap in my memory back.

Closing the article, I open the new messages. There are ones from Eliza, saying *Call me.* Finally, there's a link to an article, in a London paper. TELL ALL PAST OF SUSPENDED SURGEON, the headline screams. As I read it, I feel lightheaded. I thought things were getting worse here, and apparently the same has happened at home. Phrases swim in my vision as I read. *Old boyfriend was killed when at her family home in Sri Lanka.* Now the London papers know about that too.

After a sensationalised account of what happened here and in the surgery, there's a comment from my old sleep specialist. Apparently he isn't retired. He doesn't disclose that he was my doctor, but he comments on the case. *The condition wouldn't cause her to make the mistake. Parasomnias only strike when the patient is asleep. However, an underlying sleep disorder leaves the patient more vulnerable to the effects of sleep deprivation. This doctor should not have been allowed to operate in a sleep-deprived state. Nor should any surgeon, but especially not one with a condition like this.*

There's a comment from the hospital too. *We were unaware of the full extent of Anika Amarasinghe's medical background, or the severity of her condition. It is the responsibility of each staff member to disclose in full all medical details which could affect work performance.*

There is a final line. *The deceased's patient's family are now looking to bring criminal proceedings against her.*

Criminal proceedings? And the past that I buried for so long is out in the open, here and in the UK. Pressure builds until I can't take it. I smack the side of dressing table, next to me. It shakes, like it's about to fall. I grab it as it topples, push it back into place.

'Everything all right? I heard a crash.' It's Kavya.

'Fine.'

I reach for my phone, open on the article, on the bed, but she's seen it too.

'This is you?' she says. I can't deny it. Not with a picture of me at the top.

'It's not how they say it is.'

She looks at it, then me.

'This is why you're here?'

The sheet is twisted from where I threw it off this morning. So much has changed in those few hours. So much that can't be made right.

'I don't know what to do.'

'You said your condition was better for years, right?'

I nod.

'With all this stress you're under . . . and not being on your medication. Could it have made your condition worse?'

I look at her. I've been wondering the same thing, since the day after I arrived. I told Dinesh last night that I sleepwalk. So if I did, he would be prepared. He would have been able to stop me. Dinesh was bigger, stronger than me. But he's dead. Did I attack him? It's hard to imagine, but just like I managed to open the balcony door which was jammed shut, did I somehow manage to overpower Dinesh? If I did kill him, then I can't comprehend what my subconscious seems to be capable of. I can't risk it again.

'I need my medication,' I say.

'The one Nirmal took?'

'Yes.' *Will they have it here?*

'Why don't you get some more?'

'It's not that easy. It's rare, it's very unlikely that I'll find it here.'

'You could try in the city,' she says.

Headlights illuminate the window. It's a white car, with blue writing. Police. They park on the street. Two men in police khaki shirts and trousers get out. They stop, looking at the house.

There's a knock at the door.

Kavya looks at me.

'Are you going to open the door?'

'I can't. I can't talk to the police. What if I say something, and they think it was me?'

'You have to talk to them, eventually, Miss Anika. If you haven't done anything wrong, then there is nothing to fear in talking to the police.'

'But that's just it. I don't know. Can you please answer the door?'

'And then what? What do I tell them?'

'Say I'm not here?'

Kavya looks at me with barely disguised hostility.

'I don't want to lie to police.'

'Please. Say I just left. I'll – I'll go out the back. Then you're not lying, exactly.'

'I don't like this. I'll say you went out, but as soon as you have the medication, you must talk to them. Agreed?'

'Yes.'

She answers the door. I hover on the upstairs landing and try to make out the conversation but it's all in Sinhala, too fast for me to understand much. What I do catch is alarming enough. *Man who died on the beach. We have to talk to her.*

Kavya replies, it goes on for a while. She shuts the door and I'm relieved.

'What did you say?'

'What you told me to. But, Anika, they want to talk to you

about Nirmal's death. When they got the call to come here, they were already on the way to talk to you about that. So . . .' She blows out a breath. 'It doesn't look great, that you're involved with both incidents.'

'But I had nothing to do with Nirmal's death. Please, you have to believe me.'

'Where were you that afternoon? You were so upset when you came to my shop, I went to check on you later. But I couldn't find you in town and you weren't at the house. Where did you go?'

My eyes prick with tears. I can't tell her the truth. Hooking up with a man I barely know in the storage cupboard of his workplace is so far out of the bounds of what is okay here, it's on a different planet. She'll judge me and then she won't help me any more.

'I went for a walk.'

It's difficult to believe that was only two days ago. Dinesh was alive, and now he's gone. I bite my lip hard.

'Where?'

'I – I didn't have a route as such. I just walked. Away from town,' I add. I hope my lack of local directional knowledge will make my clumsy answer sound plausible.

But she looks even more suspicious now.

'Why don't you tell the police? Then they will leave you alone. And then you should go back to the UK. I think it's time.'

Before I left, I couldn't even go to the shop on the corner without my sunglasses on for fear of being recognised. Now all my past is public and I'm facing criminal proceedings. I can't go back to London. But Kavya is right, with everything that's happened here, I can't stay here either. But where can I go? I don't know, but I can figure it all out better when I have my medication.

'I will talk to the police, but first I need to get my medication. I can't go out there now, so – could you?' I reach into my bag on the floor, and pull out my wallet. 'I don't have a prescription but from what I remember, sometimes you can pay a bit extra and they will give it to you.'

Kavya looks unimpressed.

'You want me to bribe a pharmacist as well as lie to the police?'

'I don't want to ask, but it's the only option. It's still the early hours in the UK. Even if I managed to make an appointment to get a prescription, it would take too long. I need to get out of here, like you said. I have to leave.'

She looks like she's weighing up whether bribing the pharmacist is worth it to get rid of me.

'Okay,' she says finally. 'I will get your medication, but then you talk to the police, and you go back home. Okay?'

'Yes.' I press my house keys and a handful of rupee notes into her palm. 'Here. I really appreciate your help.'

Kavya barely looks at me as she takes them and leaves. I run to the window. Across the street, she speaks to the policemen again. The conversation goes on for some time. Then they're getting back in the car and leaving. Kavya drives off.

I close my eyes. They're gone. But my relief is temporary. Because dark is falling. I have no choice but to wait until she gets back. Until then I'm here, alone.

42

Anika

Then

'Time of death. 06:03.' The consultant's voice is weary as she makes the announcement that marks the end of two hours of trying to resuscitate the patient. Peritonitis will be the official cause of death. Internal infection, an unexpected complication of his surgery the day before. The bleeping machines turn silent. The atmosphere in the operating theatre is grim as they clean up, pack away the evidence of their futile efforts. Anika hasn't seen her colleagues like this before. This patient was supposed to go home today. Not to the morgue.

Anika wasn't in the surgery yesterday, or on the ward round that missed early signs of the fast-spreading tissue infection. In the emergency surgery to wash out and remove the infected tissue, Anika was only assisting. Two consultants took the lead. Even so, Anika can't help but feel some responsibility. Whether hers or not, losing a patient is never easy. And more than that, the powerlessness, knowing nothing she can do will change things. It's uncomfortably, claustrophobically familiar.

The uneasy feeling won't leave her, even as she exits the hospital, gets into her car and starts the drive home. She's on call tonight. She can't face the thought of going back again so soon. And she can't bear the thought of going to her empty flat.

At the next junction, she changes direction and heads for Dominic's instead. His presence is comforting, he can always make her feel better.

Central London rush hour is in full swing, it's almost eight in the morning by the time she nears his apartment block. He got back from New York last night. She hasn't surprised him like this before but he won't mind. She knows he'll be up, he always wakes early even when he's been away. She's come to know his routine.

She parks, heads up to his floor. She's missed him more than ever today, she longs to feel his arms around her. His reassurances that everything will be okay. Maybe she can sleep here today. Even if he has to go to work. In his space, surrounded by his things, it will feel like he's there. It will make her feel less alone.

She reaches his corridor and his door is already ajar. She speeds up. He'll make this awful feeling go away. No one else can.

The door opens fully.

But it's not Dominic standing there. A woman is outlined in the door frame. Blonde hair with perfect highlights, lululemon leggings. A pulse starts to pound in Anika's head. Is she his sister? His cleaner? *But he doesn't have either.*

Anika backs away from the door. She doesn't want the woman to see her. And she needs to know who she is. There's an alcove down the hall, and from here she has a view of the door.

The woman steps back, and Dominic comes out. He's in a grey suit, he looks like he's going to work.

He's about to shut the door. Then Anika hears a voice call out. 'Zach.'

Zach. Who is Zach? The pulse in her head starts up again.

The woman comes out again and puts a hand on his arm.

'You forgot this,' she says with a smile as she hands him his phone.

Her teeth, straight and unnaturally white, scream of excessive orthodontics. She has an American accent. The pulse pounds louder.

Dominic takes the phone. Anika notices it's not the one she's seen him use, in a navy case. This phone has a bottle-green case. *Maybe he got a new case,* she tells herself. Or it's his work phone. Though she's seen that too, and it doesn't look like this.

'Thanks, Ames,' he says. Then he kisses her on the lips. This isn't the passionate kiss of new lovers. It's a swift kiss that speaks of familiarity.

Anika wants to vomit.

Now Dominic is putting his phone in his pocket, shutting the door.

Anika walks quickly away, down the corridor to the lift. She can't let him see her. She runs inside and jabs the button wildly. There's no sign of him as the doors close. Then, her legs give out. She collapses to a sitting position on the lift floor.

43

Anika

Now

The lights have stopped working again. The candles are in the balcony room. All the bedrooms are tainted in some way or other now, I don't want to go in any, so I'd planned to stay downstairs until Kavya comes back. But I need the candles. So I'll brave the balcony room, for a few seconds.

A creaking noise stops me as I walk down the hall. I think it's coming from the balcony room. I tell myself it's the house settling. In the dark, the house takes on a life of its own. The house seems to *breathe*. It's been here so long, seen so much. The air feels heavy with secrets. Other people's, and mine too. The vision of Dinesh lying dead this morning, my doubts over my involvement in it, all of it merges into a horrifying cloud of darkness that feels like it could consume me. I liked Dinesh so much. I never wanted to harm him. How could my subconscious make me do that? I can't trust myself at all. I'm a danger to anyone that gets close to me. Just like I was all those years ago. I hold the wall, breathing heavily.

The stories around the house come into my head now. Lenore killed her husband and his lover by pushing them to their deaths. The locals said she cursed anyone who lived in the house to the same fate. To be unlucky in love, they said. But was it more than that for me? Did the spirit of Lenore infect me? Possess me somehow? No, I did the same thing before. I can't blame a ghost for this. I close my eyes as more memories of last time threaten. Ones I'd buried for so many years. The blood around Avila's head. The way his arm was bent at an odd angle. How my mother pulled me away. And afterwards, the funeral. I sneaked out, I wanted so badly to say goodbye. But once I was there, I wished I hadn't come. No one would look at me. His sister spat at me. They all thought I was a killer, protected by my powerful father. And I didn't know enough to deny it.

Outside, thunder crashes. Then the rain comes down, pounding fiercely on the roof. The storm pulls me from my reverie. I need to keep calm.

In the balcony room, I find the tapers on the dressing table. My hand shakes as I strike the match. It takes three tries before I get it. The candle flickers into life, casting a pool of light on the dressing table and the wall beyond. The perfume bottle catches the light. It's full, like it was yesterday. I didn't look properly before, or I imagined that it was empty.

I can't do this again. I feel like I'm losing my mind. I don't know how long it will take Kavya to come back. She said she's going home to get her car, then driving into the city to get the medication. If it's not in the first pharmacy, which is likely, or the pharmacist isn't happy to give it without a prescription, she'll be driving around a few before she comes back. This could all take a long time. I have to get through the next hour, or however long it takes. I hold the candle high and turn for the door.

The candlelight illuminates something on the wall behind the dressing table. It's a crack. An indentation in the wall. Is it a trick of the light? I shine the candle closer to the wall. It *is* an indentation, extending far down the wall. All the way to the floor. I move the candle, following the outline. The shape of a door. But that's crazy. There isn't a door here, in the wall. I balance the candle in one hand as I push the dressing table, to be sure. It moves easily enough. I push it away until the wall is unobstructed. Thunder crashes again. Then lightning rents the air. And in its bright light, I see it.

I was right. It is a door. It's around three feet high. I push but it won't move. I edge my fingers under the outline but nothing happens. Then I feel down the door and something appears under my fingers. Another indentation, small but significant. A handle. I push it, pull it and the door opens.

Ahead lies darkness. I shine the candle high and it shows a small space the height of the room beyond. It's wide enough for one person to fit. It could be another storage space. Or a passageway? The owner never mentioned anything like that. I feel the door from the other side. It's made of wood, papered over to look like part of the wall. If it is a passage, it could be another relic from colonial times. Some old houses have those. Where could it lead?

Rain pounds on the window, turning the view of the sea blurry. Under that there's another sound. A voice. Through the rain-soaked window I make out the outline of someone down on the beach behind the house. The silhouette of a man.

'*Eleata enna*,' he shouts. Come out. It's Ziman. He's back. Or he never left. I move away from the window. 'I know you're in there.'

I crouch by the window. How do I get rid of him?

'Miss Anika,' says a voice. It's Kavya.

'Thank goodness. You're back.'

She rushes towards me.

'I came as fast as I could.' She pushes a strip of tablets into my hand. It's cut from a larger strip, the plastic edges are sharp. There are four pills.

'I can't believe you found them. Did you have to drive around?'

'Luckily the first pharmacy had them. I had to hand over all the money you gave.'

'Sorry you had to do that.'

'It's okay. Here.' She hands me a bottle of water.

'Ziman is still here,' I say.

'I know. I managed to avoid him, but I saw him out by the veranda. I think he knows something.'

The veranda was covered in blood. If he was there before the rain started, he would have seen the blood. That's why he's still here.

'You have to go, Anika. You have the medication now. Why don't you take it, and then go to the police station?'

'I can't, when Ziman is out there. Will you talk to him again? Get him to leave? He's suspicious of me, because of the article. And if he's seen the blood, if he knows Dinesh is dead – he might think I had something to do with it.'

She sighs.

'I can try. But then I'm going home. I just came to check you were okay this morning. I never thought the day would go like this. I don't want to be caught up in – whatever happened here.'

I take her hands. 'Kavya, I'm sorry. And I can't thank you enough, for everything. I'll speak to the police. And after that, I'll get out of town, get the next flight out. I don't think it's safe for me to stay in the country any more.'

She nods curtly.

'Fine.'

I crouch on the floor near the balcony window, and peer round.

There he is. I see Ziman's rangy silhouette down on the beach.

'*Eleata enna*,' he shouts again. Like he saw me there. I flatten myself against the wall.

'We know you're in there,' he shouts. *We?* Oh no. Behind him are the silhouettes of more men. It looks, from the khaki colour of their uniforms, that they're police. I hope I'm mistaken, with the rain obscuring my vision.

'Come out,' Ziman shouts again, louder. The anger in his voice scares me. 'Tell us what you did with Dinesh. And Nirmal.'

'Anika Amarasinghe, we know you're in there.' A woman's voice this time, amplified like she's using a megaphone. 'This is the police. We need you to come out and answer some questions.'

Fuck, fuck, fuck. There's nothing Kavya can do about this. Not with the police there. She's best off out there, with them. Hopefully it's not too late for her to pretend to have nothing to do with me.

'Come out, Anika. We have you surrounded.' The amplified voice reverberates off the walls. I stand there in the dark and I make a decision. I can't go out there. They seem to have made up their minds about my guilt. I don't stand a chance. When I don't come out, in a few minutes they'll break the door down. My only choice is to hide until they're gone. I rush to the other end of the room. Open the door that was behind the dressing table, as wide as it will go. Holding the candle out of the way of the wood and paper, I squat down. And I crawl inside.

44

Anika

Then

Anika checks her reflection in the rear-view mirror. Her sunglasses should be enough of a disguise. The people in this neighbourhood don't know her. The only one who does is at work. But for good measure, she's added a navy baseball cap, every strand of her black hair tucked away underneath, and a dark red lipstick unlike her usual neutral colours, her lips lined to change their natural shape. Her all-black running gear is nondescript and an excuse for her unfamiliar presence here.

It's been two days since she visited Dominic's apartment. She hasn't heard from him like she usually does. She hasn't been able to sleep, tossing and turning over questions, like who is the woman, why did Dominic have a different phone she's never seen before? Why did the woman call him Zach? She tried to think of reasonable explanations. Zach is his middle name, he got a new phone. But she can't explain away his kissing the woman on the lips, with the ease borne of repetition. When the noise of all the questions got too loud, she decided to take action.

Anika scans the front of the apartment block. It's 10 a.m. and not many people are around. The block is mostly populated by young professionals, they must be at work. The neat rows of trees leading to the entrance sway as the wind picks up. It's November and the weather has turned arctic in the past week. Anika wishes she could wear a coat, but that would ruin her running outfit and with it her excuse for being here. She feels ridiculous, wearing a disguise. She's never done anything like this before. But she needs to know.

She can't talk to her friends about what happened. They're excited about her bringing Dominic to Rosa's wedding. He agreed so easily when Anika asked. The dress she bought hangs in her wardrobe. She imagined wearing the floor-length emerald-green gown while dancing with him there. She should have known it was a pipe dream.

She locks her car, checks around, then walks to the entrance. It's on an electronic locking system and she doesn't have a key. When she came here two days ago, a delivery person was coming in at the same time and she entered with him. She didn't have to buzz. She wonders now, if she did, what would have happened? If the woman had answered, or Dominic. Would he have let her in? She waits five, ten minutes, shivering under the jutting roof of the entrance. She's considering going back to her car to wait when the reflective jacket of a postman appears. He has a fob. Anika smiles at him, tries to act like she lives here.

'I forgot my key.'

'Go ahead, luv.'

He gestures and she enters.

In the lobby, the postman heads the opposite way and Anika hesitates. She wanted to find out more and the only thing she could think of was coming here to his home. She could have asked Dominic about it all, but she wants to find out for herself first. Then, when she asks him, she'll know if he is lying.

Anika walks quickly to the lift. Inside, she punches the number for his floor, before she can think about it. In his corridor, she walks to his apartment. She looks at the solid oak surface of the door, the shiny gold number five. The gold letter box. There is a letter sticking out of the slot. Anika grabs it.

The door opens. A woman stands there with a questioning expression. The same woman from the other day. Anika steps back. She grips the letter with a shaking hand. She didn't expect to be face to face – with her.

'Can I help you?' she asks.

She's been caught red-handed with the letter. To say she was delivering it wouldn't be believable, she's not wearing the uniform of a postal worker.

'I – I found this on the floor,' Anika says. She kicks herself for not thinking of a better explanation.

'Oh. Do you live on this floor?'

Anika pushes her sunglasses closer to her face.

'No. I live – nearby.'

'Okay.' The woman holds out her hand for the letter. Anika's hand shakes as she gives it back and she drops the letter onto the carpet.

'I'm sorry.' She scrambles to pick it up. The woman does too. And Anika finds the answers to her questions. The diamond that glints on the woman's left ring finger. And the letter face up on the mat. Addressed to Mr and Mrs Linden.

She hands the letter to the woman. To his wife. And she sees the necklace. Two interlocking rings on a chain around her neck. Exactly like the one he gave Anika.

Anika turns, walks fast down the corridor. There's a door to a stairwell at the end, after the lift. Anika opens it, just to get out of the woman's sight.

The door shuts, leaving her alone in the stairwell. Anika pulls the necklace from her neck. She looks again at the two interlocking rings. The same necklace his wife wears. She takes it off and stuffs it in her pocket. Then she runs down the stairs and out of the apartment block.

45

Anika

Now

It smells earthy in here, musty. Old. A passageway extends out ahead. Steps at the end lead up. Another narrow passage is at the top and I walk along it, candle held aloft. Cobwebs hang from the ceiling. The floorboards are uneven, the rafters faintly visible. I'm in the attic of the house. And as I walk, I realise I'm in one of the wings that I thought were sealed up.

Suddenly, my foot hits something. Shining the candle down I find a cardboard box. I anchor the candle, pushing it in between the boards. On the top of the box is a tote bag made of colourful material. I open it up. Inside is something small and rectangular. I hold the candle high to examine it. The light flickers off the gold logo of a British passport. An unpleasant sensation prickles up my back as I open it. On the page at the back is my photo. My name.

Why is it in here? And next to the box are three larger shapes. Three trunks with leather buckles. When I open the first, I find piles of moth-eaten dresses. Lenore's clothes. I thought Nirmal stole them. Why are they up here?

One thing buzzes around in my head like an insistent fly. The material of the tote bag is like that of my bag handle. The one Kavya mended for me. With material like this. From her shop.

I examine the hibiscus pattern on the bag. In the dim light, the red and orange flowers look a dull brown. This could belong to anyone. Many people must have been in and out of her shop. Even if business is slow now. There must be tons of bags like this out there. Especially in this town. Kavya has been nothing but nice since I got here, helping me with the pickpocket, being kind when I found his body. Trying to check on me after. Even coming over this morning with appa. And she hasn't been up to the balcony room, not without me. This bag belongs to someone else.

There are more things in the cardboard box. I rifle through the items, my pulse rising when I see what's inside. There's a photo, without the frame. The photo of me. I sit on the bare earth floor and examine it by the light of the candle. I wasn't imagining it last night. It is me. There's a bottle of perfume in the box, I don't recognise the make but when I open it the smell is the same as the one in the balcony room. A large jar of what looks like sand. I pull out the final item. A white nightdress. What the hell is going on?

'So you found the secret passage.'

I turn and Kavya is there.

'Just now.'

How does she know?

'Have you taken your pills yet?'

I take them out of my pocket, then I immediately wish I hadn't. Something is different about her. A strange expression on her face as she looks at the tablets, then me. Waiting.

She said she found them in the first pharmacy. This medication was experimental – I got them on a clinical trial all those years ago. When I sent her to look for them I desperately hoped they would be available here, but I thought it very unlikely. I check the strip for the medication name, but there's nothing there.

'So?' she says.

How did she find the pills so easily? I know then that what she gave me is not my medication. *So what is it?*

'I'll have them later.'

She frowns.

'You were so keen to get them – you made me pay off the pharmacist and lie to the police. Why have you changed your mind?'

'I – let's go downstairs. I'll have them there.'

She picks her way around the uneven floorboards, advancing towards me.

'Are you lying to me, Anika? You said you needed this medication, now you won't take it. Should I go back out and tell the police where to find you? There's more of them now. Another car came. They're waiting for you.'

Shit.

'No. Don't do that.'

'So take your pills. Then you can go and talk to them yourself. That was the plan, wasn't it?'

She grabs the strip of medication from my palm and pops one out.

'Here.'

She shoves it in my mouth before I can react. The pill sits on my tongue. I know I can't swallow it. And I know I have to make her think I did.

I hold out my hand for the water.

She hands it to me.

I pretend to take a swig. As I do, I let the pill slide from my mouth, back into the bottle.

'There.' I hold on to the bottle.

'That's better,' she says.

The small space feels unbearably claustrophobic. I don't know what is going on or why Kavya is doing this, but I know I have to get out. 'I'll go back now.'

'I don't think so.'

She blocks my way to the exit. I step back. My foot hits the pile of trunks.

I'm stuck here. I have no choice but to keep her talking. Find out what the hell is going on.

'What is all this?'

She bends to look.

'Ah, so you found it.' She pulls the white nightdress out of the box.

'I was looking forward to doing another Lenore impression,' she says. 'The first one was so much fun.'

She holds up the nightdress and I notice the bloodstains on it. Whose blood is that?

'But now I won't get to. Shame,' she says. 'Making you think you're losing it has been so much fun.'

'Lenore impression?' It wasn't a trick of the light, like I convinced myself it was. It wasn't the ghost and it wasn't Nirmal.

'That was you on the balcony?'

'Of course. It was hilarious, how easy it was to manipulate your perceptions. The locals started talking about Lenore without me even needing to steer the conversation. I knew they would. That idiot Ziman, all of them, believe the story. Then I told you about Nirmal seeing her on the balcony, the night of the boat accident. *After* you had seen her. Or rather me. I'm a little disappointed. I didn't think it would be so easy. You didn't used to be such a scaredy-cat. What happened to you?'

I stare at her. It can't be. She looks different. Her hair longer, her cheekbones pronounced. But it's been a long time. We haven't met since the funeral.

'Ayomi?'

She smiles, the smile of a predator about to strike.

'You're not the only one who changed her name, Dayani.'

'It was you? This whole time?'

She crouches in front of me.

'Oh, I've only just started. How are you feeling?'

'What did you give me?'

'Not your precious medication. I don't really know. But in about' – she checks her watch – 'two minutes, you should be dead.'

Dead. My heart pounds so loud, she must be able to hear it. She tried to kill me. The pill sits, partially dissolved at the bottom of the bottle and I tuck it behind me, out of sight. I have to pretend it's doing something or she'll realise I didn't take it. Then she might try to kill me some other way.

'What did you give me?' I hold on to the wall for support. I'm not just acting. My legs feel weak, I'm lightheaded. I had that pill in my mouth for a few seconds. It must have dissolved, it must be fast-acting.

I slump to a sitting position.

'Oh get up.' She pulls me up under my arms, so I'm leaning against the wall.

She was playing me the whole time. I fell right into her trap. If I knew what she'd given me, I could work out what kind of dose I might have ingested. If it was enough to kill me.

'What did you give me?'

She shrugs.

'Who knows. There are a few ingredients. Midazolam, some other things . . . in way more than the recommended dose. I don't really know. I'm not the doctor.'

Fuck. She really means to kill me. In the bottle, the tiny pill sits, still dissolving. Even if it is a more potent form, I only had the pill in my mouth for a second. Midazolam is a muscle relaxant and a sedative. I don't know what else was in there, but if this is the main ingredient and the dose I got was small, the reaction will pass soon. I just need to keep her talking.

I take a ragged breath.

'How did you get it?'

'You can get a lot on the black market, if you know where to look. Or the right people to pay off. As you know. You had me out bribing people for you.'

'Why are you doing this?'

'I want answers now, Dayani.'

'What do you want?'

'Admit you killed my brother. I'm sick of you using your made-up condition as an excuse.'

'It's not made up.'

'Shut up.' Something hard strikes my face. My mouth fills with blood.

Kavya rubs her fist.

'I've wanted to do that for a while. What did you do to Avila?'

I have to get out of here. But my legs feel heavy still. I try to get up, but I'm too slow. Another punch lands on my jaw, sending me to the floor. My mouth pools with blood and I spit it on to the floor.

'I don't remember.'

'Not good enough. Admit what you did. Your father isn't here to protect you now.' A kick lands on my side, winding me.

Candlelight flickers, distorting the contours of Ayomi's face. She looks deranged.

I have to do something. She won't stop. But all I can do is keep her talking until my muscles work, enough to overpower her so I can get away. Distract her is all I can do. Stop her attacking me. *Until she realises I'm not dead, like she expected.*

'How did you find me?'

'I didn't. For years I tried, but you left the country and changed your name. But then, you found me.'

'What are you talking about?'

'First, your article on robotics made the papers here, would you believe. They love to report on Sri Lankans doing things abroad, I have no idea why. You were there, smiling so smugly. Your first name was different, but I knew it was you. After everything you did, you were there, doing well, can you imagine how I felt?'

'But that was a year ago. I didn't hear from you then.'

'I tried. You were silly enough to put your email on the article. Ever wonder why the photo of the beach from the ad for this job was familiar? You'd seen it many times before.'

'What do you mean?'

'I've been spamming you with fake travel pages ever since I saw your article. I picked that photo because I know you recognise that beach, right near your father's old place. I thought you'd be in need of a holiday. I didn't bother with job ads at first, didn't even think of it. Then you appeared in the news again. Your case. They should never have let someone like you play with sharp tools.'

She kicks me again. I curl into a ball reflexively, my arms around my body. She's been trying to get to me for so long. She'll do anything, go to any lengths to get what she wants. Revenge.

'I'm not going to lie,' she says. 'Seeing you brought down like that was so satisfying. And useful. Because now that things weren't going so well for you, all I had to do was put that same photo on the ad and post it to as many different places as I could, until you caved. You must have been desperate.' Her eyes glitter unnaturally in the candlelight.

I try to ignore the pain, breathe through it.

'How did you get Mr Fonseca to go along with this?'

She laughs, an unhinged laugh.

'I didn't. He doesn't know. The caretaking job you thought you accepted? That was my job, which he offered me. Mr Fonseca has too much money to notice what happens with this place. He hasn't been here in months. The squatters you were so worried about? That was you.' She laughs. 'You were the squatter.'

'You made up all the stories?'

'About Lenore? No, that one is true. As you'll have read from the page I planted in the library.'

'You jammed the doors.'

'Or gave you the wrong keys.' She smiles. She seems pleased with herself. Like she's enjoying telling me. I can work with that. *Keep her talking.*

'You messed with the lights.'

'It's great having access to these secret passages. They go all over the house, did you know that? And it made it so easy to slip in and turn the mains off, whenever I wanted.'

Secret passages. I was worried about Nirmal lurking around here. When all along it was Ayomi.

'You wrote that message in the mirror. You stole the trunks.'

'And I planted them there in the first place. Ding, ding, ding. All the weird stuff was me. I thought you'd get there quicker. You're supposed to be smart.'

It was all her. The knowledge that Ayomi would plan all this, to get to me, sends more adrenaline pumping through my veins.

'You were trying to make me think I was going crazy.'

'Anything to make you talk.'

Will I ever get out of this place alive? I thought I'd be safer in here. I should have gone out there, to the police. Whatever they would have done, I doubt it would have involved murdering me.

'You leaked the story of what happened here to the press.'

'You've got me all figured out. *Harima hondai.*' Very good. She laughs again. She's lost it. 'Yes, I sent the story to one of your British papers, and here too. It was too easy. Fun, even. It's a bad situation, isn't it? You've screwed up back home, just like you did here.'

Eliza tried to tell me. I should have listened. Will I ever see her, Achiamma, my friends again? Hot tears blur my vision. But I can't give up now. I have to keep her talking. Feeling is coming back into my legs now. Soon, I'll be able to make a break for it.

'What happened to Dinesh? I liked him. I really did.'

'He liked you too. '

'Did you—' Tears flood my vision, this time I can't stop them. 'Did you kill him?'

'Oh, that wasn't me. That one was all you.' She grabs a fistful of my hair, pulling my head towards her. Her face is so close to me I can feel her breath on my face. 'You killed him. You pushed him off the roof. Like you did my brother. Admit what you did.'

'I can't.' Tears spill down my face. 'I don't remember.'

She lets go of me abruptly and I fall back, hitting my shoulder on the wall.

'What's going on with you?'

'What do you mean?'

'Why aren't you dead yet?' Then she sees the water bottle on the floor next to me. She grabs it. She looks at the bottle, then at me. 'You tricked me,' she says, in a quiet voice that chills me.

Fuck. But the feeling in my legs is back. The lightheadedness has cleared. She's strong, judging from the punches she landed, but I can take her. I have to. I pull myself to my feet.

There's a noise from below. Footsteps on the stairs. A shadow falls on the floor. A man. He stoops to enter.

'*Ayomi, navathanna.*' Stop.

I blink. It can't be. But it is. It's Dinesh.

46

'Dinesh. How? You fell.'

He crouches by me.

'I didn't.'

'You were dead. There was blood. The ambulance took you away in a body bag.'

Ayomi smiles.

'It's amazing what you can do if you know people who work at the hospital. As you should know.'

'*Ayomi, meka navathanna,*' he says. Stop this. I notice now that Dinesh is carrying something wrapped in a plastic bag. He unrolls it and from within the folds something heavy falls out, landing with a thud on the floor. It's a knife, with a gold hilt. '*Ay meka thiyenneh?*' Why did you have this?

'That's the knife from the library,' I say.

Ayomi rolls her eyes.

'Nothing gets past you, does it?'

Dinesh looks at her. 'Tell me, now. Why was this in your car?'

I look at her and realisation dawns. Nirmal, the pickpocket, was stabbed. And Ayomi had the knife.

'You killed him.'

'I hired him to be my in with you, stealing your bag so I could help. Get you to trust me. But then he started watching your house. Figured out what I was up to. Blackmailed me, threatened to tell you everything if I didn't pay him more.'

'So you killed him.'

'I didn't want to, but he was getting difficult.' The cold way she looks at me, with no remorse for having killed a man, chills me to my core.

'How could you, Ayomi?' Dinesh looks grim. 'He was a poor boy, trying to survive. How could you do it?'

How is Dinesh involved in this? She said they weren't good friends but they seem to know each other very well. I look at him in front of me. Solid. Alive.

'I heard you fall, Dinesh.'

Ayomi holds up her phone and plays a sound. The crash I heard, when I was dreaming.

'Sound familiar?'

I stagger to my feet. If I can get past them both, I can get out. Run out there. Tell the police. Now I know who really did kill Nirmal and that Dinesh isn't dead, they won't have anything on me.

'Why did you pretend Dinesh was dead? Just to mess with me some more?'

Ayomi smiles again. Her eyes are strange. Cold, glassy. There's no life in them at all. She's so different to how she was this whole time, as Kavya. I find it hard to believe they were the same person.

'I thought it would jog your memory. If I made the same thing happen again. I thought you would confess. But you didn't.'

'I don't remember what happened that night. I mean it.'

She lunges for me.

Dinesh grabs her arms, holding her back.

'Stop, Ayomi. She told you, she doesn't remember.'

Ayomi struggles.

'Shut up, Aiya. Let me handle this.'

Aiya. It means, older brother. That's why he's involved. He and Ayomi don't look alike, so I never guessed. But looking at him now, I see the resemblance to Avila, in the slant of his shoulders, the structure of his face. I never made the connection, because

I'd almost repressed the memory of his face. Now I realise, Avila might have looked similar, if he'd lived.

'You're the other sibling. Avila's brother who was studying abroad.'

'I am,' he says. That explains a lot. The American lilt to his accent, his secrecy.

My head is clearer now. And something else is coming back to me. The crashing sound Ayomi played on her phone triggered something. I heard that sound when I was dreaming last night. About Avila. It sounded the same. Sickeningly so. I thought I'd repressed that sound, but now I remember. What came before he fell? Reaching for the memory is like walking through quicksand. It's just out of my reach.

Ayomi twists out of Dinesh's grasp.

'Murderer! You'll pay for what you did.'

But that's it. Now, I remember. The dream floods back to me, so vivid. It's not just a dream. It's a memory. The lost memory of that night that has stayed out of my reach all these years.

'Wait,' I say. 'Listen to me. I remember what happened.'

47

They both look at me.

'I remember.'

I was on the roof. I had sleepwalked out there, I was so foggy and confused. And then –

'The night Avila died, we'd argued right before, because he broke up with me. I was so angry with him, I told him to get out, but he must have waited to check on me. I hadn't been sleeping that week, and I was so tired. Like I've never been before. I fell asleep instantly. And then sleepwalked, onto the roof. He followed me out there.'

Ayomi is still now, listening.

'I walked to the edge, still asleep. When I woke up, I was disorientated, groggy, and Avila was calling me to come back. I was right at the edge of the roof. I lost my footing. I was going to fall. Avila grabbed me. He saved me.' My face is wet with tears. That's the memory I needed. I have it now, I remember his arms around my waist. 'But then he lost his balance. He fell. It was an accident. I didn't kill him.'

It's quiet in the dark space, so much that I can hear my heart beating. Candlelight distorts Ayomi's features as she turns to me.

'How convenient, that you just remembered,' Ayomi says. 'After all this time.'

'I was dreaming about it that night. When Dinesh – but when I woke up, it was the same as always. All I could remember was seeing Avila fall. And you down on the street, shouting that I pushed him. Everyone believed you. Even me. Because that memory was gone. Repressed, I don't know what happened. But the noise you played, the crash. It sounded like that night, when Avila fell. It triggered it. Brought the memory back. I loved him. I didn't push him.' Despite everything, I laugh. 'I didn't kill him.'

They both look at me.

'Liar,' Ayomi shouts, launching herself at me.

Dinesh restrains her again, keeping her arms behind her back.

'*Navathanna me vaday than.*' Stop this now. He speaks to her rapidly in Sinhala. I make out some of it. *I didn't want to do this. Things have got out of control.* 'You heard her. It was an accident. Let her go.'

'I was there. I saw him fall. And I saw you, on the roof.'

'But what did you see?' Dinesh asks her. 'Did you actually see her push him?'

Ayomi struggles, breaks free.

'You've fallen for her too. *Modaya.*' Idiot. 'I tried to warn Avila. I tried to stop it, but she had him hooked. Can't you see? Even if she didn't push him, it's her fault he died.' She lunges for me again. I fall back.

Something acrid pierces the air. Smoke. The candle has overturned. Flames lick the floorboards. This attic, from the floor to the rafters, is wood. Kindling, in a matter of seconds.

'We have to get out of here,' I say.

I run towards the door but Ayomi blocks my way.

'You stay here.' She tries to grab me. The strength in my limbs is returning. I push her back, hard. The box overturns, the contents fuelling the fire. The flames rise higher, acrid smoke filling the air. My eyes water, I cover my nose and mouth with my hand.

Ayomi lunges for me again.

'Ayomi, go.' Dinesh grabs her, pushes her out of the open door. All three of us pile out into the balcony room. Smoke follows, my vision is blurred, my breathing ragged, my throat hurts from the fumes.

I run for the stairs, Dinesh behind me. Ayomi is still shouting, swearing, trying to get to me. The fire spreads fast, like it's following us. The smoke billows like a spectre, into the front room, out of the door. I run faster, barrelling down the front path, out of the gate and onto the road outside. I'm coughing, my hands on my knees. My side aches from the kicks Ayomi landed on me. Dinesh and Ayomi are right behind me. The police are here, a crowd of townspeople too. Behind us, the house is in flames. The balcony conflagrates, the glass shatters and falls with a splintering crash. The wooden shutter of a top floor window breaks and falls, landing in flames on the grass. It's dry in this heat, it goes up like kindling, soon the lower floor is engulfed in flames too.

Sirens wail. A fire engine and ambulance line up on the road behind the police cars. Firemen run out with hoses and blast the house with their jets but still the flames climb higher. Paramedics take us away from the house. One helps me towards an ambulance. Then lightning rends the sky. Thunder rumbles and the rain comes down in angry torrents. And behind it all, I can still hear the sea, crashing, crashing, crashing.

48

Anika

Then

Anika is drifting off to sleep when the doorbell rings. She's been trying to sleep before her night shift tonight. But sleep hasn't come easy. Not after this morning. Now, she pulls herself up blearily from the couch. She couldn't face sleeping in her bedroom today. Not with the memories of him there.

The bell shrills again, as if someone has their finger on it without pause. The clock on her phone tells her its 5 p.m. This is the worst time for a visitor. She has to leave for work in an hour. She won't get any sleep today.

She opens the door.

It's Dominic. Or Zach. Anika feels nauseous all over again. He lied to her, countless times. There is nothing left to say.

'What are you doing here?'

'What the fuck do you think you're doing, Anika?'

His hair is messy, he's in sweats like he's just been to the gym. His eyes are wild. But not from alcohol, she knows what he looks like drunk. Right now, he looks sober. This is pure, cold rage. It takes her by surprise.

Anika takes a step back.

'What are you talking about?'

He pushes past her, into the apartment, stopping next to the shelf in the hallway.

'You came to my apartment,' he shouts. 'What gives you the right to do that?' A fleck of spit hits her cheek.

So he knows. His wife must have told him, a strange woman came to the door.

'I had to know who she was. Why didn't you tell me you're *married?*'

'I didn't promise you anything.'

She looks at him incredulously.

'But you did. You said you didn't want to be casual. I wasn't sure about us, you talked me into trusting you. And you didn't even tell me your real name. Which is it, Dominic? Or Zach?' He looks up and she knows it's true. His real name is Zach Linden. The name on his mail.

Dominic smacks the wall with his palm.

'There is no us. You, this whole thing, doesn't mean anything.'

Anika stares at him. Her throat is dry. This can't be the man she thought she loved. Was it all fake? She's never seen this side of him before. It scares her, how well he kept it hidden.

'You said you loved me. You had a whole relationship with me.' She reaches into her pocket and takes out the necklace. The catch is broken from when she ripped it off this morning.

'You can have this back.' She drops the necklace into his hand. 'I saw your wife had one too. This was never for me, was it?'

He shakes his head. So her suspicions were right. The necklace was for another woman all along. He gave it to Anika only because she found it.

'Stay away from her.'

'Does she know now? Did you tell her?'

'Of course not. I said you were some girl from work. Practically stalking me.' Dominic steps closer. His blue eyes are cold. 'Don't come near me or my wife again.'

Anika's hands curl into fists. She has no intention of doing that, but she won't make this easy for him.

'If you care so much about your wife, why did you cheat on her, with me, for months?'

'I'm away a lot. And I liked the chase. The hunt. That's all it was.'

'That's it? It was just a game to you, to fake a whole relationship?'

'Look, I liked you, but I get bored easily. You were fun for a bit but then things got heavy. I was going to end it.' The casual way he says it all. This doesn't seem like the same man who said he loved her. He doesn't care about her at all. She thought she'd had her heart broken before, but this, this is something else. She wants to hurt him back, as much as he's hurt her.

'I could tell her everything. What are you going to do about it?'

Dominic gives a half-smile. Like he knew she'd say that. Unease prickles her back. Why is he smiling?

He advances, until he's almost touching her.

'I know some powerful people.' She knows he must do, for his job, but still, it feels like an empty threat.

'Like who?'

'That's for me to know.' Dominic pulls out his phone. 'If you talk to my wife, if you ever come near either of us again, I'll send this to certain interested parties. And that fellowship you've spent the last few years toiling away to get? You can kiss your chances goodbye.' He turns his screen round.

A video plays and Anika watches in horror. She's in her bedroom, the black lingerie he bought her discarded on the bedspread. She's naked. Posing for him. Doing whatever he asks. She thought she could trust him. How stupid could she be?

'You recorded it?'

He smiles again. The cold-eyed grin of a predator, about to close in for the kill.

'I always do. Call it insurance.'

Anika feels as if the rug is being pulled from under her. How didn't she see this coming?

'You always do?'

'You're not the first, beautiful.' He runs his finger under her chin. Anika shudders.

'Don't touch me.'

'If you try anything like that again? This video is going public. Why stop at ruining your job prospects, I could leak that to your whole hospital.'

Anika's cheeks flame. He could ruin her. He still might, no matter what she says.

'That's illegal. If I report you for even taking that video, tell them about the other women you've as good as admitted you videoed without consent? *You* can kiss *your* job goodbye.'

Dominic grins again.

'Oh, Anika. How could you prove any of that? Plus, my firm has access to the best lawyers in the world, if it comes to that. You don't have a chance.'

There's no way she can come out of this well. He's one step ahead of her, every time.

'You're messed up,' she says.

She reaches for the phone. He holds it out of the way. The pulse in her head starts again. Hurt and disbelief give way to anger. She sees red. The anger surges inside her, until she can't control it any more. The shelf in the hall is filled with photos, a pinboard, a large glass vase. She grabs the vase and hurls it at him. She wants to hurt him, any way she can. Dominic jumps out of the way as the vase smashes against the wall. Shards of glass rain down onto the floor, his shirt, his hair.

Dominic looks at his arm. A large gash decorates his wrist. Anika wonders if she's hit a vein. She hopes so.

'Get out,' she says through gritted teeth.

Dominic's eyes grow wilder. He lunges towards her. Then his hands are around her throat. The tang of blood from his wrist is sharp in the air. Anika grasps wildly at him, kicks out, but he's too strong. He squeezes around her windpipe. Anika tries to cry out but she can't. She should have aimed better with the vase. She didn't know it, but it was her only chance to save herself. It can't end like this. She becomes lightheaded.

Then suddenly he lets go, pushing her roughly away. She hits the wall by the shelf, which shakes with the impact. The oddments on the shelf fall with her as she slides to the floor.

'I mean it. Don't come near me again. If everything I just told you wasn't enough to convince you, look up a name. Chloe Ashcroft.'

Dominic turns on his heel and leaves, slamming the door behind him.

Anika sits there on the floor. Her neck aches, she feels dizzy. Items from her pinboard lie loose at her feet. She picks up one, a pink and green square decorated with paper ferns. It's crumpled, spots of blood mar the gold writing. *Rosa and Ravi request the pleasure of your company at their wedding.* Underneath, handwritten, are their names. *Anika and Dominic.*

Anika rips out the bit of the invite with his name on and tears it into tiny pieces.

Later, she remembers the name he told her. With shaking hands, she types it into her search engine. The top hit for the name is a news article from two years ago. The headline reads WOMAN, 29, FOUND DEAD. Anika freezes as she reads it. He's covered his tracks, the coroner ruled it was an overdose. But she knows. He as good as told her. It was Dominic.

49

Anika

Now

'You're almost good to go.' The doctor tucks her clipboard under her arm. 'When your blood results are back. Won't be long.' She pats me on the shoulder reassuringly, then leaves, pulling the cubicle curtain open. She's bright, overly enthusiastic for being at work in the middle of the night. I pull the waffle-knit blanket over my legs. The air con in the hospital ward is on high. The ward is busy, nurses are checking observations, doctors come in periodically to check on patients. The other beds in this bay are full.

As the firemen tackled the blaze, I was put into the ambulance even though I told the paramedics I was fine. I was relieved when they brought me in here and I saw that none of the patients were Ayomi. I've been here the past two hours having my carbon monoxide levels checked, even a chest X-ray. Everything so far has come back normal. If the blood tests are okay, I'll be free to leave. And then what? I have nowhere to go tonight. No phone, no clothes. No passport. All of it went up in flames. I close my eyes. The ward might be on the other side of the world but it smells much the same as any hospital I've worked in. Disinfectant with an undertone of bodily fluids. I turn on my side. I'm not tired, but I should try to sleep while I can.

Steps sound on the parquet floor.

'Are you awake?' It's Dinesh. I spring to a sitting position, wincing at the smart in my side. He walks into the cubicle. His T-shirt is now more grey than white and there are patches of soot on his cheek but he looks fine. Uninjured.

'Hi.'

'Mind if I sit?' he asks.

'Go ahead.'

He sits in the plastic chair next to the bed.

'*Kohomada dhang?*' How are you now?

'Okay. My carbon monoxide levels were fine. You?'

'Fine too.'

'And Ayomi?'

He sighs.

'She's all right. Physically. But the police came to talk to her here.' He runs a hand over his head. His arm is covered in black smudges too. 'She confessed to the murder of Nirmal.'

'Really?'

He shakes his head. 'She's not okay, Anika. She's not well.'

'She killed a man and she tried to kill me. Almost did.'

'What do you mean?'

I tell him about the pills. 'I was so desperate, convinced everything was in my head, I almost took them.'

'I didn't know.' He blows out a breath. 'I didn't know.'

The clock on the wall ticks. In the distance, a patient wails. There are so many things I want to ask him, I don't know where to start.

He leans forward. 'I'm sorry, Anika. Things got out of hand.'

'You're telling me.'

'She told me she did it all to get a confession. To get you to admit what happened to Avila. She didn't tell me she planned to – I didn't want anything to happen to you.' He reaches out as if to touch my hand, then draws back. 'I felt guilty, for being away. For not being there when Avila died. For not being there to prevent it. And now that our parents are gone I wanted to be there for Ayomi. She hasn't been right since Avila. When she said she wanted to move here and start her business I wanted to support her so I came too. It worked well for her for a while. But then things changed in the town. Business slowed down and Ayomi went back into herself. She became preoccupied with what happened with Avila again. I know now that she never let it go. The shop was a temporary distraction. Then she came up with her plan.'

He looks down at his hands, twisting them over each other. There's dirt under his fingernails.

'And you wanted to support her in that too?'

'I didn't know how bad it would get. When she told me about it she was already far in. Then you were here.'

'That's why you warned me away, the night I arrived?'

He stretches his legs out.

'It was a pretty weak warning but I had to try.'

'Was it her idea that you befriend me?'

He shakes his head.

'No. I wanted to keep an eye on you from afar because I had a bad feeling about her behaviour. That it wouldn't end well. But then you came into the shop. And . . . it became hard to stay away from you. I told myself I was looking out for you, but it became something else. Something more.' His brown eyes hold mine. 'I'm sorry for deceiving you. For everything we put you through. And for everything you went through, before. With Avila.'

My eyes fill with tears. After all this time, it's relief.

'I loved him. All these years, I thought I killed him.'

'I can't imagine how that must have been for you.'

'It was hideous. Everyone thought I pushed him. Even my family. I couldn't trust my own mind. Didn't know what I was capable of. I wished I could rewind time. Wished I could just remember. But, Ayomi's crazy plan, it did trigger something. I finally got back the memory I was missing. What I came back here for. I know now what really happened. And I don't have to feel guilty. Or to fear myself any more.'

He rests his hand on the bed rail, near mine.

'I'm sorry for everything you went through, back then. And now.'

'Thank you.'

'What are you going to do?'

'I'll go home. Face things. To be honest, I don't know how. You?'

'Same. I don't know either.'

I edge my fingers close to his. He inches his hand closer too. We stay like that, not quite touching, for a while.

It's morning by the time the test results come back and I'm discharged from the hospital. The staff, knowing about the fire, direct me to the British High Commission. They help fix me up with an emergency passport and access to my bank account. They find me a flight too, that same night.

It's hours before I have to be at the airport and there are two things I want to do before I leave. I take nearly everything that is left out of my account, in cash. Then I head back to the town. The townspeople aren't too happy to see me, until I explain why I'm there. They give me the address I need and I take a scooter taxi there. The house is in a series of dwellings with corrugated roofs, small and insalubrious. I knock on the door.

A woman answers. She's about my age, she wears a housecoat. Behind her, in the gloom of the room beyond, I see a bed. Gnarled legs stretched out on it.

I give her the cash in the envelope.

'Please take this. I'm so very sorry for your loss.'

'You knew Nirmal?'

'I – it's a long story. I know his mother isn't well. I hope this will help.'

She looks at the envelope and frowns.

'That's strange. Someone else came by this morning. He gave us money too.'

'Who was that?'

'He was about your age. Tall. He was very dirty, he had ash or something all over his shirt and his face.'

Dinesh was here too. I smile.

'I hope this helps.'

I get back on the scooter taxi. I have one more stop to make.

The beach in Hatton Bay is emptying out. Tourists are leaving, the roadside stalls are starting to get busy. The pier is cordoned off still, the tape there just like the night I jumped off it. I don't go on it this time. I hold my flips-flops in my hand and walk down the slope of the beach, stopping close to the water's edge. The sand is warm as I sit, facing the waves. I came here to this beach the day after Avila's death. I believed I'd killed him. I was near hysterical, felt like I was losing my mind. I wanted some peace. Some answers. Closure. Now I have it.

There are tiny pebbles and lots of little shells buried in the sand. Most are broken. I run my fingers through the sand, filtering the fragments through my fingers until I find a whole one. It's a bluish-white, the edges perfectly scalloped. All these years, I felt disconnected from a place that once felt like home. Because of what I thought I'd done here.

The sea sparkles in the afternoon sun, like thousands of tiny diamonds, scattered over the surface of the waves. Now, I have my memories back. I don't have to stay away, don't have to run from my past any more. The ghosts I had here can finally be laid to rest.

I breathe in the salty air and it feels like home. Part of me will always belong here. It doesn't matter how long I've been away. I close my fingers around the shell, feeling its edges. I've faced my past here. Now it's time to do the same in London. I bury my toes into the sand and make a silent promise to the beach. This time, it won't be so long before I'm back.

50

One Month Later

'You're here.' Eliza grabs me in a hug. 'What took you so long?'

I squash into the booth at the bar near our hospital. Some of my friends from work are here. I didn't want anything to celebrate today, but Eliza insisted, and invited the others. Now that the verdict is out, it seems people who pretty much ignored me for months are talking to me again.

'It's a longer journey now I'm in my new flat.'

'Well, here's to new flats and coming back to work,' Rosa says, raising her glass. They all toast, to me. The verdict from the case was yesterday. And they cleared me of any wrongdoing. The conclusion was that the cause of death was a complication of surgery. Not surgical misconduct. And not my medical condition. There won't be any grounds for criminal proceedings now. I'm free.

'Listen to this.' Eliza reads from the report on the verdict. 'Anika Amarasinghe was not given adequate support following the surgery and she should not have been put on prolonged night shifts. The management of this incident by the hospital was unsatisfactory.' She looks up. 'That's a mild way of putting it. And they haven't mentioned anything about that nurse leaking the story to the press. Or Isaac spilling it to the surgical department in the middle of your M and M presentation.'

'They're both moving to new hospitals,' Rosa says. 'Which we all know is code for, asked to leave.'

'Well, good,' Eliza says. 'The hospital were such dicks to you. It's good of you to continue working there after everything.'

'When are you coming back to work?' Ravi asks. 'We miss you on the ward. And in theatre.' The others from our ward assent.

'Actually, I'm not coming back. I've got a new job.'

'Since when?' Eliza asks.

'I got the offer this morning. It's a medical role, for a non-profit. Based in London, starting with a project in Sri Lanka.'

Eliza looks surprised.

'Medical, meaning non-surgical?'

'Yes. It will be a change. But a good one.'

Eliza looks conflicted. Then she smiles.

'And you can go back to surgery,' she says. 'When you're ready.'

My phone rings. An international number.

'Excuse me.'

I take the call in the corridor outside the toilets.

'Hey, Anika.'

'Hi, Dinesh.'

He called me a couple of weeks after I came back. We've been talking regularly, since. It feels strange to even say so, after everything. The last month, before the case verdict broke, has been hard. With my past so public, thanks to Ayomi. Dinesh was on the other end of the phone when I needed to talk about it. We're feeling our way through this. There's no handbook on how to behave in this particular situation.

'I visited her,' he says.

'You did?'

'It's an okay place. As far as prisons go. It was horrible to see her in there. I'm sorry, I shouldn't talk to you about this.'

'No, it's okay. You can.'

'I wish things hadn't happened this way. But she killed Nirmal. She confessed. There was no other way it could have gone.'

'I hope she'll be all right in there. Any developments on the house?'

The house was pretty much razed to the ground after the fire, though the garden was saved and for that I'm grateful.

'Mr Fonseca is going to build luxury apartments there. It's going to help rejuvenate the town – that's what the locals hope.'

'I hope so too.

'By the way, I got the job.'

'That's great. I knew you would,' Dinesh says. 'And you're really okay with not doing surgery any more?'

Though the case verdict went my way, I know, for me, there's no going back. Not after what happened. I didn't tell Eliza because she couldn't understand. But it's for the best.

'More than okay. It's what I want.'

'Hey, I wanted to tell you, I got a job too,' he says.

'Congratulations. Where is it?'

'I'll be in the US, where I studied. Mostly.'

'Mostly?'

'There's some travel back to Sri Lanka involved. I'll be in Colombo, sometimes.'

Me too.

'Really?'

There's silence for a moment.

'Can we—' he says, at the same time that I say –

'Maybe we should—'

I laugh.

'Yes,' I say. 'I'd like that.'

'Take care, Anika,' he says.

'You too, Dinesh. Good luck.'

I go back to my friends in the bar. Life is going to be different now. I don't have a plan for after the non-profit role ends. No more type-A expectations. Things lately have taught me to let go of control. But one good thing came out of it all. I touch the chain around my neck. On the end is a pendant I had made with the shell I found on the beach in Hatton Bay, set in rose gold. Finally, I have closure. The peace that I wanted. I know that after everything I've been through, I can trust my own mind again. And that, to me, is everything.

51

It's not easy to tamper with a surgical rota. It's a boring piece of bureaucracy and not particularly complex. Long, yes, but not complicated. But changing it is not easy. I only needed to alter one box, but it took a hell of a lot of planning. Only one person has access to it, and that's not me. It took a lot of cups of tea, pretended interest and fake conversations while leaning over the rota coordinator's desk, to learn his password. But that wasn't enough to get me into the document. That was all about having the right timing. And the key. So many things had to come together for me to make it work. From taking the keys to picking the moment when the hallway was empty, and no one saw me go into the office. Erasing the evidence that I'd been in the shared document. It took a lot of very unsavoury dark web research to figure that one out. One row switched, one deleted.

Ensuring that I was working, the night before the surgery. And that no surgeon was working the day shift.

The next part was crucial. Checking the surgical list. Making sure the patient's procedure date hadn't changed. That one was easier. The list was on the shared drive, accessible to all the team. I only had to search his name. His real name. Zach Linden.

One second is all it takes. One millimetre. A knife's edge. One moment, between life and death. One cut in the wrong place. Everything has a tipping point.

That's the thing. You don't know what someone is capable of, until they're pushed to the limit. That's when you know who they really are. But if you knew that? You might be better off not knowing at all.

Author's note

This novel explores parasomnia, a term used for a range of disorders characterised by abnormal experiences during sleep. Parasomnia can affect people in various ways. I have done my best to portray the condition with sensitivity and have consulted resources and first-hand accounts to ensure respect for the challenges people with this condition face. However, it is important to remember that every case is unique, and Anika's journey is only one possible, fictional, experience. Most individuals who experience parasomnia do not encounter symptoms as severe as Anika does. It is also important to note that parasomnia has only rarely been used as a legal defence.

This book is not intended to provide a wholly accurate or complete depiction of parasomnia. If you or someone you know is experiencing sleep disturbances, please consult a medical professional.

Acknowledgements

Writing a book is never a solo endeavour, and I am so grateful to those who helped make this one possible.

First, a huge thanks to Katie Ellis-Brown and Sania Riaz, who believed in this story from the beginning and helped shape it into what it is today. A heartfelt thanks to Isobel Gahan at Curtis Brown for your help with the first draft, and for finding it a home at Harvill Secker. Thank you to managing editor Sam Stocker, designer Dan Mogford for the gorgeous cover, publicity director Shona Abhyankar, Mairéad Zielinski in marketing, assistant editor Anouska Levy and all the team at Harvill Secker.

This novel started as a short story for Rewrite Academy and the thoughtful feedback from my fellow Rewriters Olive Ahmed, Anila Arshad-Mahmood, Patricia Burgess, Zarah Dalilah, Jennifer Enti, Fatima Luz Naeema and Lalah Simone Springer, helped me see this story in new ways. Thanks to Rachel Faturoti for your help with the edit. To Leila Rasheed, Stephanie King and all at Megaphone, to Christina Fonthes and all at Rewrite, your hard work and commitment to diversifying bookshelves helped me believe a story like this was possible.

A big thank you to some lovely writing friends: Thomas Leeds for all your help and the podcast, Tom J. Cull, My Ly, Nacho Mbele, Beth Rose for your enthusiasm and support for this story. Lizzie Huxley-Jones for the writing sprints and all the authors of the Debuts 22 group for moral support, bonk stick and Patricia references.

Thank you to some fab doctor friends: Dr Samantha Anandappa and Dr Arnold Somasunderam for help with medical aspects of the story, Dr Nitin Bhalla for advice on surgical scenes and Dr Samah Alimam for all your help and support.

To my parents, grandparents, brother and members of my extended family, my heartfelt gratitude for helping me to maintain a connection with our heritage over the years. To my mother Malini for help with Sinhala translations and auntie Kaushala Surenthiran for help with Tamil translations. Thanks to my brother Nalin and sister-in-law Purnima for the videos and photos to inspire my scene setting. In loving memory of my auntie Chumma. To my cousins Ransi, Druvi and Himashin, and my family and friends in Sri Lanka and the diaspora.

Thanks to my husband for all your support and encouragement and to our daughter Isabella, thanks for always inspiring me. The greatest privilege of my life is being your mummy.

And finally, thank you to my readers. I am so grateful for every one of you.

Read on for an extract from

Deadly Cure

by Mahi Cheshire

Prologue

Rea

'*Adult cardiac arrest.*'

My pager usually emits a bleeping noise. When it talks it only brings bad news. A staid female voice speaks amidst crackling static. '*Adult cardiac arrest. Medical team to Emergency Department, Resus.*'

I start running; out of the doctors' office, down the stairs. Matt, the on call anaesthetist, follows me, his trainers squeaking as he runs.

In the foyer, we pass Khaled, the senior surgical doctor on call. His pager bleeps. '*Trauma call. Surgical Team to Emergency Department, Resus.*'

'I wonder if it's the same thing,' I say as he starts running alongside us.

'Maybe. Either way, looks like all the doctors in the hospital are going to be in the Emergency Department.'

Our soles skid as we sprint through a dark corridor. We're on autopilot after a busy night shift, too tired to talk. It's 6.30 a.m. and the hospital is just waking up. Staff arriving for day shifts walk past us in the opposite direction, thick winter coats buttoned over their uniforms. Through the glass doors of the main entrance, first light shows in a murky grey sky. There's an off-kilter vibe, of darkness lifting over a day that's not quite ready to start. As we run my mind returns to the same thing that's been bothering me all night: Feng's voicemail, at the beginning of my shift twelve hours ago. *I need to talk to you when you're home.*

We race through the Emergency Department and barrel through the double doors into the resuscitation area. The large white tiled room is separated into four bays, the beds all empty. Light from the fluorescent overhead panels is unnaturally bright, the air smells sharp with the tang of disinfectant. In one of the bays, nurses and doctors in blue scrubs stand, chatting. The registrar, Bo, greets us. There are dark circles around his eyes.

'What's coming in?' I pull on a plastic apron and latex gloves. The powder inside them makes my fingers itch.

'Thirty-one-year-old male, cardiac arrest post road traffic accident.'

Matt looks up from his respiration equipment and whistles. 'Poor guy. What else do we know?' He fits together a big plastic balloon-like apparatus with a tube on the end which will ventilate the patient when he squeezes it.

'It's a trauma call with major haemorrhage and head injury. The C-spine isn't cleared.'

This patient has multiple problems. But the priority will be to restart his heart before we can deal with any of the other potential complications. Fractures, internal bleeding, damage to the lungs or heart, any of the things that could have caused his heart to stop. I fill a cardboard dish with equipment for a blood test – syringe, alcohol wipe, green needle. Mechanically, because I've done this so many times that arrest calls have become mundane.

The doors to the ambulance drop-off point burst open. Cold air bites into my bare forearms below my short-sleeved scrubs. Three paramedics in dark green jumpsuits appear. One pushes a stretcher in, another runs alongside it as she squeezes a bag of blood into the patient's veins. A third paramedic perches on the side of the stretcher, her torso moving up and down, dark brown ponytail swinging from side to side as she does chest compressions. The patient is largely obscured; all I can see is his right arm, long and streaked with dried blood. They come to a stop in front of us.

'Thirty-one-year-old male hit a wall at high speed,' says one of the paramedics in a matter-of-fact tone. 'C-spine blocked. He's had two units of blood and thirty minutes of CPR so far. We haven't been able to get an ID on him yet.'

The nurses and doctors shift immediately into sixth gear. The room fills with movement and noise, people talking rapidly, multiple footsteps bustling over the tiled floor. The team gather around the stretcher and move the patient to the bed. A nurse cuts off his T-shirt. It might have been white once, but now it's mostly soaked red. He attaches electrodes to the patient's chest, ready to shock, and connects him up to winding leads that feed into a heart monitor. As soon as it connects, the trace on the screen shows a haphazard, squiggly line. A dangerously unstable heart rhythm. A nurse stands ready to take over compressions.

'Twenty-eight, twenty-nine, thirty.' The paramedic counts her in in a perfectly choreographed routine, and she takes over, moving up and down over the patient's chest.

'*Analysing.*' The automated tones of the defibrillator, a machine which gives electric shocks to restart the heart, cuts through the thrum of activity.

'Everyone stand clear!' Bo shouts. The nurse stops compressions, we all take a step back to avoid electrocution.

'*Delivering shock.*'

The shock is given, the patient's chest heaves centimetres off the bed then lands with a thump. Bo feels for a pulse in his groin.

'Nothing.'

'Continue CPR.' *Bam, bam,* the compressions start up again.

I squeeze through the people pressed around the bed as I prepare to take blood to test. I reach for the patient's arm, streaked with dried blood. Then, I see. My knees feel weak. My hand shakes as I turn his wrist over, examining it. The glass front of the watch has been smashed, the silver hands hang askew, but still I recognise the birthday present I bought him last year. The needle falls from my hand. It clatters to the floor.

'Hey, isn't that one of the doctors?' someone asks. There's a sudden, palpable shift in atmosphere. People are crowding around to look now.

I need to know. I force myself to look at his face.

It's immediately obvious why it took so long for the staff who work with him every day to realise who this patient is. A C-spine collar like a huge upended megaphone obscures the lower half of his face. There are big red plastic blocks either side of his head to stabilise his neck. His eyes are swollen shut, his face is smudged with blood. His usually immaculately styled black hair is matted and there are fragments of glass in it. He looks nothing like he should. *Why is he here?* He's supposed to be tucked up in his bed in the flat we share right now, snuggled up to his boyfriend. My medic brain analyses the situation and I wish it wouldn't. Only about eight per cent of cardiac arrests that happen outside of hospital are resuscitated successfully. He's had at least thirty minutes of cardiac arrest, major trauma, head injury, blood loss. With all that, I don't see how we can bring him back. *Please, just be another male the same age. Anyone but him.*

'It's Dr Tanaka,' someone says. 'It's Feng.' *No, no, no.* Bile builds at the back of my throat. The man on the stretcher isn't another anonymous patient. *He's my best friend.* There's an uneasy buzz of voices around me now.

'I can do that.' Khaled takes the needle from me. I turn to the nurse about to finish another two-minute cycle of compressions.

'I have to take over.' My voice sounds hoarse.

'Rea, no.' Bo grabs my shoulders. 'You're too close to this. We have enough doctors, you need to step back and let us handle it.'

'No!' I fight as he moves me gently outside of the throng around the bed. The air is thick with the metallic odour of blood. The lights overhead seem even brighter than usual. I stand aside for a moment, strangely detached from my body, like I'm watching a scene happening to someone else. The team continue compressions. Matt stands at the head of the bed *ventilating* my best friend. They all keep it together, but they don't know him like I do. He was the one I cried to when I was fourteen years old and my parents were separating. I was by his side when he came out to his family. Why is he here? And earlier, what did he want to talk to me about? He'd sounded panicked in his voicemail, in a way I've never heard before. *It's about Julia.* Why did he mention her? After Julia, after everything that's happened lately . . . Not him, too. Please, not him, too.

My vision blurs, hot tears run down my face. I push closer to the bed again, reach for a blood gas syringe, but a nurse moves me away. 'Rea, get back.'

A single tone beeps. I look at the heart monitor. Then my legs give out as the trace flatlines.

I

Julia

Seven Months Earlier

June 4th

Met a hot guy. He was playing guitar in the bar on open mic night. He approached me after his set. There was something soulful about him, despite his stupid, 'ironic', Sugar Puffs T-shirt. I'm so glad I didn't bat him off with my usual, made-up excuse about a boyfriend, because he works as a porter at the London Medical Institute. I think I'm going to have to see him again.

June 12th

Turns out hot bar guy, Krish, knows nothing about what happens in the London Medical Institute lab. But it doesn't matter, because he has a porter's access card. It's been winking seductively at me from his wallet all week. Of course I want it. Question is, how to get it without getting caught?

June 14th

It was simple in the end. I suggested to Krish that we hook up at his workplace after hours. A covert flash of my new black lace bra and he was game, no questions as to why it had to be in the lab building. The promise of sex and he became instantly co-operative. Like most men. While he was putting his clothes back on, I had a look around. Now there's a picture on my phone. Amelia Perez, whoever she is, should be more careful about where she leaves her lab book. Especially as it had 'confidential' stamped all over it. Now I know what their research is about. It's bold, cutting edge, like nothing I've worked on before. I want the job more than ever. The problem is, I also now know that the presentation I had planned for interview is completely off-topic. While Rea's is exactly right. And she doesn't even have a clue. This job is perfect for me. It's just so unfair.

June 16th

Something unprecedented happened today. Almost like the universe intervened on my behalf. I just got back from dinner with Rea. She organised it in an attempt to meet Krish. I pretended I would bring him to shut her up even though I had no intention of following through. I thought Rea would be on my case when she saw that I was alone, but she arrived at La Foglia holding a huge binder and her laptop and didn't even seem to notice.

'There's not enough time,' she said. No greeting, nothing else. The aura of stress around her was palpable as she opened the binder over our menus like we were at work rather than a candle-lit restaurant.

'For what?'

'For me to memorise all this.' She started flicking through articles she'd ripped out from recent journals.

'Why do you need to memorise articles on medical imaging?'

She looked at me like I was an idiot to even ask. 'I need to be clued in on recent developments.'

I couldn't be bothered to ask her why she was so worked up about this random topic. I started eating the marinated olives that I'd ordered. Rea always comes out with it eventually. I listened to her talk me through an entire article on MRI scanning advances before ordering more food, even though I was starving. Rea had picked the place because she'd heard the food was amazing, but she hadn't even looked at her menu yet.

Finally, she put down the binder. 'Should I focus on one imaging modality for the presentation? Or cover a few?'

'The presentation for the interview?'

She rolled her eyes. 'What else?'

'But you have already have a presentation.'

'I'm not doing that anymore.'

I almost choked on an olive. 'Why not?'

She smiled like she'd been waiting for me to ask. 'Look at this.' She flipped to an article from *The Lancet* and pointed to the author. Dr Owen Ansah. Our soon-to-be interviewer. Future supervisor to whoever gets the research job.

'He wrote about the topic. So maybe it's related to what they're researching on the project.'

She was so far off course. Rea's overthinking is excessive at the best of times, but this was ridiculous.

'I doubt it. That paper is three years old.'

'I want to do something different. Everyone else will present on their PhDs or their master's projects. I'm going to show I can produce a good presentation, without having had to study the topic for years like they have.'

Amelia's lab notes flashed across my brain. *Oncolytic viruses.* Their project is on Rea's PhD topic. She has the perfect presentation already.

'I'm trying to think outside of the box. No one else will pick medical imaging. Dr Ansah might like it.'

My throat went dry and I started coughing.

'What is going on with you today? Here.' She poured me a glass of water.

I drank it in one go while Rea studied her menu.

'So? You think he'll go for it?' she said.

'I don't know.'

'It's a risky move. Is it a bad idea?'

All this past week I'd been toying with the idea of suggesting she change her topic, but couldn't bring myself to wilfully sabotage her. By doing medical imaging, she would effectively be sabotaging herself. I remembered something Mum used to say, about having an angel and a devil on each shoulder. I never believed in all that. If it were true, the angel would have screamed at me to tell Rea about Amelia's lab notes, to convince her not to change her presentation. But I really want the job. I need it more than her. Because of Amy.

'Medical imaging sounds great,' I said. I motioned to the waiter. 'We'd like to order.'

There's not much angel in me, anyway. The devil part was always going to win.

Credits

Vintage would like to thank everyone who worked on the publication of *THE LYING GUEST*

UK Editor
Katie Ellis-Brown
Sania Riaz

Editorial
Anouska Levy

Copy-editor
Katherine Fry

Proofreader
Jane Howard

Managing Editorial
Sam Stocker

Contracts
Emma D'Cruz
Gemma Avery
Ceri Cooper
Rebecca Smith
Humayra Ahmed
Kiran Halaith
Anne Porter

Hayley Morgan
Harry Sargent

Design
Dan Mogford

Digital
Anna Baggaley
Claire Dolan
Brydie Scott
Charlotte Ridsdale
Zaheerah Khalik

Inventory
Rebecca Evans

Publicity
Shona Abhyankar
Amrit Bhullar

Finance
Ed Grande
Aya Daghem
Samuel Uwague

Marketing
Mairéad Zielinski

Production
Konrad Kirkham
Polly Dorner

Sales
Nathaniel Breakwell
Malissa Mistry
Elspeth Dougal
Tracy Orchard
Jade Perez
Lewis Cain
Nick Cordingly
Kate Gunn
Sophie Dwyer
Maiya Grant
Danielle Appleton
Phoebe Edwards
Amber Blundell
Rachel Cram
David Atkinson
Amanda Dean

Andy Taylor	Lucy Beresford-Knox	Olivia Diomedes
Dan Higgins	Beth Wood	Jake Dickson
	Maddie Stephenson	
Rights	Agnes Watters	**Audio**
Catherine Wood	Sophie Brownlow	Nile Faure-Bryan
Lucie Deacon	Amy Moss	Hannah Cawse